horse crazy

ALSO BY GARY INDIANA

FICTION

Scar Tissue and Other Stories

White Trash Boulevard

Gone Tomorrow

Rent Boy

Resentment: A Comedy

Three Month Fever: The Andrew Cunanan Story ·

Depraved Indifference

Do Everything in the Dark

The Shanghai Gesture

Last Seen Entering the Biltmore: Plays, Short Fiction, Poems 1975–2010

Tiny Fish that Only Want to Kiss

To Whom It May Concern (with Louise Bourgeois)

NONFICTION

Let It Bleed: Essays 1985–1995

The Schwarzenegger Syndrome: Politics and Celebrity in the Age of Contempt

Utopia's Debris: Selected Essays

Andy Warhol and the Can that Sold the World

A Significant Loss of Human Life

I Can Give You Anything But Love

horse crazy

a novel

GARY INDIANA

introduction by
Tobi Haslett

SEVENS STORIES PRESS
New York • Oakland • London

Most of this book, some of it in slightly different form, originally appeared in
Bomb.

Library of Congress Cataloging-in-Publication Data

Names: Indiana, Gary, author.
Title: Horse crazy / Gary Indiana.
Description: Seven Stories Press first edition. | New York : Seven Stories
  Press, 2018.
Identifiers: LCCN 2018017496| ISBN 9781609808617 (pbk.) | ISBN
  9781609808624 (ebook)
Subjects: LCSH: Writers--Fiction. | Gays--Fiction. | AIDS (Disease)--New York
  (State)--New York--Fiction. | Male friendship--Fiction. | Drug
  addiction--Fiction. | GSAFD: Psychological fiction
Classification: LCC PS3559.N335 H67 2018 | DDC 813/.54--dc23
LC record available at https://lccn.loc.gov/2018017496

College professors and high school and middle school teachers may
order free examination copies of Seven Stories Press titles. To order, visit
www.sevenstories.com or send a fax on school letterhead to (212) 226-1411.

Manufactured in the United States of America

9 8 7 6 5 4 3 2 1

Introduction
by Tobi Haslett

Sex, hypocrisy, solitude, loss, the punitive affinities that swallow the self—these are Gary Indiana's themes, jingling through his books like money in Balzac. But rumbling beneath the malice is a melancholy yearning, a mind groping vulnerably for a human link.

"Affection is the mortal illness of lonely people," declares the narrator of *Horse Crazy*, whose own loneliness will froth into a mania by the novel's end. A writer in his thirties, he's just been named the art critic for a magazine he dislikes. "A new year had begun with ominously good fortune," pushing him deeper into the New York culture industry, a feudal world ruled by bloated personae and venal logic. The post is prestigious; he greets it with dread. Chained to his column, he will now be a minor celebrity and a downtown *figure*, "an object of envy, malice, and all the other base emotions that drive the majority of people at all times in every conceivable place and circumstance." Risible, then, that he wants to be loved.

And *Horse Crazy* is, by the laxest possible definition, a book about love—about a psyche smashed by what it can't help but want. The narrator—I'll call him "the critic"—is infatuated with a younger man, a twenty-seven-year-old artist named Gregory Burgess. But their courtship is pricked by a wincing imbalance. The critic is "established," and Gregory is not. Gregory is a former heroin addict who makes rent by waiting tables at a passé restaurant, an arrangement he sees as a kind of cosmic abuse. Philippe, his boss, is an erratic French freak who deals cocaine, terrorizes his staff, keeps a gun behind the counter, and has lascivious designs on Gregory (the burden, of course, of his sexual appeal).

Gregory resents the job. He also resents the critic. His column, fame, and chicly accomplished milieu make him the whimpering target of Gregory's punishments: the lying, cheating, screamed recriminations, and preposterous threats for which he is instantly forgiven, liberated from morality by his lovely face. And Gregory *is* lovely. He glitters with a mind-shattering sexiness, which he cannily exploits as he sails through the world.

His lies swirl into delusion. His compulsive manipulations grow more reckless and cruel. He might be using the critic to boost himself a bit higher in the art-world pecking order— or maybe he just likes his sexual power. Either way he's mean, demanding, stroppy, petty: a bundle of malevolent reflexes and bullying tics. "I had always wanted someone to take control of my body and soul, rule my life, fill my consciousness to the exclusion of everyone else," the critic admits. "And at last someone had, a full-blown psychopath." So we're shoved into the cage of the critic's sexual need.

But Gregory has renounced sex. The restaurant drains his vitality, so he can't possibly "give you what you want." Not to mention that his ex-girlfriend Gloria was apparently a vindictive nymphomaniac, an addled banshee whose savage appetite demoted him to the status of mere object—a theme he's started to probe in his art. Gregory spends his days ripping pages from porn magazines, extracting pictures of limbs and genitals for his "technically sophisticated" collages, which mount a critique, he says, of sex. Or rather, the gleaming *fantasy* of sex—sex made vulgar and slick by commodity culture. "Something of the zeal with which reformed sinners make themselves odious sparkled across Gregory's photographs." So his celibacy is enshrined as a virtue in a world devoured by AIDS.

When *Horse Crazy* was first published in 1989, William Burroughs invoked Genet—"Fascinating to every man, no matter what his sexual tastes"—Peter Wollen reached for Breton—"a *Nadja* for New York"—but only the radical feminist Andrea Dworkin, perhaps chastened by decades of militancy, thought to allude to Dante: "There's a circle of hell called the Lower East Side of New York where boys and girls love too much and die too soon. *Horse Crazy* is one writer's guided tour."

It was also Indiana's first novel. For three years, he'd been the art critic for the *Village Voice*—a job that placed him in the blast radius of the Lower East Side art scene, the garish bloom of galleries and "spaces" whose existence hinged on the very financial interests then dismantling the neighborhood. Trapped within this microcosm, Indiana sought to censure and expose it, cackling at its follies and chastising its buffoons. He was a canary, a Cassandra—the grimacing superego of a lurid age.

New York in the '80s. The phrase brims with myths—about art and finance, AIDS and real estate, right-wing *schadenfreude* and a jagged avant-garde. In *Horse Crazy*, the critic's ravings and sorrows are flecked with little musings, swiveling panoramas of a desolate decade. Bohemia is dying, rents are rising, and even the *luftmenschen* of downtown are gripped by a generalized neurosis and a twitching self-interest—a feeling enforced by a lethal disease. *Horse Crazy* traces the imprint of AIDS on the consciousness: its terror and humiliations, how it hardens the heart.

And mangles language. Indiana is among the best living prose stylists in English, lushly sensitive to phrasing, timing, patterns, sounds. Paul, a former lover, falls sick, "[a]nd so this body whose secret parts were my main pleasure in life for longer than anyone else's transforms itself into a fount of contagion." And Indiana summons the vocabulary of the disease with acrid brilliance: the word "pneumocystis" is dumped into an otherwise elegant paragraph, and the "fatal sarcomas, pneumonias, and neuropathies" that feast on his friends comprise a kind of brittle clinical slang.

AIDS, in *Horse Crazy*, is an assault on intimacy, a kind of hyperbole for how hard it is to connect. But it's also history—history coming into crashing contact with human life, human weakness. AIDS draws and patrols the line between people; it crumbles the body and poisons love. And the disease becomes a cynical alibi for Gregory's refusal of the critic: "The only safe sex, he says, is if one person jerks off at one end of a room and someone else jerks off at the other, both trying to hit the same spot in the middle of the floor." This has a chilling, malicious logic. Whole stretches of the novel consist of crazed thoughts and desperate calculations, as Indiana's characters stare down the barrel of the epidemic. So the psyche lunges for totems and explanations, the kind of magical thinking that needs reasons, signs, clichés:

> It wouldn't be strange to get it and then to decide as Perkins did that this one particular person gave it to you, one out of ten or fifty or a hundred, maybe because that person made you feel something special, had done wonderful things in bed or gotten you to trust him physically and mentally as no one else ever had. . . . You would naturally connect your most vivid memory of pleasure to infection and death because the others weren't remotely worth getting sick from,

just pale skimpy traces of sex crossed with thin trickles of "bodily fluids," if the two things had to be linked, better for a cherished memory of sex to connect with transmission of the microbe.

To open your life is to threaten it—to die, in effect, for love:

In any case, if you had sex now it was a matter of deciding, even if you took elaborate precautions, whether the degree of risk involved (and who could calculate that?) was "worth it," whether your need for that kind of experience with another person out-weighed, in a sense, your desire for survival.

"Who," asked Roland Barthes in 1977, "will write the history of tears?" Indiana has written the history of blood, skin, sputum, semen—and of art, lust, money, and fear. We are living, now, in a fearful time. And Gary Indiana is still writing books.

horse crazy

For Betsy Sussler

PART ONE

desire

I

Yesterday I took a miniature trip with M., back and forth on the Staten Island Ferry. The sky was clear and bright, the day was warm enough for us to stand on the deck without a sweater. Going out, we were light-headed and said a lot of silly things to each other, made fun of tourists, joked about the military look of New York Harbor. And then coming back, we felt weighted, withdrawn, ate hot dogs and potato chips in long pockets of silence, sitting inside this time as if the water and the passing sights had been used up on the first Crossing. It was fine going out, barely tolerable coming back. This problem of attrition has been creeping into many experiences lately. Things commence in reckless hope and die away in stifled longing, not that we had hoped for much From the Staten Island Ferry.

M. says the boy he's been seeing uptown is infatuated with him and mistakenly believes this is love, true love. I know what M. means by "mistakenly" but it often comes to the same thing. Affection is the mortal illness of lonely people.

I dimly recall, from childhood, a movie where a man and a woman meet on the Staten Island Ferry late at night, by chance. It's gradually revealed that one or the other, maybe both of them, had planned on jumping off the boat. But instead they fall in love, each becoming the other's ray of hope. Love, the rescuer's flashlight. Perhaps we all grow up with these salvational fantasies that never get entirely dislodged by experience.

I haven't the heart to tell my own story, and keep looking for less convoluted fictions. Love like a stone in the stomach, a penance, a noose: love like a crime. Is this about love, I wonder.

There is a wall I run up against, again and again (a dream). At times what's needed is this blank, horrendous wall. You rise up flush against its stark, gritty surface and can't move any further. Even if you thwack your skull repeatedly against this wall, becoming bloody and insensible, the wall doesn't know you, doesn't yield, doesn't pity. A pitiless wall, a pity. That's how it is. Let's say you think of leaping over it. Well, perhaps you can. But you don't think you can, which is the same as not being able to. Its too high, just looking at it brings on a spasm of fear. You think: I'll smoke a cigarette, have a drink, come back to it later. And your absence adds an inch or so to the wall. You return. My God, that's a big wall. You seek advice about methods of jumping, phone people up. They tell you not to think about it, just jump. Jump blind. Or they might say, Don't force yourself, take it easy. Jump in little stages. Or: Maybe you're up against the wrong wall. Or: Try walking around the wall. Slinking around it. Pretend the wall isn't there. Walk through the wall.

Through the wall. Like passing through an oval mirror with a peeling varnished frame, in a house where everything is running down, and the clock beats insistently while telling the wrong time. It has taken me this long to understand how dreadful it would be to say, *That afternoon, I met Gregory Burgess in St. Marks Bookshop,* planting the first stout parenthesis of a story that seems, now, really to have a beginning, a middle, and an end. I didn't just meet him, I would say, but froze in his gaze like an animal mesmerized by headlights. And it would not be my first attempt, then, to describe *his oval chin, small ears, an unbroken, elegant curve of a nose with a tiny gold loop in one nostril, full lips that break easily into smiles, lips that chap and whiten in cold weather, and often go slack in a rictus of pain that obscures his bright teeth; clear coral eyes, a face fringed with onyx hair*—I have more in this plangent vein, but Gregory doesn't actually look like this, except for the nose ring. Is his chin oval? No. Yes. I don't know. Neither oval nor square. A nicely formed chin, definitely. Memory doesn't give me this chin, and the single photograph I possess looks nothing like Gregory: it's a group shot, taken on my building stoop, Gregory's sitting behind me, his fist planted firmly in his cheek, pulling the right side of his face off its axis. Memory obscures the immediate tug of Gregory's beauty, drops the details from his chiseled face, the glinting facets in his unwavering stare. I remember that afternoon in surprisingly intricate detail, but nothing exceptional occurred.

I made a clumsy, untoward effort to meet a total stranger, met him, got his address and phone number with dreamlike ease, established some flimsy pretext to see him again, and later felt foolish. It would be part of this way of telling about it to add that I knew he lived with a woman (he got this across almost instantly, pointedly), furthermore a quite possessive woman much younger than himself; that he worked killingly long hours, in four-day stints, at a French restaurant in SoHo, a job that drove him into spells of numbed exhaustion; and that he was, like most young men in Manhattan at the time, some kind of artist.

But here things bifurcate and become opaque. I don't know how much of this I really found out that day. It seems important to keep events in order, not to run ahead of things. I've told the Gregory Burgess story to myself so many times, so many different ways, and told it to other people, too, for so many different reasons. I met him that afternoon in December, and after that I hardly thought about anything else. It really was that way. Still, questions obscure this story from beginning to end. For example: Did I go home that afternoon thinking, "I've met someone I could love." It must have been like that, but this thought was sliced apart by the feeling that such a person couldn't possibly love me, he being first of all a lover of women, secondly a physical marvel, thirdly eight or nine years younger than I was. None of which would, by itself make Gregory Burgess unattainable. But on the strength or weakness of this unforeseen, upsetting encounter, I decided, at once, that Gregory Burgess was unattainable, and I embarked almost immediately on the project of seducing him. I would seduce him by laying myself entirely open to him, offering myself unconditionally. Use me, I would beg him. People who look like him, I thought, are completely selfish. They want everything, and if they know there's something they can have, without obligation, at any time, chances are they'll take it, sometime or other. Such is the flawed logic, I could say now.

That night I put aside my fiction of former defeats, former glories, *Burma* (a country where I have never been but have always wanted to go), and began writing a letter. It began reasonably, as a sort of old-fashioned, literary coda to the afternoon. How pleasant to have met you, and so on, the kind of letter no one ever writes anymore, which naturally has its peculiar charm for the startled recipient. A courtly letter. Spinsterish but sensual. I felt in the brief time we conversed that I was speaking with someone of extremely rare sensitivity, and that you, of course, sensed my physical attraction to you, and were gracious enough to take this in stride, giving me the opportunity to show you the kind of person I am. I know it's eccentric to come right out with this in a letter, but I have been so moved by your beauty that I, that I, at this point everything floundered, I ripped the letter into shreds and started over. Dear Gregory Burgess, I began, It was obvious when I spoke with you today what I was feeling, and I'm sure you had no uncertainty about the nature of my interest. As you were kind enough to say you are familiar with my writing, I thought I would offer you my feelings in written form, regardless of the consequences. If this alienates you, I perfectly well understand. But I'm crazy about you. When I first saw your face I had no more choice about meeting you or not meeting you than, than, never mind what, I lost any idea of control, I had to talk to you, find out about you. I can't pretend, even though you seem to have a sympathetic personality (I crossed out "personality" and wrote "character"), that my attraction is any different than that of a stranger who might catch a glimpse of you in the subway or the street. I desire you, it's as simple and awful as that, and if this doesn't repulse you, despite your current arrangements, I will propose something disgustingly modern, vulgar, contrary to my own way of doing things, but: I want you. If you ever feel you want me, should you ever have a moment's urge to make love, I don't care when, you can phone me up in the middle of the night and come over, use my body for whatever you like, and if it suits you, you can then leave and never have any contact with me again. I don't know how else to present this. I'm not a subtle person in matters of this kind. I'm open to any urge you might have, however perverse or cruel. It's idiotic, but I love you.

This was, at any rate, the gist. The letter itself ran to twenty single-spaced typewritten pages, gave a long-winded account of my personal history, my circumstances, my mode of existence, and included numerous philosophical digressions, speculative passages, lyrical paragraphs concerning Gregory's blinding erotic attraction, and so on. In my early youth, I had once managed to get in bed with a rigorously heterosexual, surpassingly beautiful guy by writing him an incessant stream of flattering letters, and I supposed there was as good a chance if I kept this up with Gregory. No man is straight every minute of his life unless he is dead.

But the first version of this letter failed to satisfy me. I read it through, compulsively, nine or ten times throughout the evening, all the while drinking bottles of Japanese beer. After some readings I thought, Well, just stick the thing in an envelope and mail it, you've already made an ass of yourself, you might as well be a complete ass. On the last reading, the excessiveness of my own sentiments sobered me. What am I doing? I'm handing this person a deadly weapon, a weapon he'll use against me, he'll show it to all his friends and laugh about me with them. I'll be an object of derision wherever I walk. This was not an unreasonable fear. New York is a woefully tiny village, despite its apparent hugeness. Everyone knows everyone, everyone talks about everyone, everyone knows everything there is to know about everyone, to the extent that a simple stroll through your neighborhood often feels like a protracted crawl through a minefield, and if you are at all known for anything, a character in this city's tiresome living novel, it's especially true that you cannot go anywhere without being observed by people who then talk about you, who talk about you even more, in fact, when they do not see you for a while. Anyone who is known who isn't seen for a while is rumored to be dying of AIDS, addicted to heroin, living in another country, or dead, such is the idle chatter of New York and particularly of downtown Manhattan. And of course among Gregory's peers, the young set, in this neighborhood, a letter declaring my uncontrollable passion for him could have tremendous gossip cachet. Look here, he would tell various odious strangers, this *older writer* has fallen in love with me. I painted this scene in the darkest colors, in my own mind, casting myself as an *older writer*, a sort of

Humbert Humbert figure, and by the same token, in light of Gregory's extravagant comeliness, thinking of myself as comparatively unattractive, ill-dressed, not at all *sportif*, a natural object of ridicule for the fashion-conscious younger generation. These ruminations advanced sufficiently for me to tear the thick letter into tiny pieces. I brooded for several minutes, then rolled a fresh page into the typewriter. Dear Gregory, I commenced, dropping the "Burgess" as altogether too precious and nineteenth-century, Even though we only just met, and under such peculiar circumstances, I feel I really have to see you again, to get to know you; I rarely meet anyone to whom I feel such instantaneous sympathy and attraction, anyone of such obvious discernment and intelligence. Had he actually displayed any obvious discernment, or more than quotidian intelligence? It seemed to me, just then, that he had. But perhaps this was going too far. I ripped this up and started afresh. Dear Gregory, This is probably the weirdest letter you've ever received. I can't help that, I can only hope that even if I don't interest you, you'll find it sufficiently flattering not to despise me for it. There, I considered, I've hit the right note. I continued filling the first page, then a second page, arriving at last at a length of twenty-three pages, assuring myself the whole time that virtually any human being given such elaborate and loving homage would almost feel obligated to bestow his favors, simply out of gratitude if not attraction. I flopped onto my bed, wasted from so much writing, and noted that five hours had ticked past in a frenzy. Again I read through the letter, many, many times, and this time got up, found an envelope, typed out Gregory's name and address, folded the letter into it with difficulty (wondering if it might burst open in the mail), licked the flap, sealed it, and placed it triumphantly on my desk. It would arrive at its destination like a bombshell, I thought. Perhaps he, despite his impossible beauty, feels insignificant, struggling along as an artist while working backbreaking shifts at some loathsome French restaurant. Whereas I, in his eyes, am a published author, an inhabitant of a glamorous world he only dreams of entering. Perhaps, receiving such a letter, from such a celebrated person, will seem like a miracle. Of course he'll sleep with me. Not only sleep with me but become my lover. Not only become my lover, but the person closest to me throughout my life. We will adhere as one being, becoming so close as to seem indistinguishable. Or perhaps he'll handle this whole business with astonishing sophistication, give this adoring older guy an affectionate toss, and thereafter remain a friend, taking his particular path through life while I continue alone down mine.

I drank another bottle of Japanese beer, which turned sour and disgusting in my mouth, then tore the letter into shreds, envelope and everything. I'm not twenty-one any-more, I informed myself, I'm thirty-five. At twenty-one it seemed noble and romantic to send letter after letter to Teddy Brightman, whose name at least I haven't forgotten, Teddy who was hardly any older, who succumbed to this adulation in no time at all, showing up one afternoon in my Boston rooming house, where, after an hour's chitchat, he unzipped his trousers to reveal what he claimed had been lauded as the finest cock in Christendom by his Eurotrash girlfriend. And I remembered having thought "Christendom" a jejune word choice at the time, expressing a worldliness we were much too young to feel. Summertime with Teddy: fellating his proud Christian pecker twice that day, then again a few weeks later when he came in from Amherst for the weekend; then throughout the early summer he turned up at odd moments, developing a taste for butt-fucking, rim jobs, whatever I then had in my repertoire. By autumn his homosexual period had drawn to a close, if memory serves. I ran into him a few years later, but he'd lost the taste for it, having matured into a totally uninteresting, unexceptional-looking adult academic. By then I was twenty-five, Teddy twenty-six. Years later, at thirty-five, I was drinking through the night and writing love letters to a twenty-seven-year-old, imagining these letters could produce the same magical results they produced when I was twenty-one and Teddy twenty-two, back in the provinces. Absurd.

"People are what people are," M. says, dismissing the idea that some people, at certain times, reinvent themselves as worthier, more responsible, more thoughtful people. I suppose a person gradually becomes aware of deficiencies and virtues in others, sometimes only after decades. I think I've known "everybody" in New York at one time or another, and I have spent years weeding out the ones with truly lousy characters. You're less and less likely to be really deceived, though it's always possible for you to be mistaken. There are people you can sustain two utterly different opinions about at the same time, people who command equivocation as other people command respect or fear or sexual attention; people who've deliberately obscured the text of their own personalities, who can't be read without incredible difficulty. In the end, the hardest thing is learning how to tell a secret from a mystery.

I haven't the heart to tell my own story: but a few weeks later I was offered a job, a regular job, writing cultural items for a large-circulation weekly magazine. The offer came out of the blue, and my first impulse was to turn it down. I did turn it down, as a matter of fact. Two days later, the editor again phoned and asked me to reconsider. I reconsidered. Can I write anything I want, I asked. By all means, I was told. That's what we want you to do.

I had not been an employee for many years, and the prospect of becoming one was only slightly ameliorated by the immense prestige attached to the position. Immense as far as magazine writing goes. It was a power job, writing about the arts for a big audience. A job through which one could focus public attention on virtually anything. And in a city where nearly every person carries about with him a pathological craving for public attention, a person in such a position would, of course, be regarded as powerful, would be courted, lobbied, hounded, importuned on every front. However, *mutatis mutandis*, such a person would not be powerless. Such a person could even accomplish some conceivable good in the world, using such a position in a judicious fashion. A writer's most fundamental need is to be read by people, as many people as possible. Of course one only writes for oneself but after one has written, one wishes to be read. It was not really the sort of power I wanted or the sort of job I wanted. I had, in fact, always detested most of what appeared in this particular magazine, which had, curiously enough, ignored my existence for years. I had done so many things, and yet the magazine had never taken the slightest notice. And now I would be part of the magazine. Odd.

Soon after accepting the job, which wasn't to begin for two months, I realized my life was about to change. A person goes through life, longing for one thing or another, wishing if he's a writer to be read, to be recognized, to produce a body of work, laboring against the self-destructive inclinations which seem almost inevitably to accompany a Creative gift, despairing frequently if not incessantly because of the impossibility of doing the single thing he wishes to do, ultimately resigning himself to his obscurity and his feeble productivity, and then, as he approaches the nadir of despondency, things change. Even if they do not change very much, even if this change is not a dramatic change, the very premises upon which his existence is based turn themselves inside out.

And now, I considered, I shall truly exist in the world. Not that

I don't exist now. But I will exist in a special way, for others, too: a large and disturbing way. I will no longer be a private person, but a public figure. Not an enormous public figure, like a film star or a politician, but a modestly-scaled public figure, someone whose activities are inquired about by many people he does not know and doesn't care about, a person who takes up space, who is fated for attacks from embittered individuals, an object of envy, malice, and all the other base emotions that drive the majority of people at all times in every conceivable place and circumstance.

In that week, a kind of panic set in. A new year had begun with ominously good fortune, dragging me into a new situation as if my clothes had gotten caught by the fender of a speeding truck. I telephoned Gregory Burgess, inviting him to lunch.

It was a cold day of soiled white sky. A few hours earlier he had called, asking if I would meet him on the street, so we could then decide where to eat. I am never happy about choosing restaurants over the telephone. So at 1:30 I positioned myself in front of a drugstore on Second Avenue. Actually, I got there at 1:15, anxious not to be late. I looked at a display of unspeakable objects in the pharmacy window: bedpans, rupture trusses, ointments for varicose veins, corn plasters, for some reason this pharmacy had decided to cast its most repugnant wares into the limelight, things one finds it disagreeable to ask for, purchases for which one loiters until other customers move out of hearing range were lovingly piled up in the sooty window, shameless advertisements of the human body's wretched deliquescence. Every few seconds I walked away from the window to the corner to peer up the side street and down Second Avenue.

Gregory's apartment, which he'd recently moved into, he'd said, with his girlfriend, a woman named Gloria, was in Loisaida, down around Orchard Street. A part of the Lower East Side that had always been mysterious and depressing to me. He would undoubtedly arrive from that direction, but perhaps he'd walk up First Avenue and cut over on the side street, rather than walking across Houston to Second Avenue. He might come from either direction. I hoped to catch sight of him walking toward our meeting from a distance. Every young person of a certain height caught my attention, if he was wearing a hat or had black hair; my eyes seized on any person under six feet tall who happened to look thin in winter clothes, walking up Second Avenue or across on the side street. A man who looked like Gregory made his way up Second Avenue, becoming more familiar-looking as he came nearer, and then, still some distance off, strode off across Second Avenue, in the direction of Bowery.

I ran down Second, thinking suddenly that I'd been standing all this time on the wrong corner. I'd thought he'd said Seventh Street, but perhaps he'd said Fifth Street. When I reached the corner of Fifth Street I could see the man proceeding toward Bowery and saw that it wasn't Gregory after all, because this person was now swinging his arms while in motion, in large unnatural ellipses, and his head seemed to be jerking compulsively up and down. I raced back to my original spot, trying to recall exactly what corner we'd agreed on. I knew it was Seventh. But it could also have been Eighth. The corner of Eighth and Second is such a typical corner for meetings of this kind, perhaps we had settled on Eighth after all, having at first rejected it in favor of the less frequented corner of Seventh and Second. But should I venture up to Eighth, I wondered, in the certainty that I could see the corner of Seventh and Second from the corner of Second and Eighth, or stay put in front of the drugstore, confident in my ability to view both the corner of Second and Eighth and the corner of Sixth and Second, which suddenly seemed another possibility, from my vantage point at

Seventh and Second? I now felt less confident. If we hadn't agreed on Seventh and Second, it seemed likely that we had agreed on some place even more obscure. Certainly not Eighth and Second, the popular meeting-corner, and perhaps not Sixth and Second, either, since Sixth Street has no pertinent associations in my mind, I would never propose that corner for a meeting, whereas I might very well suggest Fifth, Seventh, or even Fourth.

By now, it was several minutes past the appointed time, according to a digital clock over a bank entrance across the street—though one could never fully rely on this clock because it tended to malfunction in the winter months, sometimes erring by a few minutes, sometimes by several hours. It now read 1:36. I had never known this clock to run fast, except when the hour itself was wrong, for example, if it happened to be 5:00 and the clock reported the hour as 10:00 or 12:00 or whatever, whereas quite frequently, the clock ran slow, in which case it might well be 1:45 or even 1:50. And if it were now 1:45 or 1:50, I most certainly had taken up my vigil on the wrong corner, had been standing at a corner which was not only wrong but so far from the correct corner that Gregory, waiting at the correct corner, whichever it was, couldn't see the corner where I stood, or couldn't or hadn't imagined it possible that I could confuse such a simple, unequivocal matter and in fact be standing at the wrong corner. In fact, if he did not imagine this, he might have been standing as nearby as the corner of Eighth and Second or Sixth and Second without even glancing at the corner of Seventh and Second, and I, so eager for a glimpse of him, may have been following complete strangers with my eyes, overlooking Gregory completely although he'd been in plain view for several minutes.

If this had been the case, and Gregory had been standing, say, at the corner of Eighth and Second and had, like me, arrived a few minutes early, he might even have surmised, as I had, that the corner he thought we had agreed on was not the right corner.

He might then have panicked, as I had, and left off waiting at his corner in order to locate me at another corner, at roughly the same moment that I had abandoned my corner to follow the man who had crossed Second Avenue at Fifth Street. I began walking back and forth between the corners of Seventh and Second and Sixth and Second, my gaze searching down the side streets and ahead to more distant corners, all the time rehashing the brief phone conversation of a few hours earlier, becoming steadily more agitated and fearful of having missed Gregory already, or of missing him now by perambulating between corners, for if it was by this time 1:45 or 1:50 or, as the increasingly plausible digits of the bank clock reported, 2:00, and Gregory had been delayed, he might now arrive and assume that I'd grown tired of waiting for him, or that I myself had been grossly delayed, or was in the habit of making people wait for unreasonable amounts of time. If that were the case, Gregory might simply have arrived, and, not seeing me where we'd agreed to meet, concluded that I was completely frivolous and not worth knowing at all, and returned in irritation to Gloria and his apartment.

Of course I had arrived early, and my defection from the corner of Seventh and Second had been momentary. Almost certainly we had agreed on that corner, and even if he had shown up, say, as I was walking to the corner of Second and Sixth, he would have seen my back moving away from that corner, would have run and caught up with me. And in any case, I walked back and forth rapidly, if he stood waiting for even a few moments at the corner of Seventh and Second I would have arrived back there myself within plenty of time to encounter him. Then, too, although I had never known the bank clock to run fast except when it told the hour wrong, I did not observe the vagaries of the bank clock throughout the day, or pay much attention to the bank clock throughout the year, for that matter, and for all I knew the clock ran fast all the time, or a great part of the time, and though it seemed I had been waiting for Gregory, in one fashion or another, for well over a half hour, my own acute anticipation of his presence may have made the time feel longer than it was.

My sense of things, at this point, told me that Gregory was merely late, delayed, probably by the hectoring of Gloria, and in all likelihood rushing from his apartment to meet me, unless he had assumed, having been held up for an egregious amount of time and unable to reach me by phone, that I would have given up by now. In that case, he would certainly have phoned my place and left a message on the answering machine. It occurred to me that my down-stairs neighbor, who has keys to my apartment, could, if she were home, let herself into my place and play back my message tape, then tell me whether or not Gregory had called to explain his nonappearance. I would have to phone the neighbor from a pay phone, tell her what I needed, wait a few minutes, then call her back. However, as I had ascertained over the previous half hour by watching people go up to them, the pay phones at the corner of Seventh and Second were out of order. The nearest pay phone, then, would be the one at the corner of Fifth and Second, so even trying to find out if Gregory had or hadn't been delayed involved abandoning the corner he might that very moment be rushing toward. It was quite possible that I would miss him in the process of trying to learn whether or not he was coming.

At last I returned to the pharmacy window. I would give him a few more minutes, then go home and take the messages myself. No accounting for this person, I thought. Maybe he feels threatened and wants me to give up on him right at the outset. And I should, I considered, staring at a gleaming enamel bedpan, give up now, he's too handsome, a monster of vanity, too sexy, and in this freezing weather, letting me stand all this time waiting is practically a declaration of contempt. Rupture belts. Imagine getting old, going flabby, and having to wear a rupture belt. I've always been thin, my body's in relatively good shape for someone who drinks and smokes and never exercises, but I should do something, keep myself fit somehow, go to a gym, work out, lift weights, if I stopped smoking my skin would clear up, it's always breaking out in strange eruptions, thank God I've got a nice face, if I were plain these skin things would make me look really ugly.

Gregory put his hands on my shoulders. He wore a black fleece hat with flaps covering his ears. His face had roses in the smooth cheeks.

I'm really sorry, he said. He said that as he was leaving his apartment the phone rang, and it was Gloria, the girl he'd been living with. Their relationship, he said, was now a thing of the past. My spirits lifted at this news. I pretended not to be irritated. In fact, the discomfort of waiting had already dissolved. He smiled, I turned to gelatin.

He suggested an Indian restaurant nearby, and in a few minutes we arrived at Shagura, a place whose festive canopy and red-and-yellow window decorations had repulsed me for years.

I love this place, Gregory declared as we pushed into its steaming interior. A pink and green paisley dining room full of squat, square tables covered with stained oilcloths. He went decisively to a table against the wall. I followed. We sat. We gazed into each other's eyes. A waiter, who seemed about three feet high, set down enormous menus and two water glasses. The menus, bound in brownish vinyl, felt clammy. The amber water glasses had a malarial cast. I couldn't keep my eyes away from Gregory's face. I pretended to study the menu. I kept up a brisk flow of bright chatter about the weather, the holidays just past. Gregory answered with matching banalities. We ordered *kurma*. The room had a thick smell of curry.

He pulled off his hat. His hair was fastidiously clipped, his fingernails tidily manicured. The black shirt and embroidered vest on his slender frame attested to careful maintenance. He's dressed up for me, I thought. He's made himself look nice for me. I noticed we were both chain-smoking.

Why does he like this hideous restaurant, I wondered. Two people live in the same area, they sometimes have the same opinions or ideas about any number of different topics, but the way they feel about various places that each one sees all the time will be drastically unalike. One will have strange emotional associations with a bar, a restaurant, a block of houses, yet for the other it's just a place. There are places I can't go because of the past, houses I can't walk past without some painful feeling. Some people conquer their sentimental impulses, their draining nostalgia, their regrets. They can live in the streets and rooms of their memories as if every day were a new day. Why is that, I wondered.

I asked him what had happened between him and Gloria. He said something quick and somehow shocking, a phrase full of words so abruptly violent it took my breath away. A moment later he described, in a perfectly sanguine voice, a pop singer he admired. It was as if a tape recording had been spliced at some jarring, brittle point and turned into sedative mood music. I didn't know where we were going but sensed that a door had been opened that wouldn't easily close again.

2

. . . and then Gregory said that Gloria, who was really just a kid, inexperienced, not at all sophisticated in affairs of the heart, had left the apartment on Clinton Street just before Christmas, a few days after you met me in the bookstore, Gregory said, she started driving me up the wall, he said that her incessant demands, her sexual demands on him, would start at four in the morning when he got off his shift at the restaurant, I'd be half dead, Gregory told me, my feet would be throbbing, all I'd want to do would be to get my clothes off and do aerobics for twenty minutes and then pass out, he said, and Gloria, as soon as Gregory came through the door, would grab at his belt trying to get his pants off she just wasn't capable of understanding that the last thing in the world I would want at four in the morning after being on my feet for twelve hours was sex, Gregory explained, in a tone of infinite reasonableness, compassionately, though an aggrieved note kept slipping into his voice, and she'd moved out, finally, actually he'd sort of kicked her out, made her leave, the thing is the apartment's in my name, he said, and now Gloria was persecuting him. He said he'd supported her for several months and even though she'd put up some of the initial money for the apartment she'd lived off him since then, he'd certainly more than paid back whatever funds she'd invested in the Clinton Street apartment, but now she's demanding that I give her back her seven hundred dollars, Gregory said, which is crazy, I just don't have it. I'm making a lot at the restaurant but I also have a lot of debts, he said, and I'm trying to get my work made, his work involved expensive photographic processes, first I make slides and then those have to be blown up into prints, Gregory explained, it's costly, my work means everything to me, right now it's the most important thing in my life, and now, he said, Gloria had launched a campaign of persecution. She had started ringing his buzzer at all hours, or phoning him in the middle of the night on his nights off walking him up, throwing pebbles at his windows, screaming up from the street at him, ambushing him when he left his apartment house, he'd taken the keys away, or changed the locks, anyway, she couldn't get in anymore, she was demanding money and also claimed he had some of her belongings in there, in fact some of her things are there, he said, she's welcome to have them back but I won't have her coming into the place, she has to set it up so I can have her stuff carried down to the street. I won't have any more dealings with her, she's insane. Gregory said that Gloria's insane behavior was beginning to make him completely paranoid and he had taken to unplugging the telephone and cutting himself off from any contact with the outside world on his days off, I bring all this food home and hole up there watching television, Gregory said, or cutting things out of magazines, I use stuff from magazines in this work that I make, I really want you to see it, he said, but I'm honestly afraid that Gloria's becoming violent, she's made threats over the phone, she says she's hiring goons to beat me up, or she's going to have this old boyfriend of hers beat the shit out of me, she says all this stuff to me and then she goes real sweet and says she'd like us to get together and just talk things over, I told her, there's no way we're getting back together again, if that's what you've got in mind, Gregory said, I can't take it, he went on, I've been through a lot of awful crap and my threshold for insanity is extremely low, if she keeps this up I don't know what I'll do. I'm having the phone number changed, he said, because the phone's in her name. You threw her out? I asked, meaning, how do you throw someone out in the middle of winter, a few days before Christmas, in New York City, someone with whom you've been sleeping, it sounded somehow off, a bit ruthless actually, not withstanding Gloria's sexual manias, I thought, there has to be more to it than that.

Not exactly, Gregory said, I mean she agreed to leave, we'd done nothing except fight for days and days and it couldn't possibly go on like that any longer because one of us would've killed the other one, she's not that crazy, besides which it's my name on the lease, if one of us was going to move out it was going to be her, I don't know where she's staying now but she found another place right away, it's not like she was suddenly having to sleep in the gutter or anything, but now that she's settled into her own apartment she's decided to make my life a living hell, twenty-four hours a day, all hours of day and night, it's incredible that anyone can throw so much energy into making another person miserable.

But this is awful, I said, what's the matter with her, if she agreed to leave and she knows you can't possibly pay her this money right away why does she keep it up? She hates me, Gregory said, she thinks I betrayed her, she's still in love with me, she won't give up no matter what. I actually feel sorry for her, the sooner she forgets all about me the better off she'll be, she ought to just find herself a new boyfriend, she's quite attractive, but she was always in love with me with that kind of clinging horrible fixity, we couldn't just have an ordinary relationship, on her side it was this major passion whereas I *loved* her but I never felt *in love* with her, being in love like that is dangerous and stupid, Gregory declared, it blinds you to everything, it's unfair all the way around, I feel a lot of compassion for Gloria but I can't make myself love her if I don't love her, can I?

No, I said, of course you can't, it sounds like she's behaving very unreasonably and this harassment is absolutely destructive for both of you, it's too bad she can't step away from her feelings and realize you don't feel about her the way she feels about you, situations like that are always horrific, you must feel really frazzled, I said, between your job and her showing up all the time, God.

I'm trying with every ounce of will to hold things together, Gregory said, I went through a really bad time a few years ago, I had to leave the city for a long time, almost four years, I got involved in some pretty sordid scenes, I got involved with a lot of people who were really, really evil, things got very rough and I had a kind of crack-up and I had to get out of here, for a while I went in and out of a mental hospital, it got that extreme, it's taken me almost four years to put myself back together again, I spent two years living like a complete hermit at the seaside, I never saw anybody, I worked as a short order cook in a little diner and kept to myself all the time, I lived in basically a shack, out in the dunes near P-town, I had a dog and that was all the company I had, Lucie, my dog's name was Lucie, it took me four years to pull my nerves together, and before that, when I lived here before, at the tail end of this truly rotten period I got into heroin, heavily involved with it, I made a lot of money back then doing interior design, which I just sort of fell into really, I had this guy who was kind of my lover who did that for a living and he showed me how to design basic stuff and do rooms, and I started doing it on my own and got all these fabulously rich clients and then I got written up in some magazines and then every rich old bag in Manhattan wanted me to redesign her apartment, he said that someone in the same business was in love with him at the time and turned him on to smack "and later when I was all fucked up and strung out this guy told me he'd got me hooked so I'd get into a condition where nobody else wanted me," Gregory let this statement sit there for a few moments, his eyes wide and horrified, as if he'd unveiled the nature of true evil, then went on, within six months his business went bankrupt because he'd gone through about a hundred thousand dollars in drugs and dissipation, buying drugs for himself and buying them for everybody he knew, and then he'd gotten severely strung out and sick, also, I finally went home, he told me, first they put me in a dry-out hospital but on the wrong ward, they put me in a ward for the criminally insane, I almost got killed in that ward and raped and everything else you can think of.

But you're all right now, I said, touching his hand on the table-cloth, thinking he looked as normal as anyone else, that in fact he seemed bursting with health and sounded entirely lucid about it all. Yes, he said, but this is after cleaning out up there and fucking up all over again when I was living at my mother's, I got completely out of control twice and finally my mother even threw me out, drove me out to the Interstate and pushed me out of the car, after that I checked into another hospital and they assigned this counselor who actually finally put me straight, I went into her office and started mouthing off about all this bullshit about how great I was and how I had been at the head of my class in college, which actually I was, and she just looked me straight in the eyes and said, You're nothing but a scummy little junkie, Gregory, and until you get clean that's all you're ever going to be, Gregory asseverated that this initial encounter woke him up, and from that moment on he began really working on himself, I started seeing all the ways I'd found to deceive myself I never had acknowledged my basic patterns, Gregory stated.

One thing that had profoundly affected him without his ever really understanding it, he said, was this trouble between him and his father, not simply between Gregory and his father but between the mother and the father, and Gregory's sister and Gregory's brother and the father, and between Gregory and his sister, and Gregory and his brother, and in a completely different way between Gregory and his mother, and perhaps also between Gregory and his Yugoslavian grandmother, relations on the Yugoslavian, that is to say on his father's, side of the family. On that side of the family, Gregory claimed, lay mania and depression. Everyone on the Yugoslavian side of Gregory's family was a chronic depressive given to periodic bouts of mania.

Not only had the children, that is, Gregory and his siblings, inherited the congenital manic-depression of these despondent Yugoslavs, but living with the father for almost twenty years had reduced the mother to a nervous wreck. The father was, had been, a compulsive gambler, whose fortunes—and therefore the family's fortunes—had oscillated wildly from one week or month or year to the next, sometimes they were, according to Gregory, "incredibly well off" whereas, at other times, they "suddenly had no money," life "was either a feast or a famine" in the Burgess household, during Gregory's entire childhood. At some juncture in the middle past, Gregory didn't stipulate precisely when, the mother had divorced the father, after years of torment, Gregory assured me, my mother crawled through hell for that man, all they ever really had in common was their physical attractiveness, she tried every minute to make a *good home*, and all he ever cared about was gambling, and now he's living in a car, selling pencils on the street in Meriden, Connecticut, right near where my mother works, sometimes if she walks to the office she has to walk right past my father selling pencils, Gregory said, or sleeping in his car. He's a complete derelict, Gregory said, whenever I see my sister she says, I wonder if we'll all end up like Dad.

Now, he said, the main problem in my life is this job, it sucks away all my time and energy, it's unbelievably draining. Philippe, the guy who owns the restaurant, is a certifiable lunatic, a total coke freak, he's completely out of his mind, he throws fits, sometimes he takes out the gun he keeps under the bar and goes into the basement and shoots at targets, while these hordes of trashy Europeans are upstairs gobbling up his lousy nouvelle cuisine and swilling alcohol at the bar, everybody who hangs out there is a coke freak, they get it from Philippe, in fact his main profession is selling coke, he only has that restaurant so he can socialize with other coke freaks. He's even beaten up a couple of waitresses, one of them took out a lawsuit against him and she's been getting death threats from him over the telephone. When Philippe gets high he's either effusively and suspiciously friendly or homicidally paranoid, he swings from one mood to another without a moment's warning. He likes me, he's never actually attacked me. Gregory said that before he'd made all that money in the design business he'd waited tables for Philippe in the same restaurant, Philippe had been just as crazy then, or possibly a bit less crazy, since Philippe's insanity was obviously a degenerative disease.

I almost despise myself for going back there, Gregory went on, he's always had this sort of sick affection for me. There's this odious bond between us. I think he wants to fuck me. He's not openly gay or anything but he's always grabbing me and saying, Dah-ling, you are ze only one who is worse anysing, and planting these big slobbering kisses, right on the lips, he's such a pile of shit, really, a total psychopath. Everything Philippe does is completely criminal, he's never even paid taxes on that dump, and the people who eat there, these braying bosomy pigs and their oily gigolo boyfriends, oinking swine from Ibiza or Goa or wherever they come from. You can't imagine what torture it is serving them food, and when I'm bartending they're all the time coming on to me, telling me all about their repulsive sex cravings or who they're fucking and what getting their dongs into so-and-so's twat is like. Just human garbage basically. I hate the way they eye me behind that counter, I feel like a fucking monkey in the zoo fixing their cocktails for them. And waiting tables, unbelievable, the way they dawdle over the menu and make what they imagine are sexy remarks, sometimes it's the same cruddy, pawing assholes from one night to the next, after a while they even think they've got some type of personal relationship with you, before you know it they're inviting you up for threesomes after work.

But why, I said, do you keep on working there? There are a million restaurants in Manhattan, they aren't all run by maniacs. That place is notorious, I said, everybody knows what a trashy clientele hangs out there, I mean, I've even heard about Philippe and the drugs and all that. I used to go there years ago when I was more or less employed by this heiress, she had a lot of friends and family connections who were the type that goes there. I can't imagine you working there, I continued, not for a minute. It's the kind of environment calculated to drive any sensitive person into Bellevue. I said that I knew several perfectly civilized people in the restaurant business and would gladly try to find Gregory a more agreeable place to work.

The problem is, Gregory said, lighting a cigarette, which suddenly drew my attention to the mess of butts that had accumulated over lunch, I'd never make as much money, Gregory explained that part of his odious bond with Philippe was the tacit understanding that he, Gregory, along with Philippe's other underpaid employees, would rob various amounts every night from the house till, pocket checks from certain tables, neglect to ring up various bar receipts. Philippe knew all about this furtive rake-off, according to Gregory, and didn't care about it at all, except sometimes, while throwing one of his absolutely inevitable yet invariably surprising fits, Philippe would accuse one or another waiter or waitress of robbing him, the accusations typically accompanied by blows, and not infrequently by threats with the gun, Philippe had in fact on one occasion pistol-whipped a bartender, who had quit on the spot but had later, somehow, been lured by Philippe's honey-tongued, lying promises of higher wages. Philippe's fits and accusations and assaults took place in full view of the clientele, usually when the restaurant was jam-packed, during the stylishly late dinner hour. Philippe's fits were a grotesque entertainment for the customers, Philippe's tirades had seasonally driven off any normal habitués, the place was mainly crawling with Philippe's drug-crazed friends and acquaintances. But precisely because Philippe was this kind of monstrous, criminal exhibitionist, Gregory felt no particular ethical qualms about peeling off anywhere from eighty to five hundred dollars from a night's receipts. This money enabled Gregory to get his real, that is, his photographic, work fabricated, at decent laboratories. The success of Gregory's art work absolutely depended on using the best laboratories available.

But he was, he said, caught in a Catch-22 situation, since the job deprived him of the time and energy required to go at his real work full steam, so to say. Gregory's artistic aims, he elucidated, were impossible to achieve through half measures. It was, he emphasized, integral to his work that it resemble the most technologically crisp sort of advertising images. He was, he said, deconstructing the media in his work. The satirical qualities of Gregory's art could only be perceived, he said, in mental contrast to contemporary advertising, and therefore the technical level needed to be as high. For the moment, he said, he had purchased a Nikon, and on his days off he made transparencies of his little cut-out tableaux, which he would later have blown up to giant size. I've spent a fortune just doing the slides, Gregory said. Until I get a show, sell some works, I'm going to be stuck at the restaurant. I don't see any alternative. I would never steal from a place where I was treated decently, and if I worked in such a place, I'd never make enough to get my career going.

Gregory said that the expense involved in becoming a contemporary artist had almost discouraged him from pursuing any such endeavor. He had started making these little images, deconstructing the media and so forth, on Cape Cod, purely for his own amusement. At first he'd lived with his friend Pugg, and the dog Lucie, Gregory said, You must meet Pugg, he's so brilliant, he's in art school now, Pugg had been wonderful to live with, but immature, confused, a bit too demanding, I worry about him now, Gregory said, he sleeps around a lot, and with this AIDS stuff, I mean, he gets fucked up the ass quite often, picks people up in bars, French types, boy model types, *Comme des Garçons* types that give it to him up the poop chute, and he's such a great guy I worry all the time what could happen to him. When Pugg left Cape Cod for New York, Gregory remained with Lucie in the shack, until the dog died from chewing lead-based paint off the molding, of which Gregory's despicable lesbian feminist landladies had been entirely culpable, when Lucie first began gnawing on the molding Gregory went to the dykes insisting they strip the toxic old paint and repaint the place with harmless latex, the dykes then told him to get rid of the dog, they weren't going to all that effort for a cocker spaniel, and, besides, he owed them several months' arrearage. If Gregory paid the arrearage they would consider repainting the place, but not before then, so consequently, by the time Gregory had slaved double shifts at Helen's Truro Hash Palace to settle the arrearage the dog had already ingested lethal quantities of lead, gone into convulsions, and died. It was one of Gregory's ugliest memories. Then after that he met Gloria, which at first seemed the kind of placid, mutually nourishing relationship Gregory needed as a check on his excessive tendencies. Gloria didn't smoke or drink, didn't take drugs, her only major problem was wanting her pussy full of Gregory's juicy whang every time he turned around, but this hadn't been as much of a problem at first, up there, as it became later, down here, since Gregory was learning from Gloria about screwing women for the first time and was entranced by the novelty of it, and of course it had proved interesting, even from a clinical perspective. I'd always been the fucker with guys, he laughed, but a cunt feels different from a rectum, it's real squishy inside and it really clings to your meat, I'd probably be straight if guys had cunts instead of assholes.

Then last summer this old friend of his, Bruno, visited him for a couple of weeks. You know Bruno, Gregory told me, Bruno runs that gallery. He named the gallery. I did know Bruno. Right, Gregory said, well, I've known him for years, he came up to Truro and saw the pictures I was making, Gregory said that after that he'd started getting letters from Bruno full of encouraging remarks, urging Gregory to move back into the city, even inviting Gregory to stay with him until Gregory found a job and an apartment. In the letters Bruno said that the art scene was opening up for the type of work Gregory was doing. Bruno implied that he could help Gregory "launch himself" in the coming year.

Gloria sensed danger. Bruno's letters also conveyed a restrained but unmistakable romantic attraction to Gregory. Gregory said that Bruno's interest in him had been simmering unobtrusively for some years, but had suddenly churned to a low boil during those two weeks in Truro. How can he do this to me, to us, Gloria wanted to know, poring over Bruno's twice-weekly semi-love letters to Gregory. Bruno's invitation did not extend to Gloria. He said in his letters that his apartment was much too tiny for two long-term guests, besides which, as Gregory well knew though Bruno's letters didn't say so, Bruno loathed Gloria and everything about her. Gregory knew that Bruno had told Pugg that Gloria was a vicious destroying cunt. He had told Pugg, according to

Gregory, that Gloria was ruining Gregory. Bruno had contacted
Pugg, evidently, to check up on Gregory, was constantly calling
up Pugg for news of Gregory, grilling Pugg about Gregory's relationship with Gloria, looking all the time, Gregory said, for some
little crack to drive a wedge into, Pugg reported all of Bruno's calls
directly to Gregory with bemused exasperation.

As things turned out, the heinous lesbians who owned the shack
served him a thirty-day notice to vacate for the arrearage, which
he hadn't paid, finally, because of the dog's death, which had been
entirely their monstrous fault, and they also hated him because he
was fucking Gloria, whom they were both vainly trying to get their
squalid mitts on, and the tourist season was winding up, which
meant that business at Helen's Hash Palace would soon begin dropping off and he'd either have to move to Boston, a dead place, where
everyone he knew was a heroin addict or an alcoholic, or go back to
his mother's house in Meriden, where, despite his slightly improved
relations with his family, he remained an object of intense suspicion
and constant anxiety, since his greatest behavioral excesses had actually transpired there after his initial removal from New York and
his first unsuccessful rehabilitation at Silver Hill. Ultimately, given
this array of dreary options, Gregory and Gloria devised a scheme,
wherein Gregory would move into Bruno's apartment while Gloria
stayed with Pugg in Pugg's sublet on Macdougal Street, keeping
Gloria's presence in the city a secret from Bruno, until she and
Gregory found an apartment. In that case, Gregory wouldn't be
subject to Bruno's whim, at least with respect to Bruno's sexual
jealousy of Gloria; and later, when Gregory and Gloria turned out
to be living together once again, Bruno would be compelled, by
his own principles, to continue supporting Gregory's work, on the
basis of his expressed admiration and friendship, since he, Bruno,
was too honorable in his dealings to stop promoting an artist simply
because he hadn't been able to exploit the artist sexually.

Which was, Gregory said, putting it too crudely, really, and if my part of it sounds calculating, he said, you've got to understand that Bruno's infatuation with me was and is a thing quite separate from our friendship, and it would've been very wrong of Bruno to invite me here just to get me in bed. And don't forget, he went on, if he did invite me here only for that reason, he himself was deviously planning to smash up my relationship with Gloria.

Which, I pointed out, had gone kaput anyway, just as soon as they moved in together.

Yes, Gregory said, but for completely different reasons. That doesn't have anything to do with Bruno.

3

Who knows what hearts and souls have in them? On the answering machine a message from Victor, who tells me when I call him that Paul, long ago my lover for two years, is sick. People use a special tone of voice, now, for illness, that marks the difference between sick and dying.

I've heard he's sick.

And so this body whose secret parts were my main pleasure in life for longer than anyone else's transforms itself into a fount of contagion. Paul passes over into the territory of no-longer-quite-alive, and I calculate that if he got it five years ago, the general incubation period, he must have been infectious on each of the fifty or sixty occasions when we slept together, giving me a much better than average chance of being infected.

He wants to see you. He's asked for you.

I haven't seen Paul in over a year. One day I saw him on the street with the man he's been living with, a tall, gangly man, whereas Paul has a rugged, packed look about him and that face, the map of Macedonia. We said hello goodbye very pleasantly and I considered that if he hadn't had a continual need to fuck all over town we might've moved in together and had a normal relationship, if there is such a thing. He liked having someone at home, waiting for him. I never could wait for people. Victor says, he came back from abroad and his roommate found him the next morning bleeding from the mouth.

Maybe it's because we didn't love each other that we broke off without any rancor, without even really breaking off. We met every three or four nights in the corner bar, the one near my house where I still sometimes drink with Victor. Paul and I never made dates or anything, and some nights we saw each other there but went home with other people, if Paul didn't feel like doing it with me he would say: Let's get together real soon.

How long has he been sick.

We stopped sleeping together when people still referred to "gay cancer" and thought it came from using poppers. For a long time I moved back and forth from Europe, each time I returned the thing had become more of a subject, I heard of this one that one getting pneumonia and fading out. Paul said once: It's getting scary, it's getting close. He'd met Jason years ago and they had made it once in a while, Paul told me, when it wasn't you it usually was him, and then he and Jason moved into a place on Cornelia Street, signing a joint lease, which was practically marriage.

They've had him in the hospital for two weeks.

At first the people who died were people I barely knew, or people from earlier lives who'd been in a lot of the same rooms, their deaths were disconcerting but seemed to happen on a distant planet. At first people would say: Well, he must have been leading a secret life, taking all kinds of drugs and going to the Mineshaft. Because at first, most people who got ill did seem the same ones who never finished an evening at four A. M., piled into taxis together when the regular bars closed. And then of course there was this other thing with needles, if it spread by blood and sperm, people who used needles would naturally get it.

The worst thing is, I can't feel anything for Paul. I'm too scared for myself.

But you'll go see him, I hope.

Of course I will.

Except that I am, in this particular business, a bigger coward than I'd like to be. Victor and I used to drink with Perkins when Perkins turned up in the bar, and when Perkins got ill, I didn't go to the hospital, he had one bout of pneumonia and the now-familiar remission, and Chas, who lives in a building behind my building, called raising money to get Perkins a color TV, since he had to stay in all the time, and I never gave any, I promised to, in the early autumn, and one mild afternoon I saw Perkins at Astor Place, looking all of his fifty-four years which he never had previously, he said, Call me sometime, and the next I heard it went into his brain and they brought him into St. Vincent's raving, Victor went four or five times, I said, My God, Victor, what do you say?

The thing is, Victor said, when he feels all right he doesn't feel as if he's dying, the worst thing is acting morbid and stricken about it. You just go have a normal conversation with him. But it's too late now because he isn't lucid for more than a few minutes during any given visit. At first he's his old self and then he babbles.

I never thought I'd be so chickenshit about anything.

But this new situation, with Paul, what does it mean? And with Gregory? Another thing about Perkins: he had, for a time, a comely Irish lover named Mike, a slender boy with soft brown eyes and a small wisp of a mustache, they were together for a while and then they weren't. Mike fucked everything that walked, one night we found ourselves using the toilet in Nightbirds when it was still an after-hours joint and I let him piss in my mouth, then we screwed at my place the whole next day in every conceivable position. He called a few days later and warned me his doctor thought he had hepatitis B, as it happened I'd just had a typhoid shot for my visa to Thailand and got a bad reaction, my pee turned red, then it passed on and Mike phoned just before I left to say his results turned out negative.

Mike moved to California and then Hawaii for several months and when he came back he lived with Perkins again but soon after that he started looking spectral and then stopped going out and then everyone heard that he had it and a few months later everyone heard that he died. That was four years before Perkins came down with it and when Perkins came down with it he told everyone he was sure he got it from Mike, though how Perkins could be sure, since Perkins took it up the can as often as possible from anyone available, was a mystery. Yet he insisted that Mike had been the source.

Until now Mike has been the only person I know I've slept with who later died from it and I used to think that because I recovered from the typhoid shot, which I got after I slept with him, that meant I hadn't caught it from him, and I also rationalized that maybe Mike caught it in California or Hawaii and then gave it to Perkins when he moved back to New York, in which case Perkins' incubation period may have only been a year or two, or rather four years, I keep getting dates mixed up, I went to Thailand in '81 and I think I'd already stopped sleeping with Paul, so if I didn't get it from Mike possibly I didn't get it from Paul either. But with Mike I could only have been exposed once, and some people think repeated exposure is necessary for the virus to take hold, so if it had only been Mike I could now feel fairly confident though how can anyone who ever did anything with anybody feel at all confident, and with Paul, of course, the case is quite different, his dong has been in every hole in my body hundreds of times squirting away like the Trevi Fountain, I've rimmed him too, and once when he cut his finger chopping up some terrible cocaine he bought in the Spike I even sucked his blood.

Now, of course, everyone's conscious about the problem, but as somebody said in the paper the horses are out of the barn, how can you possibly know if, back in the days of sexual pot luck, someone you met by chance and screwed and never saw again wasn't a carrier? Not that I've had so many in the last few years, but they don't really know if numbers are important, even if I don't have it I probably have the antibodies and if I have the antibodies I'm probably a carrier. So if I do it with Gregory I risk infecting him. And then, I don't know about Gregory, either. He says he hasn't taken heroin in five years, but junkies who do manage to kick usually fuck up several times before they get off it, maybe five years isn't so precise either, in addition to that Gregory looks like a magazine cover and I can't imagine he hasn't satisfied all his sexual appetites regularly, in fact he's alluded to dark periods of the past, hinted that when he used heroin he did some hustling here and there, he's so well-spoken and smart it's hard to imagine him peddling his dick on the sidewalk but who knows what people will do. Anyway, I threw myself at him in less than a second after seeing that face and I'm shy, there must have been hundreds of opportunities. Thousands.

Victor says he'll go with me to see Paul.

I realize that I really am in love with Gregory.

These have to be peculiar times.

It wouldn't be strange to get it and then to decide as Perkins did that this one particular person gave it to you, one out of ten or fifty or a hundred, maybe because that person made you feel something special, had done wonderful things in bed or gotten you to trust him physically and mentally as no one else ever had. Mike for example had miraculous talents because his sexual demands were flagrant and overpowering, he was socially rather genteel but I remember in the bathroom at Nightbirds and later too he talked dirty and tough, Kneel down, bitch, suck that dick, he actually said things like, Yeah, you want that big dick, sure, you wanna get fucked with that big prick, and of course the pissing, which had introduced itself as a specially filthy surprise, but the way he insisted on it made it seem like an ordinary thing people really ought to do. Mike was an incredibly complete fuck, he exhausted your imagination and wiped out your memory of other fucks, when Perkins remembered making love perhaps he only thought of Mike and things Mike did to him. You would naturally connect your most vivid memory of pleasure to infection and death because the others weren't remotely worth getting sick from, just pale skimpy traces of sex crossed with thin trickles of "bodily fluids," if the two things had to be linked, better for a cherished memory of sex to connect with transmission of the microbe.

In any case, if you had sex now it was a matter of deciding, even if you took elaborate precautions, whether the degree of risk involved (and who could calculate that?) was "worth it," whether your need for that kind of experience with another person outweighed, in a sense, your desire for survival.

When I think about Perkins in that fifth-floor walk-up watching the color TV his friends gave him, I imagine him measuring out his life in half-hour segments, telling time by the flow of images and the chatter of voices, his thoughts melting into the TV. As he wasted away the set continued entertaining him, keeping his mind off things. It showed him funny pictures that weren't really funny and brought him news of catastrophes that were somehow beside the point. The TV made his death feel vicarious and filled his bedroom with another world he could enter when this one ran its course. A quilt covered the bed, the same bed he'd slept in with Mike, the room was big and chilly with a thin musty carpet covering the wood floor, brown velour drapes hiding the arched windows. His bedside lamp had a pink shade, the square table near his pillows had pill bottles and a water glass on it, he didn't feel as though he were dying, Victor said, he just knew, intellectually, that his death was coming sooner rather than later. Sooner than expected. But does anybody expect to die? Even when one is quite old, it must seem a fantastic event, if you're ninety you can still imagine living, say, till ninety-five.

M. is lying in the darkness of his own bedroom, a plywood cubicle within his vast loft, near the southern tip of the island. He's talking into his cordless telephone, which gives local calls the scratchy echo of long distance.

We live in large and small boxes in buildings on regularly shaped streets. We see each other seldom because we are busy. Nothing happens to us except dinner parties and visits to the dentist and work, our lives have the generic flavor of deferred pleasure and sublimation until we fall in love or die.

M. is thirty-six, rich, successful. He's a closer friend to me than Victor but I haven't been in his apartment in years. When you're busy you use the telephone.

Contamination, he says, through the telephone crackle.

Like water, I tell him.

Water, blood, sputum, spit, urine, semen, any kind of fluid. It's all in the food chain, M. declares. You have to imagine particles, like from Chernobyl, settling into the water table like—like little dissolving snowflakes. They sink into the ground when it rains, go into the water, everybody drinks it. Some people get a little bit, some people get a lot. Or maybe it gets eaten by a cow or a pig, it grows into grass and some *swines* store it up in their tissues, and then you pop into the local deli for a ham sandwich with a little mustard, on some nice rye bread, presto you've got AIDS.

And what if I die, right away instead of later on, if for instance I take the blood test, it's positive, I'll never finish anything important, I won't leave anything behind. Or just a few things, of no historical interest. On the immortality front I will fail, ashes to ashes, and no health insurance either, I'll become a ward of the city and be put in one of those wards where the doctors and nurses shun you for fear of catching it, and none of your friends comes to the hospital. Libby would come, M. would come, Victor would come, my friend Jane would definitely come, but how would I die, what would I be like, and how lugubrious for them, if it's a big ward there's bound to be others dying in the same room, dying with the television on, perhaps they make them wear headphones but when the ward got deathly quiet at night I'd hear the little bug noises in their earpieces. Is that the point, to leave something behind, it's really a silly ambition, if you're dead what difference does it make. Of course they say it's why people have children, they can remember you for a time, though mainly they remember pain, pain from their terrible childhoods, even if their parents loved them, it's usually so twisted it's as bad as hate, and even when it isn't, the other children torture you and make fun of all your little quirks and debilities, you try to escape into fantasies but those are poisoned from the very outset, while you're still in first grade they've already turned you into a monster, you spend your whole adult life trying to wipe out all the things they've taught you to do, trying not to hate yourself.

I never talk about my childhood because I only remember pain. And then I keep meeting people like Gregory who think they're as they are because of the father or because of the mother, he seems so clear about it, my father did this to me and my mother did that, therefore I am. I don't know what either of my parents did. My mother says she regrets slapping me too often and I can't remember ever being slapped. Maybe she remembers wrong. When you go into psychotherapy they teach you to invent false memories of childhood beatings and sexual abuse, people become addicted to these simple explanations of why they're monsters.

And now everyone is going to die before they figure anything out, I'm going to die before I can be truly loved, I'll die with every sort of bitter memory of my last lover's coldness and Paul's faithlessness, though really that didn't matter with him, I'm not bitter against him, but why couldn't I have what I had with him with someone who loved me, and I'll die before I can make Gregory love me, I can see I'm fated to cash it in without a single memory of real happiness. What is real happiness. Is it this business of living with another person, I never really lived with anybody, I thought no one could stand it. You think you'll have a long life, so you do everything at a snail's pace, before I tried to write *Burma* I started a book about a family, one sister was a socialite, another was crippled in a wheelchair, the brother was a fag actor in Off-Broadway, the parents had been murdered in their townhouse, I only wrote two scenes of that book, the sister in bed with her boyfriend and the brother getting drunk on the set of a soap opera, not bad, oh yes and one scene with the sister racing through the townhouse in her wheelchair, she'd had special ramps built so she could get around. Before that I tried something like a love story based on me and that California surfer type I fucked a few times when I lived in Boston, a shoplifter. Nobody shoplifts any more, I remember when everyone did it, it showed your contempt for the capitalist system. Everyone worships capitalism today. Look at this obscene medical system. If Paul doesn't have insurance he's probably in a room full of other people's contagion, they say the patients with AIDS go into Sloan-Kettering perfectly healthy and pick up diseases in the waiting room, it's how Michael got pneumonia, I almost forgot about Michael, his apartment windows used to be right there, the windows still are there but he's dead.

Maybe I'm dying anyway, faster than others because I smoke so many cigarettes. I try and try quitting and nothing works. I can lay awake at night telling myself, You will not smoke a cigarette tomorrow, your body doesn't want you to smoke, when you go to the hypnotist he makes you close your eyes and tells you your brain is going down a steep flight of steps, that you're on an elevator going down, deep down into the hypnotic state, it sounds like a car salesman, and when you emerge from hypnosis, he says, You will have no desire for a cigarette, all cravings for a cigarette will have left your body, and whenever you feel a temporary urge for a cigarette you will tell yourself "I need my body to live. " The impulse only lasts for ninety seconds, he says, after ninety seconds you will no longer crave a cigarette. I ought to go back because I did stop for six hours, thinking the whole time, I'm a nonsmoker now, since telling myself I'm a nonsmoker now was one of the hypnotic suggestions, and even while I smoked the first ten cigarettes the same night, I still thought: I'm a nonsmoker now.

They say if you're infected and have the antibodies you might not come down with the fatal syndrome, therefore you should build up your immune system, which I'm tearing down with cigarettes and alcohol, sometimes I drink nothing for weeks and then for reasons I've never figured out I'll get drunk at a party and then drunk again the following night, sometimes for as many as six or seven nights running, then stop again, though I never stop smoking, I wake up wanting a cigarette, it's crazy, but then again, Perkins went into AA two full years before getting ill, he stopped smoking at the same time, he began looking wonderful, his skin all clear, the bags around his eyes vanished, he'd always been youthful anyway but then he became spectacular again, young again, and immediately got sick. And Michael the same story exactly: he gave up drugs and alcohol and cigarettes, toned himself up at the gym, etherealized himself like some ideal sexual object, but without screwing around because even then he was frightened of catching it, and perhaps a year passed before Michael's glands mysteriously swelled up, he woke one day in a high fever, they treated him at St. Vincent's for pneumonia, he recovered, then I saw him out and around, he said he felt normal and the only difference was you suddenly know that anything can kill you. I despised Michael but near the end he wrote a hilarious story about assholes, assholes taking over the world, assholes that turn into mouths that breathe and talk and kiss, it wasn't original with him but so what, he laughed right to the grave about the whole thing, which I can't help respecting, really, he died his own particular death without any pietistic nonsense or feelings of solidarity with anything, least of all the social contract, he'd had a good time while he was here, lots of laughs, plenty of weird scenes, his one full-length film which somebody somewhere has, Michael didn't want much in life besides kicks, I don't think death found him with a lot of plans pending for the future. Whereas Paul, this can't possibly feel natural to him, something further, quite a few things further were supposed to happen, he's always gotten acting work, always a play, a movie, something, never a starring part but it would've happened eventually, Michael had had plans once upon a time, but then his wife went through the windshield on the Ventura Freeway, after that Michael wanted a good time and eons of forgetfulness, but at the very least, he must have wanted to live. Life doesn't care about what anybody wants.

I see Gregory again, for five minutes, on his way into work. I'm walking along lower Broadway, deciding about shoes.

I've got to see you real soon, he tells me. I really want you to see my work.

When he speaks I fall into a terrified ecstasy. I'm losing my will to this man, who embraces me on the corner of Prince and Broadway and purrs: But mainly, I want us to become very close. I feel as if we are already. I've been walking along here thinking it might be the route he will take to the restaurant today. I'm not saying anything about Paul, though I want to tell Gregory everything I'm feeling and thinking. Not yet. If ever.

He has a beautiful smell, a faint nicotine funk mixed with some essential oil, opopanax or civet, in his fur-flapped hat he looks like an expensively bred animal, the thick nose a sexual warning, a carnal threat. And he looks as if he might dart away from me, slip out of my grip, jump to someone else like a fickle cat. He's interested in everything that doesn't interest me when I'm with him, little events in the street, what other people wear, how other people look, window displays, marquees, he dates everything, clocks everything, he's obsessed with defining this minute, this period, this era, he savors details and tiny nuances, he knows about what's on television and all the new movies and every song that's played on the radio, his fixation with the inessential, the passing moment, also makes me feel he'll slink off to someone else, almost unconsciously, to whatever offers him momentary pleasure without obligations. I pretend an interest in his interests, wanting to seem modern and up-to-date, and in fact all this junk he likes bores me silly. But I try seeing it through his eyes, I begin learning what something will look like to Gregory. Magazine pictures start falling apart when I study them, break down into sex messages, sales points, prescriptions of what people are supposed to be in this time, this place. He has more energy, more appetite than I do. As if the world were still offering him unlimited possibilities, endless options. As if he'd been born yesterday and still had a whole lifetime to make choices. His face lights up like a child's when he sees, for example, a stunningly well-dressed Puerto Rican girl.

I need him and I need money. The editor who hired me at the magazine offers an advance of $400, which I take. We've been friends for a long while before this, long enough for him to say: Just imagine, this time you know you can pay me back.

I call Gregory at home, on a day he doesn't work: Let me take you out to dinner. His voice is withdrawn, not exactly irritated but not expansively friendly, as it's always been. I'm dead, he tells me. I need to be alone, I'm so fucking wired from working. I didn't mean to bother you, I say, coolly, and he says: Please don't be like that, don't get an attitude just because I'm exhausted.

His voice sounds like it's wrapped in flannel, but it suddenly turns genial and clear. I really can't see you tonight, he says, then he tells me stories of the job, what happened last night, which customers insulted him, Philippe's latest outrages, all with eager irony, as if to say: Look how well I put up with such insanity.

We talk for an hour, about everything and nothing. Something keeps getting shunted aside. He throws himself into amusing me as if this will compensate for not seeing me. I wonder if he's seeing someone else. He reads my thoughts. If I could be with anybody right now, he says, I'd be with you. Try to understand, I always need a day or two completely alone, just to stop my nerves jumping all over my skin.

I don't dare say: I could help you. After all, Gloria thought she could calm him down by opening her body to him, and she was obviously wrong. I don't want to blow it with him. But why has it always got to be me who's worried about blowing it. Days and days go by without seeing him, I know he's thinking about me but he doesn't want to come closer. Maybe there's something about me he's afraid of.

I wake up with tears running down my face but I can't tell if I'm crying. Nerves. Plastic coating on the parts that feel.

They say the outer surface of the virus mutates rapidly from one host organism to another. It's difficult to fix a clinical picture of the virus. You can kill it, said a health worker, with ordinary ammonia.

Who was the disinherited nephew, Libby asked, who swallowed the bleach?

What have I learned? He smokes a lot of grass. He watches Friday night videos without fail, alone, and he's stood me up three times in two weeks. We make a lunch date and he does show up, forty-five minutes late, somehow smoothly talking me out of my irritation by saying he's intimidated by me, that I'm a celebrity and he feels like nothing in comparison, a fucking lousy waiter in a sleaze bag restaurant, he's afraid I'll find his afraid I'll find him boring, or stupid, if he stands me up, he says, it's because he's terrified, the job makes him so depressed he's sure he'll alienate me by complaining about it, he wants so much to give me the best of himself he only wants to see me when he's feeling good about his life.

This is already more than I know how to deal with. I tell him it doesn't bother me if he's depressed and wants to complain and that listening to problems is a normal part of a friendship. I say that my so-called celebrity means nothing to me and isn't as enormous as he imagines, and even if it was it wouldn't have anything to do with how I feel about him. I explain that I know he's "more than a waiter," that I don't think of him as "a waiter," but even if all he wanted to be in life was a waiter, even if that was all he did, I'd love him the same way. He says this is unfair because he wants me to love him for who he really is and he doesn't think of himself as a waiter, he's repulsed by having to be a waiter, and if I think I could love him if that's all he was, then I obviously only love him for his looks because that's all being a waiter requires, his looks. I say that I don't define people according to what they do for a living. He says that really clever people don't waste their lives doing menial work. I tell him there are lots of kinds of cleverness and I don't particularly respect the kind that devotes itself to making money, that it seems to me it takes as much brains to be a good waiter as it does to do anything else. He says I've obviously never been a waiter. I tell him that's true, but I've been a gas station attendant and a busboy in a cafeteria and an office clerk and I've also sold popcorn in a movie theater, I know what menial work is like, I know it's exhausting but I think his reaction to it is a little bit extreme. Everybody who doesn't come into the world with a trust fund, I tell him, finds they've got to do stuff like that for a few years. It's nothing shameful or unendurable. You just get through it however you can.

You don't understand, he says. He then describes a sensation of vertigo, of falling into a bottomless black pit, of knocking off his four-day shift every week and immediately becoming hyper-sensitive to noise, to touch, to voices. In this vulnerable state he goes into, the touch of someone's hand feels like a razor ripping through his skin, or an electrical shock. I know, he says, that part of this has something to do with Gloria as well as the job. I can't stand being grabbed ahold of. I don't think I can have anything to do with anybody physically for a while.

I decide to be brave and tell him that if he isn't physically attracted to me, he should tell me. He says if he told me that I wouldn't want to have anything further to do with him. I say I'd probably feel bad about it but I'd still want to know him, but even if I decided not to, he'd have to take the risk. He says he can't risk losing me because he wants to be part of my life. I say I want him to be part of my life but I also want him physically and if he doesn't want me physically I want us both to be clear about it. He says it isn't that he isn't attracted to me, but his present mental state makes it impossible to feel anything sexual about anybody and I have to understand this and if I refuse to understand it I'm just being horribly unfair and cruel to him.

We leave each other in the street. Walking home I realize he's made me feel like some elderly lecher. I remind myself that I'm only thirty-five and look pretty good for my age. I hate his guts, I tell myself; he's a manipulative little creep. Three weeks ago he was fucking Gloria every night and suddenly he's frigid, it's some twisted sort of power trip. What does he want from me. Ego gratification, no doubt. He wants me to desire him. He enjoys feeling worshipped. I ought to drop him right now, put him out of my mind before it's too late. I can see where this will lead, more misery. He knows I've fallen in love with him and I could be useful to him somehow, he keeps harping on what a big celebrity I am, which I'm not, maybe he wants to meet famous people and attach himself to someone with money. I think he mentioned he once let some rich guy take him to Egypt, some old queen I believe he said, back in his hustler days. Obviously I'm not in any position to help him financially so maybe he thinks I'm a stepping-stone to bigger opportunities. If he strings me along . . .

He said Gloria went from being great gash to a pain in the ass in no time flat, that "great gash" business really bothered me. He thought she was a convenient hole for when he wanted it. And when she wanted it he thought she was predatory. Now he says he can't stand being touched but he touches me whenever he pleases.

Maybe he's sick, though, anemic or something, and when he works these long shifts he really does get abnormally drained of energy, it could even be mononucleosis or leukemia, today he looked quite pale, even a little cheesy, gorgeous as ever but his forehead was sweaty. He didn't actually say he wasn't attracted to me but he obviously isn't, he simply doesn't want to say it, he thinks it'll hurt me, but really it wouldn't hurt to know it now, while I can still get him out of my life without going nuts, because I'm getting a little crazy, I can feel Gregory talking over larger and larger areas of my mind, I think about him incessantly, lately I need to know or at least feel like I know exactly where he is and what he's doing every minute of the day, if he's not with somebody now I'm scared he'll meet somebody he wants to sleep with, but how do I know he's not already fucking five different people, ten for that matter, if he doesn't want me to know there's no way I'd find out without actually spying on him, which would be truly crazy.

He might even be right, I'm making all kinds of unfair assumptions, for instance, because he attracts me sexually I assume everyone else is after him, and further assume that because he's beautiful he also has a raging sex drive, that if he found me attractive he'd automatically want to sleep with me right away, and because he hasn't, he's not attracted to me. So I'm reducing him to a sex object when he may very well be this highly sensitive, caring person with leukemia or mono or a severe vitamin deficiency. After all, he says he wants me to love him, so he wants me to be attracted to him. But then again, knowing I want him physically, he should give me what I want or leave me alone, if he does care about me, because I don't want just a friendship. It's too frustrating that way. This feels like a movie I've seen before.

4

A big furry black and white malamute races across the arctic snow, breaking the gelid crust with his fat paws, heaving sprays of soft flakes as his chest barrels up and down, like a dolphin stitching through breakers. A helicopter slices the air overhead, firing blasts from a rocket gun. The pooch tears along with his mouth hanging open in a doggy smile, tongue lolling out comically, as scientists on the ground call to him. The helicopter crashes and explodes. Charred bodies tumble from the wreckage, making long steaming holes in the snow. The scientists lead the dog to a kennel, where the other dogs instantly start howling, petrified. When the humans leave, a strange look colors the dog's whitish-blue eyes. His jaws open impossibly wide, tearing apart his head, revealing a stumpy magma of bloody tissue and dripping bluish viscera that wiggles arterial tendrils in the direction of the other canines. A monster inside a puppy.

Gregory says he's had a tiring afternoon with his models. First they went to Los Angeles, then flew to Montego Bay for a shoot. They're so featherbrained, he says in his "bright teenager" voice. So vain. Forever arguing over makeup and which is their best angle. I know he means the magazine models he clips out and pastes on cardboard backing, but he maintains this fantasy for so long, with such adorable earnestness, that it sounds like the story of a life he should have had. Gregory enters his fictions with awesome concentration. I'd like to segue back to reality, though the suspension of time and the zero gravity of these playful longueurs seduce me. I have nothing clever to contribute. When he offers the names he's given the models, I try to play, referring to them familiarly. But Gregory contradicts whatever I say, changing the game. "Dave isn't like that *at all*," he declares. Or, when I hint that Bobby is difficult, Gregory protests that he *adores* working with Bobby.

He can linger in flight for hours, spinning out a movie script world where no rough edges obtrude. He calls nearly every morning now, after his shower and coffee. I picture his apartment in my mind, picture him in his apartment, drying off with a Cannon bath towel, brushing his vigilantly serviced teeth, dressing himself with a pedantic sense of street language. One morning when I miss his call, he leaves an obnoxiously long message on my machine, plaintively wonders where I could be at ten in the morning, describes the wonders of personal hygiene he's performed while trying to reach me: an inventory that conjures a vivid underground film of his naked body, complete with toenail clippings, Q-tipped earwax, snips of pinkened dental floss.

A second message follows the first: I've had my coffee now, I'm cutting up some magazines, pretty soon I have to leave, *where are you?* The days begin with candied daydreams. Gregory invites me to China, all expenses paid, ticking off possible itineraries. Or wails about the technical gaffes committed by his brace of assistants.

I haven't visited his place, and he's never been here. I would prefer meeting him in the flesh, since our phone calls mainly transpire in his imaginary interzone. The dialogue barely touches ground, floating instead through Gregory's dream castles. He talks about how life will be "after my first show," admits that he expects his work to be "popular," perhaps unavoidably so, for the wrong reasons, since it "deals with the body," though his work, he says, is really a critique of "sexual images," it also displays these images, it might easily appeal to people "on an uncritical level," he worries about that. In any event, he says, suddenly hypothesizing public indifference, I'm not interested in becoming rich and famous, all I want is enough money to go on making work, I'd be completely satisfied with that. Once he's free, once he never has to see Philippe's stupid face and its protruding lower lip, never has to serve another malodorous *plat du jour*, never has to interrupt his projects or enslave himself to keep food in his stomach, Gregory will feel contented. After I've established myself he tells me, we can really be good for each other. Not that we aren't now. But I know my moods exasperate you, the trouble is I can't control them as long as I'm this indentured servant working my butt off

Hours crumble away. We could have taken a walk together. It's a bright day, with false traces of spring softening the air. The buildings in the window are mottled from the snow that's melted off the rooftops. If I came out to see you, it would eat a big chunk of the day, he says. I'd have to dress and then come back here and get ready for work. You could just dress for work, I suggest, but he says No, I couldn't, I'd have to carry a bag full of work clothes and they'd get all wrinkled. And I like being in my place just before I leave.

When I think we're finished talking he opens a new conversation, something about Georges Bataille: have I read *Blue of Noon*? Oh, of course, I tell him, I read it when I was sixteen, before it was translated. This slips out needlessly, casting me as the pedantic older role model, the "admired" one. There is the danger, when Gregory strays from the movies and pop singers he consumes, mentioning a book, that my years of incessant reading and dormant intellectual snobbery will poke forward with spines attached, that I'll become overbearingly cerebral, detached, argumentative in a way that stings his ego, underscores our age difference, and reminds him unpleasantly of his long history of wasted time and his aimless druggy past. He's told me he feels unequal, that he needs to catch up lost time. I've wasted twenty-seven years, he says, while you've made a name for yourself you've gotten things done, you're in the public eye. I've let my talents stagnate. Now, he says, he can't afford wasting any time at all, that's why this work of his is so crucial, it will make up for his nervous breakdowns and his horrific family background, the heroin, the hustling, the ugly behavior which he still feels paralyzed by guilt about, and of course, even now, after five years, there are times when Gregory must cross the street, avoiding people he treated wretchedly or ripped off when he was a junkie, quite a few people actually, though he also experiences a rush of inner pride when he encounters some of the scum buckets he used to hang around with, when he sees them playing the same old sordid games they ran on him years ago, because now he's having none of it, he's clean, he can look them straight in the eye without any embarrassment. It's just that certain things he did will never be forgiven by the people he did them to, it's sad, he says, it's actually tragic, but there it is, when he catches sight of those people the only thing Gregory can do is make himself scarce.

Gregory says: I should've known you've read *Blue of Noon*, you've read everything. Then he says: That's what I want to be, a person who's read all the books. One of the smart boys. Like you and Bruno.

On certain days these phone calls last half the afternoon. I never find the will to say I've got work to do. It's always Gregory who suddenly decides he's got to press a shirt, mail a letter, run out for groceries or art supplies. The conversation tapers down to a flutter of gentle noises. We're like two fragile little birds preening each other's wings. He longs to see me as soon as he can. He'll call

me tonight if the restaurant's slow. He buffers his goodbyes, as if
assuaging my unreasonable need to keep him on the telephone.
It's true, his voice has become a hypnotic drug, a bed of caressing
hands. I'd stay on the phone with him around the clock. When he
hangs up I feel vacant and useless.

And yet, I remind myself and yet. I "have a life," a role to play.
The way I've arranged my life strikes me as extremely dangerous.
Instead of having a job and someone who tells me what to do,
I've got to make everything up on my own and tell myself what
to do. Even though I've never got any money, the money I need
always comes to me. I sell an idea, Or a piece of writing, or else I
borrow money from M., mainly M., though I owe huge sums of
money to twenty other people, somehow everything gets paid, I
manage to eat and also to buy books. Any extra money goes for
books, despite the fact that there is almost never even the slightest
amount of extra money, I somehow always save enough for a book
or two. I don't even really need money, since I never buy anything
except books. I haven't, for example, bought clothes in ten years.
All my clothes were given to me by friends who tired of wearing
them. People undoubtedly imagine that I spend lots on clothes
because I have expensive things, when the fact is, I have never,
in ten years, purchased a single article of clothing besides socks
and underwear. Nor have I frittered away money on furniture.
The furniture in this apartment, which scarcely can be called furniture, all came from various acquaintances who moved away or
grew tired of the furniture they had, now I have it, I've never given
a single thought to furniture, or to clothes, or for that matter to
anything else associated with the home, with the home environment. The objects and appliances associated with the home environment, which occupy and even obsess other people, have never

exercised the slightest fascination for me, and in fact, I have always found other people's mania for cluttering the home environment with objects and appliances grotesque. This mania, which I have observed in many of my closest friends, amounts to a psychosis, as far as I am concerned. When people begin talking about their latest acquisitions, their tables and lamps and stoves and sinks and whatever else they've managed to fill their homes with, I immediately think, Now the psychosis comes out, the buying mania, the replacement mania, the remodeling mania. A person may seem intelligent and reasonable, full of interesting observations about life, show an unusual understanding of human psychology, human foibles. A person may seem refreshingly sympathetic, strong-minded, subtle, well-informed, and then, without any warning, he's chattering on like a maniac, describing his home and everything in it. My couch, he tells you, I've had my couch done in vermilion leather. And next it's my chair, my table, my lamp, my desk, my stereo, my television, my carpet, my refrigerator, my microwave oven, I'm replacing my this with my that, and of course this passion for inanimate objects extends to the world of art and culture as well, people yearn to own all the products of the inner life, as if the inner life were comparable in value to their chairs and sofas and dining room tables.

We can only expect this degenerate mania for possessions in a culture where everything and everyone is for sale, a malignant disease of a culture like ours can only acknowledge the existence of the inner life if it too is for sale. By the same token, in such a malignant disease of a culture, only an inner life which is for sale has the slightest chance of survival, since those who keep their inner lives locked away and bolted up against the depredations of the public marketplace soon find their inner lives overwhelmed and colonized by the inanity of this culture. This culture cannot rest, until every inner fife that is not for sale has been consumed by the inanity and violence around it, while the inner lives which are offered to the cultural marketplace become part and parcel of this inanity and violence. Everything we do, every effort we make to express our disgust at this situation becomes an integral part of this situation, all our pacific intentions and reasonable acts are transformed by our vicious culture into more inanity and more violence.

Therefore, I considered, the so-called freedom I enjoy, in contrast to Gregory's servitude in his menial job, his status as a wage slave, only makes me more aware of the impossibility of any freedom, since everything I do contributes to everything that oppresses me and everything that oppresses him. Furthermore, it's dangerous because, being somewhat more free than he is, I'm more liable to waste time, especially since I dread my own work, knowing perfectly well that anything I do simply adds to the general ruin, *despite my intention to do otherwise.* If I write and publish my writing, I end up selling out my inner life in order to remain alive, everything that lives within me becomes something for sale, therefore the more I write the less existence I have, consequently my freedom diminishes the more I produce and expands if I write less, the less I write the freer I become, but in order to remain free it's necessary to sell my writing, and so, the less free I am, the freer I appear to be.

Naturally I could not sustain these thoughts for very long. Such thoughts lead only to despair, the type of despair I've heard so often in Gregory's voice. He's drowning in self-pity, I thought, letting every minuscule irritation destroy him. He spends half his time in despair, the other half in a fantasy world. What am I to him, I wondered. What is he to me, and what am I to him? He resents it when I tell him he's attractive, and I resent it when he praises my intelligence. He hates the beauty of his own face, he says his father's looks brought him everything without any

effort, until he started losing them, and then he took up gambling, dropped all the family money at the races, later on in poker
games, blackjack, ultimately craps. Gregory's father never stuck
at anything because his face could charm the skin off a snake.
The other day Gregory told me his friends used to call him the
cutest boy in the East Village, evidently he's worried about losing
his charms the same way his father did. I want him to like how
I look, he never says anything about it. He can't see me over the
telephone, in any case.

I rolled these conversations around while trying to think my
way to some activity. I found it impossible to recall much of what
Gregory said. His voice carried the cloudy atmosphere of a steam
bath. It had a playful tone and a somber tone, a tone of distance
and a tone of intimacy, it ranged freely back and forth, giving
out or drawing back, marking boundaries or rubbing them away.
But what is happening here, I wondered. If Gregory is depressed,
I enter his depression. When he's in a good mood, I'm elated. I
shouldn't feel what he feels. His life isn't my life. I have as many
problems as he does, furthermore I'm seven years older, I haven't
the time to waste that he does. He's selfish about time, whereas
I'm wastefully generous. I have more to do, yet he's the one stingy
about meeting, or giving himself. Perhaps I'm crazy and doomed,
after all my efforts in the opposite direction. I'll ruin myself over
him, and he'll get anything he wants handed over by a bunch of
fools like me.

Crowded blocks of retail markets and one-room shops, then a passage of high, cross-shaped public housing flats. Snow shrinking in
grimy pyramids between the parking meters, stubbled ice pools
glistening with livid opacity in the roadbed. Sunlight catches
every harsh angle of the street, streaks across car chrome, explodes

against store windows. Time has stopped, or paused, to frame a sore picture of things, on one of those frozen afternoons that sits dead in a person's vision like a jade lizard squatting on a plastic leaf. The occasional tree has been flogged bare by blasts of wind and stands rotting in its square of incongruous earth.

The side avenues end at a wide boulevard that is crossed by flat concrete islands dotted with high metal stalks with glazed lights curled over at their tips. A gas station in the center of its own tar arcade sports an immense crimson "M," broken at a slant for design allure. Behind it a cyclone fence barricades more stripped trees and a row of vacant tenements, row after row of shattered windows like broken teeth in a swollen mouth.

Gregory looks different today. His body seems more organized than before, small and sinewy and animated by controlled, tottery movements, like the body of a life-size puppet. Tight gray and black jeans, thick black ankle boots, a voluminous black sweater and a thin denim jacket. He moves determinedly, on his way to an exam he knows all the answers to. He likes these squalid streets, they're "his," he's used to them and they're used to him. I haven't walked over here for much of anything in years, too many shitty memories, though it isn't far from my house. One of the shabbier zones of the Lower East Side: bodegas with yellow and red plastic awnings, a Nedick's, over there a wan-looking tar playground with a basketball hoop and some smashed-up orange swings. Across the street, a boarded-up synagogue. On Gregory's corner, there's a cocktail lounge with a sloped pink roof and jalousie windows, shaped like a roadhouse in an upstate village. We walk past it to the fifth house on the block, past a maroon monolith that used to be a day-care center, past a gap in the block full of uncut gravestones, past a monument showroom—Gregory lives in the monument district—to a place with a short, scarred stoop, double black doors with rectangles of iron mesh bolted over grimy inset glass, the wood splintered and gouged around the lock. Like the other buildings, this one has a fire escape jutting down its face, an architectural scar that jumps out at me as Gregory points to the buildings across the street, waving at the nearest: That's where Bruno lives. Bruno doesn't care for this area, Gregory says, insinuatingly. He can't believe I go exploring down these ratty side streets, Bruno hates all this poverty and ethnic clutter, but I'm really moved by it. I like checking out all these tiny shops, listening to ordinary people talk. Bruno's so out of touch with real people, he just stays in that constricted world of art and artists and never comes in contact with anything real. When you watch and listen to the people down here, Gregory says, you realize each one of them has a life, full of particular things.

Gregory pushed open the door and walked into the hall. He peered into the mailbox grille. The stairwell had dim fluorescent circles coloring up the sickly green walls and the warped, rotted stairs. I followed him up while he talked, perhaps about the neighbors or the drunken super or the landlord, or he may not have spoken at all, possibly we climbed the stairs in the crackling silence that often swallowed us. Silence like: We're normal together, everything's normal. I'm in your mind, you're in my mind. Silence like: Now we're content and steady. This is how it's supposed to feel, being together. Ordinary silence, which is to say: a silence that can change character when one or the other does something unexpected, gets an abstracted look in his eye or stands a certain way, fails somehow to follow the unknown laws of this particular silence. With Gregory this happened easily, a content or approving silence changed into a doleful or an angry silence, and I would find myself outside the charmed circle of Gregory's approval, Gregory's interests, becoming a chunk of petrified rock obstructing Gregory's path. When Gregory had had enough of somebody, he had none of the usual gift for concealing the fact.

He might say in one breath that I was the most important person in his life, and a moment later behave as if I were an importunate, vague acquaintance from whom he tore himself away with a gelid apology. It could happen in the course of a phone call, a dinner, a walk through the neighborhood.

A few days earlier I had gone to visit Bruno at his gallery. We not only knew each other but had been flirtatious from time to time, in a desultory way. I had considered Bruno the best possible choice for a boyfriend until meeting Gregory. For a time, even after meeting Gregory, I continued flirting with Bruno, in hopes that if Gregory proved as refractory as he seemed, Bruno would fill the void. And then, naturally, I discovered that Bruno too was infatuated with Gregory, though he had drawn back from his infatuation, found another boyfriend, and now kept Gregory at arm's length, emotionally speaking. I hadn't wanted to ask Bruno about Gregory. Bruno was never especially loquacious. Bruno favored epigrammatic, slightly irrelevant answers to almost any question. I don't understand Gregory's behavior, I once told him against my better judgment. What behavior do you mean, Bruno asked. I like Gregory, I hastily qualified, he's an exceptionally nice person. But, Bruno said, encouragingly. Yes, I said, but what, exactly. What is it with him. Why is it that one minute I feel I know him and we're close to each other, intimate, practically lovers, then without warning it's as if I were oppressing and torturing him, smothering him, using up all the air in the room, why does he call and arrange to see me and then keep me waiting for hours, sometimes not bothering to call, sometimes never showing up, when the whole thing was his idea, not mine, why can't Gregory just say, I'd rather not see you today, instead of making an urgent point that he wants to see me, and if he does show up, acting as if I'd begged him to meet me and he's only enduring a situation which is *actually killing him*, reversing the whole thing?

And if he injures my feelings and I tell him he's treating me badly he whines and moans about how unacceptable his life is, that I'm his only reassurance, his only true friend, the only person he can turn to, how wounded he is that now I seem to be turning against him like the rest of the world, so suddenly I'm the one abusing him, before I even know what's happening I'm plunged into a bath of guilt, when it's all his fault.

This sounds disgustingly familiar, Bruno said, but I don't want to puncture your balloon.

But what, I wanted to know. I thought: Bruno's so much less complicated than Gregory, why did I give him up when we were just becoming friendly?

But, everything you just said will seem comparatively charming, if you get deeply involved with Gregory. If you put any expectations at all on Gregory, be prepared for the worst. He wants everything his own way. He's a child. People have always wanted him, and he's always exploited anybody who got close to him. The trouble is he's so fucking convincing. He could make a million dollars in Hollywood, he's such an incredible actor. But then again, if he ever came close to a real opportunity he'd fuck it up big so he could still feel like a victim. He'll never compromise with you even the slightest little bit. He's destroyed people for his own amusement. He's a rotten monster, if you want to know the truth.

But he's so bright, I said.

Oh, bright, Gregory's too smart for his own good, Bruno said. He's really brilliant, really charming, and he's really, really beautiful in a sleazy sort of way, and he's totally seductive.

But, I said.

But, yeah, he's so fucked up I can't even talk about it, Bruno went on. I don't really want to discuss this, if I tell you any more you'll just resent me for it until you find out for yourself.

Maybe, I said, you just took the wrong line with him. The wrong approach.

Bruno made a sour face. I didn't take any approach, Bruno said. That's his thing, not mine. Approaches. Lines.

Oh, well, I said, thinking: Now Bruno thinks I'm nuts.

Look, Bruno said, I'm only going to say this once, but if you want to get along with Gregory . . .

Uh-huh . . .

Never believe a single word he tells you, ever.

As he turned the key in his door, Gregory said: Bruno said he saw you the other day.

He looked at me over his shoulder, one eyebrow raised.

The apartment door swung open.

Did he say what we talked about?

We entered a long room. It contained a recently installed kitchen area, a sleeping area, a work area, a shelf area, a closet area. All these areas, in a single, not terribly large room. Next to the door, a tiny bathroom with only a toilet inside and a red light-bulb over it. A metal shower stall beside the stove. Adjacent to the toilet, a deep, empty alcove, painted black, with a stuck-looking window staring directly into another apartment across a thin air shaft. Along the lower wall of the alcove ran a panoramic poster of night-time Manhattan, snapped from a helicopter.

He threw his keys on the shelf of a built-in cabinet, into a bowl full of change. I noticed a stack of opened mail, some photos in cheap paper frames.

No, he said, but I suppose you talked about me.

So, I thought: This dinky place holds his life. No wonder we all lose our minds in this city. Like kids playing at adulthood, living in these rabbit warrens with ugly floors and chipping ceilings. And areas instead of rooms.

A little, I admitted, striking a playful note which soured

instantly as Gregory smirked and walked to a small metal desk festooned with eviscerated magazines.

Do us both a favor, he sighed. If you want this to work out between us, don't discuss what happens between us with Bruno. Or with anybody else. I don't discuss you with anybody, but especially not with Bruno. I can just hear the things he'd say. In case you hadn't noticed, Bruno hates my guts. He's deeply embittered because I never went to bed with him, which I would've thought it was my privilege not to, so now he thinks he's been swindled out of something he deserves. He's convinced himself that I led him on. So he tells people I'm untrustworthy, says I'm a lousy friend, he tells everybody this. Imagine what that's like for me. Look out for Gregory, he'll fuck you over. I know what Bruno spreads around about me behind my back. He's probably freaked as hell that you and I are in a relationship suddenly. To my face he's a friend, actually sometimes we can be friends when it's about art or ideas or day-to-day practical things, but periodically Bruno gets on his high horse about what I did to him, and if you want to know the absolute truth, I never did anything to him. He played this whole manipulative number with me and when I failed to play along, get seduced by him or whatever, he decided I was the root of all evil.

Gregory sifted out grass from a plastic bag, pinched it between his fingers, let it spill down the seam of two stuck-to-gether rolling papers. As he spoke he rolled a joint, lit it, sucked on it, and held it out to me. I hate smoking dope. A few minutes later I sat on the floor, laughing uncontrollably, while Gregory put on several black wigs he'd pulled from the closet. He had switched on the stereo, and with the wigs aped various singers. With female hair he looked like a costly, big-nosed prostitute on her day off. As he discarded each wig he tossed it to me and I put it on, feeling acutely conscious of my face. My expressions tightened and lost their spontaneity whenever I knew he was looking at me.

You look really foxy like that, he said, I'd love to put it inside you right now. He rubbed his crotch. He sprang up and danced around the room.

Let me show you my Tricia Brown, he said, lifting one knee to his chest, lowering his leg, lifting the other, gyrating on his heels. See? Like she's dropping the world's biggest turd, in an artful fashion.

Gregory took off his boots, and then he was lying on top of me, grinding his hips against mine. It felt gestural rather than erotic.

Fuck everything, he said. I love you. Is that enough for you, or what?

Of course it's enough, I told him, noticing that I was hard but he wasn't. He kissed my forehead loudly and rolled off, jumped to his feet and began slicing the air with his elbows in time to the music. He was still wearing a shoulder-length wig.

I gotta get a shirt, he said, flinging the wig off. I just have to finish up something here, he said, waving at the desk, then go buy a shirt. You want to wait? Or maybe it's tedious for you.

I'm not bored, I said. But I felt time slipping past in a senseless drift and knew that hanging out would later make me feel guilty. He settled down behind his desk and sorted through sheaves of paper cutouts, his office chair wheeling and squeaking as he worked. I lay down on his leather futon and stared at the dingy wall. Why do I feel like I'm cracking apart, I wondered.

A radiator hissed under the window. The room looked chalky and provisional under the bare ceiling bulbs. As if Gregory could clear off with an hour's notice. His clothes were shoved away in the closet, cardboard boxes of packed-away treasures splitting open in there. Dishes and cookware his mother must have given him, stacked in the cupboard. Miles of albums under the turntable, a few books arranged for display: a boxed set of Calvino, probably unopened, piles of art magazines, lots of current theoretical writings in paperback.

And a picture on the wall, over the stereo: a familiar picture, blown up big. It was an arrangement of six snapshots, reproduced on a single large sheet of white paper, six different male types, all handsome, some clean-shaven, some bearded or semi-bearded, with various hairstyles, various styles of clothing: college preppie, Kennedy-type young lawyer, bohemian, blue-collar worker, and so forth, in age ranging from about twenty-five to somewhere near forty. The significant peculiarity being that these faces all belonged to the same person, and had all been taken within four years, a so-called serial killer who had raped and murdered his way across the United States a few years earlier. A man who had impressed everyone who met him as extremely charming, sexy, intelligent, sensitive, possibly brilliant, definitely middle-class, an exemplary neighbor and concerned friend, buckets of fun on a date. Ted was typically described by horrified ex-acquaintances as "a real all-American," a "golden boy." Which, in fact, is a description not entirely inconsistent with raping and murdering upwards of thirty women, though press accounts had found it particularly rich in ghoulish irony that Ted struck everyone who knew him as an all-American, even when he'd completely run out of control, sometimes murdering two women at the same time, abducting one and tying her up somewhere, driving off and finding another, then raping and killing the first one in plain sight of the second, who then would be raped and murdered in turn, or running amok in a women's dormitory with a baseball bat, cracking in the skulls of as many women as he could locate. Such is the ambiance of American society, that a person who runs out of control in this manner can effortlessly impress those he meets as a paragon of desirable national qualities. Even after being apprehended, an event that occurred a ridiculously long time after Ted had been identified, thanks to the professional rivalries and murderous laziness of various law enforcement organizations, Ted attracted flocks of admirers of both sexes, fans who attended his trial every day and wrote him adoring letters full of blunt sexual propositions and marriage offers.

And here, on Gregory's wall, are the six faces of Ted. He notices me noticing it and says: That's my first large-scale work. He resumes clipping pictures from *GQ* with an X-acto knife. I think: What does this picture indicate here, about Gregory—no killer, he? Of course, it's obvious: he tells me every day, in one way or another, that he's not what he appears to be. He reproaches me, in fact, for what he calls fetishizing his looks, and what I call being attracted to him. But that's not me, he says. That's not what I am inside. He says: I think I'll eat everything I can lay my hands on and grow immensely fat, then you'll see how much you love me for who I really am. Are you immensely fat inside, then, I asked. Perhaps, he said, you never know. One day, when we noticed an elderly woman begging on the street, Gregory said: I think when I'm old I'll have my dick cut off and pass myself off as an old woman, they've got more style than men.

Bruno had been working on a pencil drawing throughout our conversation in the gallery. A sort of castle tower, with macaroni-shaped lines flowing down from the top. He worked with a green-hooded lamp shining on the paper. Whenever the discussion of Gregory flagged or went dead, the tip of his mechanical pencil claimed his attention. I smoked and flipped through an issue of *Vogue*, feigning interest in Gaultier's spring line. Nice jacket, I remarked, hoping I would sound less than totally obsessed about Gregory. Gregory spoke to his drawing. "But if a body falls from a certain height . . ." he murmured, then stared with pale lips pursed, as if the thing before him had assumed a troublesome identity of its own. He cocked his head and shot me a quizzical look, which he does again as he watches me walk to the cupboard. I study his odds and ends, poke a finger into the bowl of buttons and keys, pick up one of the framed photos.

Is this you, I said.

No, he said, he's my younger brother. He's in school. I saw him in a play they did, you could see he'd be dynamite on stage. He sang and danced and everything, I could never get up in front of people and do that, not if my life depended on it. And what a heartbreaker Joey is, huh? If you met him, you'd drop me in a second. You'd say, Forget that Gregory, this guy is boyfriend material.

What an odd thing to say, I said. Gregory does sing to me sometimes: *I'm your private dancer*, he sang the other day, and crossing Astor Place last week he sang, lips close to my ear, *I've got you, under my skin*. He played the accordion as a child, his mother loved for him to play the accordion and sing for her, *Goodnight, Irene, goodnight, Irene, I'll see you in my dreams*. His mother's name is Marina.

That other picture is my parents, he said.

Smiling, gorgeous, dated faces: Marina, and Jerzy-that-got-changed-to-Jack.

They're beautiful, I said. Well, he said, they certainly thought so, in fact that's practically all they ever thought about. I said that people often get together for mysterious reasons. Gregory said he didn't think it was so mysterious in their case, but you could apply that to a lot of other situations. What, I said, you mean like ours? That's something else again, he said.

Has Gloria still been pestering you, I asked. He said he'd gone with her to a coffee shop in the West Village to talk things over. I said, Why doesn't she leave you alone, thinking if he'd agreed to see her perhaps she'd also got him to fuck her. Gregory said it wouldn't be normal not to have a chat, that he showed her slides of his work. Gloria had asked why none of his pictures showed any women. I had to explain, he said, that this work is about men, I'm not a woman, I have no right to use images of women, I'm trying to figure something out about male sexuality, she didn't get it of course, Gloria's dense when she wants to be and anyway it was obvious what she was driving at. Why doesn't she give up, I said, with irritation. He said: She's still pissed off and you know something, I didn't treat her so wonderfully if the truth be told.

She should grow up, I said, why don't you tell her you're going out with me? At this stage, he said, that would hurt her terribly, and I've already done enough damage to her, she's still in love with me, can't you understand, she doesn't have any choice, she's under a compulsion, she'd follow me around like a dog in the streets if she didn't have to work every day.

Well, look, I said, that's all well and good, but enough's enough, and also, I said, I find it pretty odd that you've gone on for weeks and weeks telling me how malign Gloria is, how she's given you all kinds of grief, and now you seem to be getting indignant because I don't feel much sympathy for her. I'm insecure enough without that cunt hanging around.

He said, It's tacky and mean to call her a cunt, you don't even know her.

No, I screamed, and I don't want to know her, either.

Well, he said, I'd like to introduce you two sometime, she read some stories you wrote and said she thought they were quite good.

I don't give a shit what Gloria thinks about my stories, I said, is she some sort of literary critic suddenly, besides being an interfering cunt?

Is the reason you're calling her a cunt, he said, now his voice shot up though he didn't rise from the desk, because you're jealous she had my dick? That isn't worthy of you, that's mean-spirited and shitty, she's a nice girl, she wants to be a writer in fact, it's so unfair to hate her just because she had something you didn't, I mean, you don't have to worry, she's never getting it again, and I told her so.

It must be something pretty special, I said, since you seem to get everything you want with it.

He laid the knife down and said, That's what you really think of me, isn't it. I said: I don't know what I think. You confuse me, I said. Everything you do confuses me and makes me feel crazy. Maybe so, Gregory said, but if you didn't think about me every second you wouldn't imagine me doing all sorts of things behind your back. There's nothing going on between me and anybody else, he said. And anyway, he went on, even if there were, what rights do you have, what claims do you have over me? I don't ask you, he said, if you fuck other people, and frankly, he went on, lighting a cigarette, I think it might be healthy if you did.

I said, You're saying it wouldn't bother you if I were sleeping with somebody. He said of course it wouldn't bother him because he didn't expect me to deny myself anything on his account. Oh, for Christ's sake, I said, I suppose by the same token you'd sleep with anybody else if you felt like it.

Gregory's voice thinned to a cool, crackling undertone. How many times, he exhaled, how many different ways, do I have to tell you I don't want to sleep with anybody?

Then why are we together like this, I demanded, fooling around with each other and talking on the phone as if we had this intense relationship? Why do you act like you're my boyfriend? Is this how you are with other people?

I'm not the way I am with you with anybody else because I love you, Gregory said, though you don't seem able to accept that idea. There's nothing I'd like better in the world than to be able to fuck you into a coma so you wouldn't feel so *deprived* all the time. But I can't. I just can't. I can't force myself to, either.

Why can't you? I said. Am I that repulsive to you?

Gregory winced. He crushed out his cigarette and put his hands over his face. He said, It's got nothing to do with you, and I'm running out of ways to tell you it's got nothing to do with you, you keep insisting like a child, how can a person as smart as you fail to understand something so simple?

Because, I said, it's not simple. He said anyone except me would think it was. I said I knew he wasn't impotent. He said: I never said I was. He said: I prefer not to. He said: Haven't you read *Bartleby the Scrivener?*

In other words, I said, this is all about your free will.

Gregory said, I'd like to see you happy. Obviously I can't make you happy if you define happiness as getting my cock up your asshole. Don't be vulgar, I said, in any case I'm not expecting to be happy. Well, he said, I am. I'm older than you, I told him. He said, That doesn't mean anything. I said yes it did. He said, What, for example. I said, Things about death, what you want the rest of your life to be like. Gregory sneered. I suppose, he said, you're referring to some greater awareness I wouldn't have acquired from shooting smack for two years. I said that some things don't happen until you physically age, that I hadn't exactly been a drug virgin in my twenties either, that the thing about drugs is you don't really learn anything from taking them.

You were never an addict, Gregory said. Since you were able to stop using horse, I said, I assume you never were, either. That's a creepy, mean thing to say, he told me, it took me more than a year to get clean. I stole money, I sold my ass, guys paid me to jerk off in their faces, he said, do you want me to list all the degrading shit I did before I reached something vaguely resembling sanity?

I suddenly felt ashamed and in the wrong; and I felt as if I'd become trapped in the mix of some top 40 song about the pain of love. I said: I'm sorry. I've been alone a long time. It's hard to trust situations like this.

But, he said, that's because you're not giving this a chance to develop slowly on its own time so we can have something that's worth it. Look, he said. If you really want *that*, I'll take my clothes off right now and dick you right there on the futon and then you can go home and forget all about me.

That isn't how I want things, I said, I want to make love with you.

And I can't, he said, do you really want me to when I don't want to? You decide. I can get it up for you. Sure, no problem, tell me which hole you want me to put it in and how long you want me to keep it there, God knows I've gone through the motions enough before, I'm sure I can do it again.

Look, I said, I didn't come over here to get laid, I just want to be with you. I'm sorry I said that shit about Gloria, it's not that I'm jealous. If I dislike her it's because everything you've told me made me think she was hurting you and adding to your problems.

I know, he said, I know, that's the thing, you can blow off at me as much as you like and I'll just wait quietly until you're finished. The real you doesn't want to get mad at me, in fact the real you hates the other you when that happens, because the real you is terrified of losing me. But see, I can tell those two people inside you apart. The other you can't hurt me because it's not the real you.

He crosses the room, plants his hands on my shoulders, squeezes me. He touches me: there. I say: Why are you touching me? He says: I want you to feel good. I say: I feel good but now I feel manipulated. He steps away, back to the desk, sighs, sits down. He rolls his chair back. He smiles the smile he knows is irresistible. Anger-proof.

I refuse to fight with you, he says. That's very clever, I tell him, because I have the feeling I'd win. But I smile and show him he can always melt me down between my legs and this will always draw a bead on anything he doesn't want to deal with.

Oh ho ho, he laughs, you can't win with me, haven't you figured that out yet? I suppose, I answer, if I've learned anything from this relationship, it's that.

Yup. You'll never get the upper hand.

Everything's going to be on your terms.

That's the way it's got to be right now.

Its nothing to brag about, really.

Come off it. Don't. You should actually feel good about it, because basically you don't want the upper hand. That would make it boring. Now come on. Come here.

I stepped over and stood next to his chair.

Look, he said, your hands are shaking. Relax. You know what I'd like? Kiss my . . . collar. Not my neck, honey, my collar. Gregory doesn't want his skin touched today, just the collar. Twenty kisses. One, two, three, four . . . kiss my sleeve, all the way down, down, kiss just along there, down to the cuff, twenty kisses . . . kiss that button. Oooh, that feels good. That's so nice. Now the belt. Stay away from the buckle area, you can only kiss the side there, where the loop is, kiss the loop. Now the knee, just the left knee, kiss it thirty times . . . very nice, sweetie, real nice. Oh, all right, do the other knee too. You know something, you're an angel, you're all warm and soft like an angel. Your hair feels like an angel's hair, it's so smooth . . . kiss the leg of my pants, all the way down, now kiss my socks, kiss all around my feet, kiss under the toes, twenty kisses . . . do my insteps, that's so beautiful, you're really my slave, aren't you, it's funny because, do the heels now, thirty kisses each heel, if people only knew you're a complete slave to me, now around, up to the ankles, people would be so surprised, I bet people think I'm your dumb little trick. Lick with your tongue, sugar, taste the whole sock, go ahead, put my toes in your mouth. People think I'm your little dog, but you're my little slave. Wouldn't Bruno freak if he saw you right now, like that. You're an angel slave. You're the most beautiful angelic slave I've ever had.

An hour later, tramping again through the cold streets, the sun blotted now by cloud cover, walking beside him but feeling, in the immense pauses between his bursts of chatter, as if I'm several feet behind him, like a Japanese bride. He walks even faster than me, races along like a keyed-up robot toy. Houston to Broadway, Eighth Street to Sixth Avenue, over to Seventh Avenue, up Seventh into the twenties, then even further west, near the river, breath steaming in the chill. People like blurred rag heaps, snatches of skin. The air has the bluish pall that sets off shop lights like clusters of stage jewelry. The first trickles of snow drift listlessly down, bits of leftover confetti, melting to brownish muck as they kiss the sidewalk. We're both powdered with clingy white specks.

This is quite a distance, really.

Not far, he says.

My boots soak up slush. He says it's only a few more blocks, but we're already in the low thirties. The wind off the Hudson gnaws through my serge jacket and nibbles under my scarf. Gregory shakes. Neither one of us has thought to wear gloves, or a hat. I notice, as if for the first time, Gregory's emphatically tapered, mutton-chop sideburns, extending to an inch or so above his jawline on either side. I notice the oddity of this facial topiary, cocky and sleazily suggestive. Gregory's hair is blacker than onyx, and these paddle-shaped whiskers belong on a gigolo in some Nebraskan microcity. Like the ring in his nose, the side-burns go with the look of a man who wants to attract women, women of a certain type, drunk and not very bright women in cocktail lounges.

In the vast, musty Salvation Army third floor where I wait for Gregory to zip through rack after rack of stale-smelling garments, I understand what oppresses me: the way he presents himself courts sexual attention from the widest possible constituency, male and female. Bluntly, brutally. He flips through dozens of stained, frayed, torn, superannuated shirts, trousers, vests and neckties, exclaiming at choice monstrosities. The place is like a penitentiary for old clothes, ugly and dust-bound as a welfare office. Yes, I think, it's the style, the look: it makes being attracted to him feel pornographic.

For someone who doesn't want it, Gregory talks about sex more than anyone I've ever met. Usually in a deprecating way, but he's still immersed in thoughts about it. He despises homosexuals who "can't control themselves," ridicules anyone who vaguely conforms to a type. He waxes sarcastic about the obviousness of people's cravings: certain women who show up in the restaurant bar, also fags he meets in a bar on Second Avenue when he pops in for a nightcap. He describes these sex-hungry barflies in close detail, nastily, as if their loneliness were criminal instead of merely pathetic. Even so, he cultivates this penis-on-legs look calculated to attract these very people.

The shirt and tie he settles on are ghastly. Blue and white broad stripes on the shirt, with a bone-white wingtip collar. The tie a yellow and red psychedelic antique. At a scarred wooden counter, an octogenarian cashier of drastically blurred gender rings them up and stuffs them in a soiled bag.

But they're awful, Gregory.

Hideous, he laughs.

Why don't you find something that suits you?

Darkness outside. Motes of snow falling in heavy veils.

I don't wear things I like to the restaurant, he tells me.

Yes, but it looks like stuff some pimp would wear.

He cocks his head, squints, pushes out his lips and nods. The look says, Now you're catching on.

He's so impudently eccentric, suddenly it's very funny. His revenging joke on the louts. The clothes complete something blank and sexy people expect to find waiting tables and serving drinks. Gregory acts the part, detached from his body by way of his clothes. At this moment he becomes something new for me, a noble soul, trapped in a widely desired form. He has something everybody wants, but for him it has no value. A complete artist. A dandy of sleaze.

You're fantastic, I tell him, laughing, brushing snow from the fringe hanging over his forehead.

He screws his face into the mask of a Gallic clown: Philippe. He recites the menu of daily specials in a raspy accent. Gregory's an incredible mimic. He's almost frighteningly adept at changing into people he's casually observed, his visual memory of bodies, faces, pictures, and rooms startles me when he plays it back. I walk around oblivious to things, blinded by my ruminations. Gregory drinks things in.

I feel around in my pockets for dollars. We should take a cab, Gregory, it's getting late and it's wet. My teeth chatter. You're freezing, he says, here, here's a hug, don't freeze. We walk. Now I'm wet from his snow and my snow. On Seventh Avenue I flag a taxi as we slog to the corner, running ahead, stepping into a crater of slush. I pretend we've agreed to take a cab. He gets in without comment, though taxis and similar expenses are awkward for us. If he can't pay, he feels deficient in the husbandly role he's assumed, my protector. We are exactly the same height and same slender build, but Gregory emits this honorary manliness around me, a pretense of greater strength and practical resourcefulness I gladly defer to because he's small and not so tough and needs to feel strong and needed. When he says: I'd kill anyone who tried to hurt you, the absurdity of Gregory killing or even slightly injuring anybody moves me inexpressibly.

Now, he says, I've got to iron this shit. He pulls them out of the bag. Some days they have a tasty item or two with no wrinkles but these are a little far gone.

It's so far out of your way, I said. You know there are thrift shops over your way, four or five of them.

This one generally has the best stuff, though.

Do they make you wear something different every night?

The streets are crawling, the usual mucky swarm. January. A death month.

Look at them all, he says. People. He looks at the shirt. I can't stand putting these things on more than once.

Yes, I said, you have to wash them and everything. I'm lucky, I never have to dress up. Blue jeans and sweatshirts. But maybe you want me to be glamorous now that I have a job.

The windshield turns the gleaming taillights and walking figures into a melt of drooling colors. Wipers slash the glass, returning things to their solid forms, dapple again with snow, pour into each other.

I take this stuff in with me, I wouldn't wear it on the street. At the end of the night I stuff it in a trash can.

The cab stutters in traffic. We pass a pet store. Gregory leans over me. Our legs brush. For a moment I feel his weight against me.

What great puppies. I really miss my dog.

You could get one.

I'd never find another Lucie. That dog loved me so much. I'd come in, her little tail would be wagging, she cheered me up.

You throw your clothes away every night?

I have to . . . I don't want them crapping up the apartment.

You don't buy different ones every day, though. You must stock up for a week or so . . .

This is taking an eternity, he says, I'm really getting shit from Philippe if he's there. Well, fuck him. No, I go buy something every day when I have to work. It kind of puts me in the mental frame of working.

But Gregory, you don't go way over there every day.

Most days I do. Sure.

But it takes your whole afternoon . . . it's too much, you're always saying you have no time.

He takes out a cigarette, taps the end of it on his thumbnail. Gregory's nails are unusually wide and stunted-looking, incongruously lacking in elegance. The nails of a Serbian peasant. He offers a sharp, strained smile, a look of irritation. His eyes narrow into curved slits, he's looking into his private thoughts, I'm not there any more. He lights the cigarette, sitting closer than he did before we passed the pet shop, now he links his fingers between mine, but my hand is a bobbing mooring hook, his mind is a boat drifting to the end of its line. The remaining minutes are glazed, quickened in narrowing intervals by his impatience, there is no room left in this taxi for anything but anxiety about what Philippe might say or do to him when he arrives at work, something characteristically insensitive and menacing, no doubt, or, worse, he'll greet Gregory in expansive, coke-zonked spirits, feel him up in that obscene way that he has and then make some typically insane demand, sending Gregory out to pick up his, Philippe's, dry cleaning, or buy magazines at the kiosk in Sheridan Square, these are a couple of Philippe's standard, psychotic orders, and there are others, sometimes requiring Gregory to get things from Philippe's apartment at the other end of town, or to deal with wholesalers at the Fulton Fish Market, or to "deliver packages" to various addresses, packages which almost certainly contain coke or smack and for which Gregory is obliged to collect money, thus involving himself in a felony, all things entirely outside Gregory's professional obligations, outside Gregory's job description, tasks that have nothing to do with waiting tables or bartending but instead are connected to Philippe's criminal depravity and insanity. However, should Gregory refuse to do these things, Philippe will fire him.

I leave the cab at Second Avenue, in front of Gem Spa: we don't even kiss goodbye, it's all perfunctory and sour, and as I walk home my mind fills with horrible scenarios, pictures of what may befall Gregory. And since what usually befalls him at work results in his becoming incommunicado for days, unplugging his phone and vanishing from my life, and since he increasingly reports sensations of extreme despondency, hints that he can't hang on much longer with the kind of depression he has, feels himself sliding towards the edge, turning the mental corner, believes he could easily lose his sanity, contemplates suicide much of the time, "goes blank" for longer and longer periods, finds himself snarling at and insulting customers, refusing to wait on certain individuals, often thinks there is no hope in the world for him, I fill the time when he's out of contact with fears, especially with mental pictures of Gregory dead, his beautiful face when he's dead, like the face of a viciously slain animal lying in a field of pissy snow.

The next time I went to his apartment, Gregory showed me a card that Gloria had sent him shortly after New Year's. Not a store-bought card but one she'd made, on a square of gray cardboard, with cut-out photos. It showed a pair of ample tits, and glued between them a meaty, erect la la. Just the tits and a bit of model torso, the prong and its wrinkled scrotum. Happy New Year, she'd written at the bottom, in infantile script. He rolled his eyes while exhibiting the card. So that was what she liked with him.

He still got stormy calls and letters demanding cash. On a whim, she'd appear in front of his building, as he left for work, planted on the stoop with too much cadmium lipstick on, a lovesick cow imagining herself a femme fatale. His finding her not just resistible but weirdly enervating bewildered her. Hadn't they been lovers just a few weeks before? Hadn't he put it inside her, come between her breasts?

He said she'd heard he was going out with me. He had refused to confirm or deny this rumor, since it was none of her business. I let this go by, although it obviously meant he hadn't decided if he was going out with me or not. At any rate, "going out" would have been a strange description of what we were doing. We never went anywhere.

5

I'm living in hell, Richard told me in the steam room. Victor's so heavy. I'll be working on a painting, you see what I mean, really into it, he lets himself in with his key now, any time of day or night, hoping he'll surprise me in the middle of a fuck. When we were actually together that way he'd never dream of coming over without calling up and asking.

So, Richard said, I got into this thing, I met this guy from Cleveland, a banker, loaded, married with three kids, and some guys, no matter what they look like, out of their clothes it's like there's nothing but you and him and the universe. He's into, like, the best wine, the best food, gentle sophisticated vibes and he's in love with my schlong, fifty sixty million bucks with a nice family and everything, and of course real guilty about the whole situation. If you saw this guy you'd laugh, but I'm in love with him, and now it's over with, I just never got hurt like this, somehow.

It isn't like he broke things off or anything, but I just couldn't stand it. Like, we could never have anything normal, just pieces. Always if he was going to be in town, and what if he suddenly changed his mind, I was always at the mercy of his whims and his priorities. Victor's been really supportive through this whole thing and tried being a loyal friend, like he put his jealousy over in storage in New Jersey. So, I'm always going to be, you know, grateful for what he's been for me during this heavy period, but now it's like he's assuming all this intimacy again, protecting me from myself and, in other words, knowing every move I make.

You know Victor's the nicest person, he'd cut his balls off for a friend. But after a while that can get pretty heavy, too. I'd like to be, like, responsible for my own shitty messes instead of thinking Victor will clean them up for me. I mean, I know I have this tendency to put myself into extreme situations sometimes, with guys I don't know too well, there's been some psychotic shit going on over there, that's why I want to cut out drinking, because my judgment breaks down and I get looped and wild and I let go, like with Randy, that kid I had helping me for a while, I'm sure Victor told you about Randy, at first I thought, here's a really built, hung kid who likes doing shows, that was when I had all that mirrored effect in the bedroom, well the mirror got smashed one night when I was porking him, Randy was ready for anything. I'd get him to sit on a broomstick or that Brancusi copy I have, or with cowboy boots, when I got those fancy boots in Marfa and came back I said, Randy, wouldn't you like getting fucked with these boots? It felt funny, kind of sexy. I mean I slid one into him right up to the heel. And he turned out to be like a complete psychopath though he dug getting fucked with almost anything that looked like a cock he also liked getting zonked on angel dust and taking a razor blade, first he made these cuts along his thighs and all across his chest, and this turned into something I couldn't handle at all and Victor was the one who threw him out finally, I mean, with my permission and everything but it was heavy. I only want to work any more. No more scenes. It's not the period for that, right? Just work and fuck the rest of it.

I had let Richard talk me into joining the health club. It had something to do with Paul, and the strange things which now appeared nearly every day in the newspapers, the tumult and confusion of the times. When I saw Paul in the hospital, he showed me oblong, puffy red lesions on the heels of his palms, and one of the white socks he wore had a damp pink patch around the shin. It was a drab room with a view of Roosevelt Island. Paul's hospital gown reminded me of a convict's uniform. Someone had brought him lilacs.

I told him stories about my life, wrapping them up in bemused petulance, as if to say: Well, what can you do about things? He listened too closely, watched my face too fixedly, I could tell he evaluated every visitor's performance, measured the precise degree of discomfort each one experienced in the theater of his distress. He lay on the bed with his head up, extracting private wisdom from the situation, and was clearly pleased when I seemed to forget what he was doing there. I made him laugh, once, when he asked what Gregory was like and I said, very much as an aside: Oh, Christ, that's all fucked up, too.

If I hadn't had Gregory distracting me, I probably would have noted the sudden omnipresence of death with greater clarity. Instead, the fatal sarcomas, pneumonias, and neuropathies reached me as isolated incidents, or manifestations of an abstract social problem. I convinced myself that since I'd been sexually unhappy for years after breaking off with Paul, this unhappiness conferred a special immunity against the virus that I suspected, nonetheless, must be floating around inside me. I reasoned: If Paul's sick, wouldn't I be sick by now, if I picked it up from him? This made no real sense, Paul could have gotten infected long before our relationship, infected me in the middle of his incubation period, by which token I might fall ill in roughly the same time after we broke up that Paul got ill after his initial infection, and then again, perhaps the thing developed at different rates in different people, with one person getting sick a few months after infection while another falls ill years afterwards.

I shunned as much information as I could. People talked a lot about "safe sex," usually in a derisory way. Victor informed me that sodomy with a condom, which he'd tried out on his occasional Japanese boyfriend Hiroshi, never proceeded very smoothly. You could never quite lose yourself in lovemaking, since foreplay no longer led directly to insertion, but rather to the peeling of a foil packet and the usually clumsy rolling of the latex down the length of the penis, which quite often shrank if you didn't slip in on right the first try. Blowjobs with a condom on the penis were really not worth bothering with. Licking the penis without inserting the head into the mouth was like eating the cone and throwing away the ice cream.

On the other hand, Victor expatiated, sodomy without a condom had always had a lot of little glitches too, if the person's asshole was too tight, or too dry, and you didn't happen to have the Vasoline open and ready. I remembered that with Paul, who always tried putting it in using spit, he often found the target constricted. He would ease himself off the bed, pad out to the bathroom for the K-Y. Of course, we were so high most of the time that these little interruptions heightened the excitement, in fact, Paul enjoyed pulling out, rummaging around for a bottle of poppers, and sticking his cock back in while holding the bottle under my nose. Once he spilled it directly into my nostrils and I spent ten minutes with my face in the sink. Now they say you should never drink or take drugs if you have sex because it breaks down your inhibitions and you find yourself "going all the way," getting come down your throat or up your ass and then you're paralyzed with fear the next morning.

So, Victor concluded, if you do it as you're supposed to, both people are completely lucid and therefore completely self-conscious, and any break in the continuity makes the whole business seem ridiculous and arbitrary, and, on top of that, five out of six times the condom snaps or mushes up, at the end of the night you've got scads of wet latex sticking here and there all over the apartment.

Some other people: there was Rainer, who'd given me an acting job in a film he shot in South America, a film that wrapped only a few weeks before I met Gregory. I had known Rainer for five or six years, first in Munich, later in Paris and Berlin, during a period when I didn't think New York would be my fate, a time when I was desperately broke but managed to hustle airline tickets everywhere and got little acting jobs with avant-garde directors. For six or seven weeks at a stretch I'd have a paid hotel room, free meals, and an honorary sort of salary. I never seriously considered myself an actor. It was just something I knew how to do. I saw more and more of Rainer in those years of restless motion, in New York and all over Europe, and by osmosis we became close friends. Rainer was one of the only people from the European otherworld I sometimes lived in who ever met Gregory. A privileged witness to my distress.

In March or April, I can't remember exactly, Rainer phoned to say: Willie's dead. Willie had been his lover of ten years. Rainer said: I take a strange inhuman comfort in the fact that the worst that could possibly happen has already happened, and what I'm now left with is the intelligent planning of my suicide.

There was Martha, a photographer who lived uptown, a friend I hardly ever saw. These intermittent friendships and their contents, like flashes of lightning, illuminate moments of that time and leave the rest in darkness. Even though people were beginning to drop like flies, we all acted as if we were going to live forever. The weeks were littered with unreturned phone messages, stupid feuds were sustained endlessly for no good reason, and very often the slight effort needed to maintain a sense of connectedness proved altogether beyond one's strength or willingness. It was something quite strange. You would hear, for example, that X had died over the weekend, but no one could definitely confirm or deny the rumor. You would not ask anyone truly close to X because if it were true you would be intruding on their grief and if it weren't they might go into a panic imagining that it was true and they somehow hadn't heard about it. Then you might mention it to someone who believed that X had died months before. And just when you concluded that the whole thing was a rumor, X turned out really to be dead. Or, just when you'd received absolutely certain confirmation, you'd walk into a party and find X standing there.

Martha had started looking after Todd, also a photographer, after his first pneumocystis episode. I heard news of Todd when Martha came downtown. A couple of years before, we had had a minor difference of opinion; he'd stopped speaking to me altogether a few months before getting ill, and after he got ill it became clear he planned on taking his anger with him to the grave. The thing that was special, she said, the way we could talk about pictures together, it doesn't happen any more. And it never will again. I go shopping with him and if I watch him picking out a sweater, I know if this happened to me of course I'd go on, taking care of myself as long as I could, but it requires such hideous courage. Sometimes I'm over there cleaning up the dishes, and I'll stop for a whole minute, thinking: Why on earth wash another dish.

It didn't matter, in the wider scheme of things, if running into someone in the street caused a couple of moments of awkward-

ness and a stream of ugly thoughts, though a fifteen-minute conversation could have cleared up the entire business. But one of
the unpleasant little ironies twinkling on the periphery of my day
was this: in an abstract sense, I thought what was happening to
Todd was horrible, but in a different sense, after he rejected a few
conciliatory overtures, I began loathing him. I assured myself that
I did not want him to die, but drew a weird satisfaction from the
fact that I knew he was going to. He had never been a close friend,
but over the course of his illness he acquired a heavy symbolic
power. I wondered what he would feel about it if our positions
were reversed, wondered if I would join him in the kingdom of illness before he died. I wondered why if death is such a conqueror
it has no effect on pettiness.

We're mutating, M. said. Becoming something new. A species at
the end of its run.

I'm scared, I told Jane. I really want to live.

Hey, she said, it's the only game in town.

Libby said her grandmother gave her three pieces of advice at
her college graduation, about how to have a successful relationship with a man: listen to everything he says, constantly tell him
how smart he is, and worship his penis.

If we seldom spoke of it directly, it must have been because Gregory's art project presumed certain evils inherent in pornographic
magazines, lustfulness, and even the body itself. He greeted the
news of my health club membership with superior irony, as if it
implied a vulgarly death-defying attitude toward my physical envelope. His collages had begun featuring porno models, spliced into
settings that heightened the absurdity of their smiles, their fore-

grounded erections, and their brazenly offered buttocks to a pitch of supreme ugliness. I laughed when he showed them to me, one morning when he fixed breakfast at his place and seemed, for once, relaxed and happy. His anxiety for my approval put me on guard. It pleased me that Gregory could make technically sophisticated pictures, ones with a strong content that his peers wouldn't despise. But what Gregory craved was my complicity in his message, his ridicule. Something of the zeal with which reformed sinners make themselves odious sparkled across Gregory's photographs. His physical poise that morning, as he briskly arranged plates and coffee cups and orchestrated a continuous medley of irritating albums on the stereo, reminded me of some keenly deluded junior architect unveiling his plans for demolishing the red-light district.

There were times like this when, unplugged from the erotic current that usually ran between us, I saw Gregory not as someone unusually developed in matters of the heart, seasoned in "relationships," but as someone painfully unversed in the art of survival. As we ate he fretted over "which pictures to put in the show," how the public might receive them, whether or not there would be copyright problems with the porn magazines. I asked him if he thought the porn industry vigilantly monitored exhibitions in obscure East Village galleries. This stung, but only for a moment. Gregory explained that he was thinking ahead, because "just objectively," he felt, his images were destined to shock people and hence to acquire a certain fame. Maybe so, I said, but look, you've only done four of them, I think you've got plenty of time to worry about lawsuits or what you're going to include.

He seemed positive that Bruno would eventually offer him a show, though Bruno had expressed to me a certain skeptical distance from Gregory's activities, saying that what he'd seen looked clever but not especially difficult. But how firmly did Bruno draw the line between his opinion and his desire? Bruno was currently dating a fashion designer, but he still had an unfinished lust that drove him to pop in on Gregory all the time without warning. Perhaps he would feature Gregory's work in a group show, holding out the prospect of a one-person exhibition later on. Then Gregory would amplify his charm in proportion to Bruno's munificence.

When Gregory put something into his mind, if it didn't conform to practical reality, he searched the corners of his daily life until something, or someone, offered confirmation of his fantasies. And so a few days later, he reported to Pugg, the mysterious Pugg, whose rather flaccid *bons mots* infiltrated Gregory's jumbled accounts of people in his life I hadn't met, this Pugg had agreed that "there could very well be problems" concerning the rights to these skin pictures. Artists who used images from existing sources, thus spake Pugg, had often run afoul of litigation. And Pugg had further said, according to Gregory, that people would "flip out" when they saw Gregory's pictures, meaning, in Gregory's interpretation, that the photographs were so "transgressive, " so bound to strike a raw nerve, that Gregory was fated to erupt upon the art scene like Vesuvius. Hadn't I been a trifle . . . abrupt in my judgment? A teeny bit thoughtless, possibly even . . . slightly *envious* in my temperate advice? No, I told him, not at all, I just don't want you to get worked up and then disappointed. I said, Things don't always arrive on a serving tray, just like that. You've got to prepare yourself for some difficult struggles, some hard times, some setbacks, it could take several years to establish a career, and even then, I pointed out, no matter how good something is, everything passes in and out of fashion, think how many things used to be shocking, this culture absorbs everything. Don't be negative, he told me.

I wanted his scenarios to come true for him, but when I encouraged him to cultivate reasonable hopes and a degree of resignation, just in case reality didn't match his fantasies, he assumed that I wanted to cripple his ego and lord it over him. He also assumed that I was eaten up with jealousy when I didn't know what he was doing. He clung ferociously to this idea, though I would have been much happier to know he was home fucking someone on the myriad occasions when I imagined he'd killed himself. He seemed unusually vulnerable to all the varieties of mischance the city has to offer, and although nothing really terrible ever seemed to happen, Gregory found ordinary living so oppressive that I expected disaster to find him at every corner. I imagined him kidnapped, mugged, shot, stabbed, raped, and dumped in the river if I didn't hear from him. This worry refined itself in stages; if someone had seen Gregory *the day before*, I felt less panic than I did if I could only find someone who'd seen him two days earlier. If he was out of sight for three days, I pictured his body decomposing in a dumpster, or in that lurid apartment, killed by a common housebreaker.

He called one morning and asked if I'd come for breakfast because he was scared, the landlord had these guys installing storm windows and one of them seemed particularly interested in his apartment. The guy came in here, Gregory said when I arrived. He came in? Yeah. They had the outside window off and he just stepped down into the room, this black kid about eighteen, he looked around at everything, especially the stereo, I gave him some coffee and he acted polite and all but I didn't trust his look, now I'm afraid to leave the place. But if he works for the landlord, I said, he wouldn't dare— Who knows, Gregory said, the landlord runs a pretty shady crew of people downstairs. Anyway half the landlords in New York are gangsters. I mean they can take what they want, but what I'm afraid of is, somebody comes in when I'm sleeping and I wake up and, you know, get killed or something.

I hugged him. Cascades of rough fabric. I wish I could protect you and take care of you all the time, I said, and he said, I feel the same way about you, I want to take care of you and never let anything bad come near you. I'm small, he said, but I'm strong.

After breakfast he wanted to walk in the streets. I said, Aren't you worried about the guy coming back? Oh that, he said, surprised, as if he'd forgotten all about it. And then I realized that he'd manufactured the intruder, or dramatized an innocuous encounter with the window installer, for the pleasure of seeing me worry about him. Well, I thought, he's still trying to figure out if I really do care about him. Which should be obvious by now. But he's been wounded by people in the past, so it isn't obvious. I felt grateful for the chance to offer proof, only vaguely troubled by the disruptive frequency with which he tested my affection. In a room together, physically together, everything he did to drive me crazy erased itself from memory.

When he saw me reading the paper someone had left on the back seat, the cab driver, an Egyptian with long, thick fingers, said he was a Virgo, and please would I read his horoscope. It cautioned Virgos to anticipate certain snags in their business relations by getting their feelings mixed up in matters of strategy.

In the hospital pavilion, the blue-gray linoleum floors had colored lines trailing across them in different directions. The cancer ward was cerulean, dermatology red, cardiac unit and X-ray yellow, green led to emergency services, and so forth. A wooden maquette of the hospital rested under a sort of oblong cake-saver on a platform near the information desk, complete with tiny trees, drive-up horseshoe paving, miniature nurses and doctors and visitors, a model ambulance with paramedics wheeling off a gurney and life-support systems.

Whole chunks of the actual hospital moved about on wheels,

metal instruments and dialysis machines and people on stretchers with cloudy IV bottles plugged into their arms, people with nostril tubes clamped in place with white tape, clutching the padded arms of wheelchairs, all dappled with the greenish yellow aquarium light which flooded in through the atrium windows and gave the procession of medical technology a floaty underwater logic. I thought: That's what happens, you creep over to the other side one morning, suddenly a chair takes on an incredible solidity, it weighs what it would on Mars. Lying down becomes a complicated negotiation. Even if your body feels normal, you know the slightest unconsidered movement will shake something vital loose or shift something around, this big elastic bag of flesh you've carried around in total confidence for years and years falls in love with its own demolition and starts courting randy microbes, loose viral particles, plaques and embolisms and alien cells, it offers bits and pieces of itself for any invader to nibble on, you watch as your body entertains your enemies at dinner, its loyalties divide between you and them, and after a while you become hypnotized by the disappearance of yourself.

I took the elevator to Paul's floor, where nurses passed in every direction. No one questioned my presence. I wondered why, in a city where so much violence had been directed against people with Paul's disease, patients weren't guarded against the much-touted general population. But of course the people with the most to say about the illness would never go near its actual victims. All such people are ruled at any and all times by cowardice and a staggering capacity for abstraction. Me too, I thought. Had I thought I'd catch it if I visited Perkins, or had I really kept away because I had nothing hopeful to offer him? I have nothing much to offer Paul, either. He's standing in the alcove near the elevator, smoking a cigarette. That's him. He doesn't look himself. It takes him an effort to walk from the room, he's looking at me with those deep eyes, I smile but I smile differently than I would if he weren't dying; tighter, as if it wouldn't be nice to look happy. He doesn't exactly smile, he adjusts his body on the wooden bench after sitting down in a way that insists that he's physically there, still in his body, even though he's lost about thirty pounds, his face used to be so broad it really beamed when he smiled his devilish smile, now it's tightly glued to his skull.

Don't look at me like that, he says. Why would I need to give up smoking now?

I've been determined to kiss him on the mouth, but I forget in the crucial moment when I should. Now it would seem histrionic and "brave" instead of natural. I light a cigarette instead.

You don't look so bad, I tell him.

No, he says. I think we've got quite a ways to go yet.

I look at the tip of my cigarette as if I expected it to talk to me, then touch his arm, glance out the window. The Roosevelt Island gondola crosses the air in the middle distance. Have you ever wondered, I say, what sort of people actually live on Roosevelt Island? Not many Roosevelts, I don't imagine, Paul says, looking at me instead of the window. They've taken me off the protocol, he says. Until the other day, I was getting the biggest dose of DDC of anyone in the world, but now I'm having this problem, he continues, rubbing his temples, with my face, he says, they think the virus went into the nerve endings around my cranium, into the facial tissue, here, and here. Insidious fucking virus, isn't it? It's torture moving my head right now, if I don't seem very animated it's on account of that. They think they can treat it, he says, they're giving me doses of this anti-seizure drug, bit by bit, they think it will gradually eliminate the . . . the neuropathy. Other than that, it's just the Kaposi's, but Jesus Christ, it's amazing when you get a *new* pain, first you think your whole consciousness has been taken over by one pain, then you get a new one. They're not giving me anything for pain, because they've got to figure out if this other drug is working. If they add anything to your treatment, even an aspirin, they've got to take you off the protocol. It doesn't seem to make any difference at the moment, but then again I'm not infected with anything, a lot of people get this thrush business, in the mouth, I've even heard of the most incredible sorts of rectal pathology. Knock on wood.

I think: If he knocked on wood he'd probably break his hand. I search for something to say, acutely aware that most of my current conversational stratagems involve complaining about Gregory. It's really offensive to complain to a dying person. Paul asks about him. He asks: Is he nice with you? I think he tries to be, I say, he's someone with a lot of problems. Paul says: Well, we've all got our problems. After a patch of silence we both erupt in malignant laughter, scaring two paramedics coming off the elevator. I look into Paul's eyes. He's a shit, I tell him, choking on my own giggles. An absolute total shit.

You always head straight for the shits, he says, waving a fresh cigarette at the window. A city with ten million beautiful well-adjusted guys, and you'll ferret out the one shit like your life depended on it.

I protest: Well, you weren't a shit. It's not like I'm asking for it.

And look where it got me, Paul says, right *in the shit*, can you feature it?

It's all shit, I tell him bitterly, grabbing his hand and instantly letting it go, remembering the lesions. I'm sorry, I said, did that hurt you?

They don't actually hurt, he says. They just suppurate.

We listen to the hum and throb of the hospital and watch the soundless river shatter light into thousands of white drops. It isn't fair. We used to say: How can we live like this? And now the question really is: How can we die like this?

PART TWO

Pornography

6

The weather turns at last, the new restaurants on Second Avenue plant their tables on the sidewalk. Are we racing forward, into the brave new world? Someone dies in an apartment three floors down, a week later the place is gutted by beefy Polish workers, three weeks later the place rents out to a prosperous, starched-looking couple for $1200 per month. People who sail out the door every morning carrying matching briefcases, dress for dinner, complain to the landlord about the opera singer on my floor who rehearses in the evening, have the hall bulletin board removed as a fire hazard.

M.'s phone now can do conference calls, and he doesn't need to hold the receiver. The entire studio and living space next door are miked. He ambles through his cast-iron kingdom, touching up a painting, fetching Cokes from the fridge, talking all the while as if other people were in the room with him. A Peeping Tom would suppose that M. talks to himself all day.

Richard's new answering machine has its own voice: Hello, you have six messages. I will save/erase your messages. That was your last message. It even says: I have detected a malfunction. I.

Libby's phone has a hold button and call waiting because Fred's a musician and if a booking agent calls and the line's busy, the agent will just contact another band. Libby wants separate phones. Fred feels separate phones would indicate that they're starting to leave each other. It's only the first step, he tells her. Next it will be separate televisions.

Jane has a "friend line" and a "business line." The "friend line" stores numbers up to ten, for her ten best friends she only needs to press a single digit. Now, she told me, to call you I simply push "Auto" and then "Two." Oh, I said, hurt. In that case who is Number One?

Gregory rings me out of an alcohol-heavy sleep, from a recurring dream in which the architecture of a vast hotel continually shifts, revealing unexpected suites and corridors inhabited by figures from the middle past, along with the peripheral gnomes of everyday Manhattan. I've started my job. This has already brought me too much attention. I am terrified of failing in public, drying up, having nothing to say. And now there are countless people out in the black space of the city thinking about me, craving my attention, writing letters to me. It is a strange role to play in the lives of others, writing things they read standing up in the subway, at their morning desks, in moments of distraction. When I see my first magazine page in print, my name in blocky letters under a not terribly funny, punning title of the kind the publication favors, I read through the article and think: I'm not him.

I'm not him. He is a personality I don't really like: a bit stiff, a little too intellectual and too moralistic, not hip enough. His voice strikes a middle register between my voice and the voice the dutiful employee inside me thinks is reasonable enough for the audience. He approaches everything with a lot of inner fidgeting. When I read what he's written, I see the lonely, awkward child he once was, someone who never quite managed to live in his own body. He expects someone to hit him at every corner, and he can't dance unless he's had a lot to drink. No, I'm not him.

The hotel is an expanse of pink and white gingerbread next to the sea, right on the Atlantic. The scene is briny-smelling and Whistler-gray with a chill skimming off it; a flag flaps on the lawn mast. Massy formal gardens, in the Italian manner, are laid out in back. Sometimes the hivelike innards of the hotel mutate, changing into pieces of the Luisiane in Paris, the Locarno in Rome, the Gramercy Park in New York. The figured patterns of the carpets shift, rooms shrink and expand. The dimensions of the elevator cages change from scene to scene. If the dream ever played out entirely, all the people in my life would show up in one room or another, in unimaginable combinations. Even the dead could carry on a second life in the onyx-and-ormolu dusk of the cocktail lounge, regaling each other with posthumous adventures.

When I wake from this dream, the true extent of the hotel is just about to reveal itself, but it never does. Gregory needs $60 to ransom two Cibachromes from the lab. Instead of asking for it, he describes his current situation in Byzantine detail, implying that even if he manages to pay the lab, his problems are so wearying and tangled that it's almost asinine for him to go on making pictures, or doing anything, really. When I offer the money, Gregory's voice squirms, dissatisfied. He doesn't want me to imagine he's calling just to borrow money, he's calling to let me know how miserable and hopeless things are, and how little my loan—which he's unbelievably confident that I'll give him—will affect his unhappiness. As Gregory dilates on this theme, I remember myself as an adolescent, the incurable discontent I lobbed at my mother whenever she tried to improve anything. Now I have become her, or rather Gregory's mother, the place where he lodges his complaints and demands restitution for life's little injuries.

Except Gregory's injuries are never, in his mind, little. He makes it sound as if he's doing his work, making his pictures, only to please me, against his own better judgment. I want to

say: Suit yourself. But this would unleash a torrent of accusations. It's easy for you, he'll tell me, you've got a fantastic job
and prestige and you don't have to slave in some menial position where you feel like an asshole all the time, you're so unfair,
you don't understand, you're always demanding things I can't
give you and yet you're not even sympathetic to me. I've learned
that the gentlest suggestion that Gregory's feelings of persecution might be exaggerated brings instant, crushing retaliation,
threats to end our relationship, intimations of suicide. He tells
me I'm insensitive, selfish, incapable of really loving him. If I
loved him, apparently, I would succumb to his mercurial but
bottomless depression. And to some extent I do. Gregory's a pro
at ruining an evening, a day, a whole week.

I'm happy to give him money, although I can't really afford
it. And I'm afraid he'll resent his indebtedness before long. But
Gregory doesn't simply want money. He needs my emotional
involvement in his need, to feel I'll be unhappy until he's contented. I recognize the tone of voice, the note of unslakable griev-
ance. I can't just hand him the cash. I'll have to monitor his trip
to the lab, call to find out how the prints look, ask if the money
covered it, and offer more for his living expenses. What on earth
does he do with all the loot he pockets at work? He's always brag-
ging about how much he steals, then never has a cent. Maybe
he exaggerates the thefts, to seem bolder than he is. He tells me
things he says to rude customers, always things so cutting and
elaborately insulting that I know he never says any such things,
I know because I ask: Well, then what did he say?, and Gregory
draws a momentary blank, or tells me, Well, what could he say
after that, he just gave me a look.

These lies have a youthful charm, they protect his ego and he
believes them. But they break the continuity. How often lately I
want to ask: Who exactly are you, Gregory?

He keeps me waiting a half hour in a coffee shop, refuses to sit for five minutes, looks agitated and vaguely scared about something, won't hear of me going with him to the lab, accepts the money with a bleak smile and promises he'll pay me back tomorrow or the next day, apologizes for his nervousness, tells me he feels shitty about everything but knows this will pass when he's taken care of some details, and seems the whole time to be talking to someone else, someone he needs to convince. Then he disappears, stuffing the money into his shirt pocket. I pay my check a moment later, rush into the street, and look for him in every direction. Gregory moves fast.

One afternoon when I had cleared away every distraction, mailed out the phone bill and the rent check, written letters to Europe, tidied up my desk, and settled down at last to work on *Burma* after weeks of inactivity, Victor called. Victor made cheery, inconclusive noises, hemming, hawing, it seemed he had time on his hands, didn't quite know what to do with himself, Victor's habit is never to propose anything, never to extend a concrete invitation, but always, invariably, almost abjectly, to make these noncommittal noises via telephone, ending in what is often called a "pregnant" silence, in hopes that I will pitch some palpable proposition into the furry static of the telephone, which on this occasion carried two faraway metallic voices, one male, the other female, chirping away along a glitched connection.

So now, said the man's voice, she's using the kids to speed up the court order.

Oh Hank, said the woman's voice, she's cutting up her nose to spite her face. And the sick part is, she knows it.

I says to her, the man said, you already found out we're not getting any overtime. I mean, she knows we're not delivering a full week any more and if the local walks off next Monday I'm a monkey's asshole on the picket line for the next six weeks.

It's what I'm telling you, the woman said, Sylvia's letting Annie lead her right by the nose. She thinks because Annie got that big settlement from Frank, all she needs is powerful attorney over your paycheck.

Using my kids, the man said, that's what frosts my ass.

Can you hear that, Victor said.

This phone sounds funny, the woman said.

What Sylvia tends to forget, the man said, Annie's case was open and shut, she had "before" and "after" pictures of her face.

Frank is prone to violence, the woman said, which for one thing, you're not.

Try telling that to Sylvia, the man said, she makes a mountain out of a molehill.

Do you want to meet somewhere, I asked Victor.

Something's funny with this phone, the woman said.

Well, said the man, it's fucked.

Swat I told you, the woman said. Hank, I hate to say this straight out but Sylvia's nothing but a little whore.

Yeah, the man said, but she's the mother of my kids.

That's the tragedy, the woman said. She was damned lucky, Hank, very damned lucky to land a man like you in the first place, and now she's cutting up her nose to spite her face to destroy you.

So what if I come over, the man said.

I'll come over, Victor said.

This phone's wacky, the woman said.

An hour later Victor showed up, holding a quart of Ballantine ale in a soggy brown bag. A bad sign, I thought, once it starts with Victor, it never stops until we're sloshed and maudlin. I'll lay out all my insecurities and frustrations, and he'll tell me stories about his hillbilly relatives, all those shitkickers in the Tri-State

area, shitkickers and general practitioners and county patholo-
gists and federal circuit judges married to his sisters and cousins.
Or else, we'll get on to Richard somehow, and Richard's quirks,
and how phony and superficial the world Richard moves in is,
Victor will describe some recent uptown dinner he's been dragged
along to by Richard, and how he, Victor, repelled some errant
snottery or inane comment from one of Richard's dim-witted,
filthy rich chums, stopping the person's mouth dead in its tracks
with a penetratingly candid observation, such is Victor's conversational agenda. Or, he'll explain in Gothic detail why he admires
my integrity and my mind. Victor can be a regular little toady
when he works himself up to it. And yet we do amuse each other,
hardly ever does an evening spent with Victor seem humorless in
retrospect, even when there are lugubrious patches of self-pitying
exposition, on his part, or my part, the real problem with Victor,
as far as I can tell, is that Victor's never carved out a place for
himself, never entered the fray, the city grows harder and harder
to live in yet Victor maintains his low-level equilibrium, he's
never focused on anything, never said to himself, I want X, Y, or
Z, I'll do whatever I need to get them. Instead, Victor has been
content knocking out custom furniture, sedating himself with
manual labor, standing on the sidelines of my career and Richard's
career, Victor extracts his sense of himself from his intimacy with
Richard or his friendship with me, he wins points in that bar he
spends so much time in down the street, Richard and I experience
all the real conflicts of life, and Victor gains simply from hanging
around us.

Richard hasn't slept with Victor in years, or rather, he's slept
with him but hasn't made love with him, Victor's become a sort
of honorary consort to Richard, who has all kinds of desperate
sick affairs with insane people while Victor lolls around, cleaning
Richard's loft, cooking Richard's food, doing Richard's chores,

making the world safe for Richard, who says Victor's hanging around drives him nuts, that it gives him a false sense of security, and Richard's too lazy and too comfortable to do without it so the guilt he feels gives Victor a further wedge. Richard tells me: I love Victor, he's one of the nicest people in the city, but the fact is, he's too nice for his own good, I can't shake him off because he's like this overgrown puppy, and the sex part has been finished for years, Richard says. Frankly, he says, it wasn't anything so wonderful to begin with, Victor has a sweet Italian face but his dick is tiny and he doesn't know how to use it to excite anybody, that's why he flips out over Orientals, they don't expect anything gigantic in that department, Victor's all cuddly and soft like a pussy, Richard reports, he's so gentle you want to kick his ass. It's strange, Victor works out every day, his body's perfect, he's built like a brick shithouse but in bed he's a pussy.

With me, too, Victor assumes a subservient role, somewhere between a friend and a valet. He opens the ale, pours it, carts the glasses into the living room, plants himself down on the floor and looks at me with puppyish expectation. It's my job to decide what to talk about, he's not exactly brimming over with news, and so, naturally, I tell him I'm rattled by my new job, it's eating up all my productive time, the hours leading up to my deadline are hours of pathological anxiety for me, I sometimes think I'm having a heart attack, but of course it's also bringing in money, right now I need money, I suppose I will always need money, and once you have money, it's impossible going back to having no money, here I've been scraping by for seven years, begging and scratching for chump change over the phone, whoring out on little acting jobs, little rewrite jobs for little independent films, selling the occasional slender essay to ill-paying magazines, whining to rich friends about the unfairness of it all, especially to M., who gets a commission whenever someone flushes a toilet in North America, and now, at least, I'm getting a regular check,

I can fix this flat up, go to the dentist, start *really living*, but then, now that all my time won't be consumed by begging and borrowing, I'll discover that writing for the paper chews up every second, making it impossible to finish my book.

Oh, Victor says heartily, once you get this apartment under control, you'll find yourself using your time more productively. The clutter of all these unshelved books and papers everywhere distracts your mind. You really only need a few shelves, and a file cabinet, fix this leaking plaster, paint the floors, in fact, he says, what you need are tables, and a proper bed, get your life up off the floor, you'll be amazed how it changes your entire attitude.

I nod stupidly as Victor gurgles on about beds and tables and shelves and file cabinets, we both know perfectly well I'm not going to do anything. Richard often says: Have you noticed that Victor's paranoid about smelling bad? It's true. Victor thinks he smells. Sweats from labor and then smells, or sometimes for no special reason Victor says: Jesus, I really smell today. I've never noticed any odor coming from Victor, but for a while now Victor has been advertising the idea that he gives off a miserable smell. I wonder why he goes on about it.

Richard has no body odor, no body insecurities either. Richard dances his nuts off whenever he goes out, Richard's all body, it probably works his nerves that Victor's so stiff, so uncomfortable with himself. And Victor wears these ugly square glasses that ruin his face, thick frames that make his jaw seem more square than it is, though they do hide the softness of his blue eyes, which are so soft and watery they retreat into his skull when he takes his glasses off. When he takes his glasses off, Victor looks like a weepy little boy who's just wet his pants. Victor has a black belt in karate. I don't know what he gets out of it, developing this complicated skill he can't use, when he never develops any that he could use.

I read Victor my recent notes for *Burma*. Except for the early pages that flowed so lyrically, all I have are notes. I am never entirely sure if I am actually writing a book because of the huge spaces of time that have interrupted my progress. The narrator travels to Rome or Venice, probably Venice so that something important could occur on the Rialto Bridge, just as the morning bells toll and echo across the canals, though maybe that's too stagey, and from there, he catches the slow night train to Ancona, meeting in the pitch-dark compartment a coffee-skinned boy named Antonio who wears a red beret, who takes him into the WC, where they clumsily have sex as the train lurches back and forth. In Ancona, the friends who had been living near some caves on the Adriatic have vanished, he's stranded suddenly with $40. He hangs around the public square, loitering under the spiky palm trees, waits for someone to pick him up. No one does. He wonders if he's beyond the age when other men will protect him. In Rome, his bank wires New York, it takes ten days to answer, when the wire comes the account's empty, the friend he thought he could trust to deposit checks hasn't done it, he now ends up sleeping in the Termini, guarding his pockets, woken every few hours by the carabinieri's nightstick, placing collect calls during the day from the phone center under the station. He has enough lira to shower at the station every day, checks and unchecks his luggage as he needs clothes, washes his feet in all the fountains. At a big fountain near the station a Brazilian guy invites him up to an expensive hotel suite, treats him to an all-afternoon fuckorama that leaves his ass bleeding, then shows him a green chamois sack full of square-cut emeralds. You'll never have things like this, the Brazilian tells him. You're a loser, a wimp. Good for fucking and that's all.

He tells the Brazilian he's a lousy fuck, that his dick tastes like goat cheese. Later the same night, they meet up again, in the cruising park near the hotel, he gives the Brazilian another long BJ and this time lifts the guy's wallet from his pants, which are bunched around his ankles. The guy comes, with histrionic groaning and panting, then as he's pulling up his pants the narrator runs from the park, runs past the Termini into a part of Rome he doesn't know where lots of mammoth ruins are brooding in the moonlight, runs till his lungs ache, wonders how a vast city can be so still and quiet and full of eternity at night, the eternity of sex and blood and death, and finally he sleeps under a bush near the Teatro Marcello. Under a carpet of stars. The next day he buys a ticket for Munich with the Brazilian's dough.

It all really happened, I tell Victor, but it's becoming fictitious as I write it down, I don't believe in it anymore.

These things that happen between people who don't know each other and never see each other again might as well be fantasies. The big problem, I say, is getting him from one place to another, so far this book is stalled, stalled in South Hampton that summer with Rita when it all began, my adult life, five or six or seven years ago when my adventures started. We've gone for more drinks, the bar on Avenue A features dark mirrors set in smoked wood and tables full of magenta-haired teenagers in spray-painted black leather jackets. Some of these kids have soft, kind faces. Others are puffy with a strange fascistic rage. Behind the bar, a chubby youth with a dozen studs in one ear, a wrinkly shaved head, and oddly endearing bad teeth—at least one flaw that isn't self-inflicted. The kids and the bar are among the things that have taken over the neighborhood. Hardly the worst things.

Maybe the story is too complicated, Victor suggests. That train stuff, this travel from country to country. Then you have to paint in this vast panorama full of precise details. Why not make everything happen in your apartment?

Who would want to read what happens in my apartment, Victor, virtually nothing, not that anything has to happen in a book, but you'd think I could put all my adventures to use, a lot of people never even have any adventures, whereas I've had many, many adventures, just think. If they die on the vine I'm going to feel like a terrible . . . vagrant.

Victor asks about Gregory. This unleashes a Niagara of complaint, to my own astonishment. I realize I've been storing up anger like a dry cell battery. Gregory's invariable lateness, our canceled dates, the casual contempt that flashes through his behavior like the metallic threads in that vest he's always wearing. Gregory adores himself with such incredible ardor, and yet he hates himself too, and so hates anyone who adores him as much as he does. I've acted like a masochist before, I tell Victor, but no one's ever quite picked up the ball the way Gregory has. Victor has heard this catechism of lamentation before, he doesn't even need to say: You see the pattern here. Two days on, three days off, one day on, four days off. The guy's a fucking flake. It's because he smokes so much grass, I suggest, defensively. And he used to shoot heroin, Victor reminds me, right? Yeah, but he doesn't do it now, I protest. This I'm sure of.

In the street, I suddenly feel that Gregory is much better than I've painted him, I rue having poisoned Victor against him before they've even met. At first I would only tell my friends that Gregory made me happy, but now he scrambles my feelings every other day and I don't know what to think, really. Since my friends don't know him, the only picture they have is the one I give them, and I'm continually retouching it according to how he treats me. I'm sure I'm getting tiresome. I burst into tears in front of my building, blubber and drool against Victor's shirt while he whispers that I deserve better than that little crud, that he can't stand seeing me so upset. As Victor says this I get the creepy feeling that Gregory has somehow overheard every word of this conversation. In fact, I never say anything about Gregory without imagining he's inside my head, listening to everything. On some deep-down level where I can't conceal anything he knows me, knows when I panic about this thing between us, knows when I'm hating him, he even knows when I've forgotten to think about him. And of course the prudent thing, the grown-up thing, is never to discuss the intricacies of a love affair with anybody. But what lover, abandoned time after time without warning or explanation, can sustain himself on prudence?

Three in the morning. An iodine breeze scuds off the river, the streetlamp rakes flecks of mica in the sidewalk. The middle-aged homeboys who usually occupy all the stoops on the block have crawled back into their flats like tuckered-out cockroaches. A skinny, fiftyish leather lady marches past with the *Times* under his studded sleeve and his Afghan on a rhinestone leash. I remember that I've invited Gregory for dinner on Friday, that I need Victor's help to clean the apartment. Now, after bad-mouthing Gregory all night, I can't very well ask. So I make up something. I just remembered, Victor, I've got these important people coming Friday, I hate to ask you, but it's business, and I'm busy all day tomorrow, I won't have a minute between now and then to clean. Please, as a friend.

What people? Victor wants to know.

Oh, publishers. A couple.

You didn't mention this.

Well, I didn't want to say anything until I got a firm deal, in case everything falls through. Anyway, you see why it's important for me even just psychologically to have a clean house when they come over.

Sure, he says, no problem. Shit, he says, it's about time something comes through for you.

Thanks, Victor, I tell him, I think so, too.

7

A memorable lie, as it turns out. On Friday Victor arrives two hours late, adding to the senseless panic I feel when I wake up: Gregory's coming here, at last. If he sees what a slob I am he'll have all the more reason to despise me, we've got to get everything spotless, and how is that even possible, there's no place to hide all these years' worth of idiotic accumulation, all these books, newspapers, it's my mother's fault, she's never thrown anything out, at home there are thousands of shoe boxes full of receipts and notebooks and family snapshots, I'm just like her, with Gregory I'm actually turning into her, why has it always been so strange between me and my mother when I'm exactly like her, and Gregory, Gregory's a bit like my father, clever with his hands, anyway, this is the trouble with getting involved with people, they don't know what they're supposed to be with each other so they turn into their parents. Dear Christ, this place is filthy. It's a wonder I'm not insane. Victor can somehow manage all this brutal organizing, what stops me, exactly? I'm afraid of this piled-up crap everywhere. It's my life, it's stronger than me.

I don't mind watching Victor clear everything out of here. It's less of a decision if he does it. I've lived here too long. You can't have your own life in New York except if you're rich. For years and years I've been going through this door, down and up these stairs, in the door again, the mailbox has brought me millions of pieces of waste paper, most of them still lying around in disturbing clumps, stuffed into shoe boxes, Victor sweeps through the apartment swabbing down surfaces while I yearn for a garbage dumpster big enough to swallow the entire past. Books, books everywhere. I suppose this is my life, my books. Virginia Woolf and Leopardi and Henry James and Joseph Conrad, Thomas Mann and Heinrich Mann, Chekhov Turgenev Dostoevsky, Jane Austen, Charlotte and Emily Brontë and George Eliot, Defoe and Fielding and Swift and Pope, Byron Shelley Keats, Hazlitt, Herzen, most of all Nietzsche, Sartre, Darwin, Lévi-Strauss Plato Plutarch Pliny the Elder Pliny the Younger, Seneca's *Letters*, Olga Freidenberg's letters to Pasternak, Brecht, Euripides, *Don Quixote* (both versions), Dante, Ford Madox Ford, Swift, Kleist, Kafka, the *Fugger Newsletters*; these are the memories I've ended up keeping, Herodotus, no snapshots, Emerson, no souvenirs, *History and Class Consciousness*, some day I'll regret not holding on to other things, mementos, when my parents die, though of course now there's every chance I'll die before they do, how strange that must be, thousands of children dying before their parents do. Libby says she wishes she had tape-recorded her father's voice, because now she finds herself forgetting what he sounded like. Next time I go home I should tape them talking, though they never do say anything worth remembering, never open up, I've never had the faintest clue what either of my parents really thinks about anything, I don't even know if they're happy or miserable or bitter or resigned. Nothing worked out as they wished, not with me, anyway. They did get all the money they wanted, nothing outrageous, enough to live the same as everyone else, of course they slaved for it their whole lives and chopped off their childhood dreams and wishes, and now they *do nothing*, if I had to say what they enjoy in life I would have to say *television*, television and *shopping*.

It's true, I've lived here too long. The person who lived here before was a ribbon queen with a degree in Arabic languages, for years I sublet from him, surrounded by his thrift shop furniture, his winter clothes, his camp treasures, and then, somehow, a legal problem arose between us, the landlord offered a choice between a joint lease and eviction for both of us. He refused to sign, so the landlord evicted him *in absentia* and made me the legal occupant. And then I got threats, tirades, accusations, on blue airmail paper from Paris, weirdly mixed in with poetic descriptions of his Arab lovers, of paintings he'd seen in the Louvre, of unforgettable meals. Look here, I had written him, you've dumped me in an impossible situation. We'll both get thrown out unless you come to an agreement. And months later I received a fuzzy assurance, again on blue airmail paper, that he'd consulted a lawyer and nothing at all could happen. By then the thing had already gone to court. But his stuff stayed in the flat for a year, two years, finally I said, Enough. Libby helped me cart everything down to the sidewalk, on three sizzling afternoons in August, and six months later the former occupant, missing for three years, showed up on the roof of the building next door, like the ghost of Christmas past, demanding his spaghetti heels and Chianti bottle lamps and the rest of his junk. He wore a powder blue suit and looked like a sort of embryonic Daddy Warbucks, balding, with giant freckles, bulldog mouth, eyes glowing with the fixity of rampant self-deception. He'd already come to look the way he would at sixty. I called the police. They made no special effort to flush him from the adjoining building, but instead searched my place for drugs. A year later our paths crossed, in a local bar. He claimed he had a razor in his pocket, that he'd been "waiting to kill me" for three years. Well, then, I said, tonight's your lucky night. He backed off. And then I had the embarrassment of telling him all his belongings had bitten the dust.

The apartment still carries the faint musty smell of that faraway time, and other times. An era of pickups and bizarre micro-affairs with boys whose points of reference belonged to another planet altogether, the underbelly of Young America. Disturbed youths and borderline schizos harvested off Second Avenue in the doldrums beyond midnight, lean bodies and adorable faces that evaporated in daylight or loitered for days in a carnal stupor, living out of the refrigerator, sometimes helping themselves upon departure to small, electronic objects or pathetic amounts of cash. The Valium salesman who shaved every hair off my body and kept an erection for three days, afterwards calling from Bellevue: I dropped acid at the Ritz, he said, and I don't remember anything after that. And Dickie Dwyer, who liked fucking standing up and later went out on a speedball. Paco with the enormous balls: Suck it again, baby, drink all a my come. Lots of damaged children have fluttered through this place, surly moths on their way to distant bonfires. That whole scene tapered off wound down, whittled itself into disgusted chastity, long before the disease made sexual loneliness healthy. I lost the energy and zeal for seduction. The script became too familiar. The real sex of our time is fame and money, and all sex is negotiated through the porthole of those ambitions. Even with Gregory. We never get through a day without rooting around for equilibrium between his potential and my reality, what he feels entitled to and what he imagines I already have.

Hours and hours of epic cleaning: for him. I leave Victor mopping and scrubbing and rush to the Associated on Second Avenue. What does Gregory like to eat? A chicken, possibly. A stuffed chicken: mushrooms, onions, crumbs. But maybe he'd like a fish. All their fish here is frozen and greenish. I could run to the place on First Avenue before they close, pick up a pound of scallops. Vegetables. I'm sure he's fiber-conscious, probably likes broccoli, too, the one vegetable I really hate. Jane also likes broccoli. Jane really enjoys food, whereas I have trouble with it. I can't always get it down, especially first thing in the morning. It's the cigarettes. When I travel I have a better appetite. In Japan we got pickles for breakfast. It's funny how food has its own special hours. You eat this for breakfast, that for lunch, something else for dinner. They say you metabolize fruit much better in the morning. M. goes to a nutritionist. Jane was skinny for years and now she's expanded. I'm forty, she says, I'm going to eat what I want for a few years.

If he loves me, will he pretend he likes what I cook even if he doesn't like it? When you're seeing somebody you eat to humor him. Friends too. M. made a horrible omelette once, with all the gristly parts of a take-out chicken, I gag just thinking about it. Some people can eat every edible part of anything. Even marrow out of chicken bones. Turnips, forget it. No one eats turnips, or parsnips for that matter. What I hate are funny things in meat, those little beef veins that look like suckers. We shouldn't eat our fellow creatures. When you walk through Chinatown you see fish gasping for water in those wooden bins full of bloody ice, the Chinese are cruel, no more cruel than we are, but we hide everything. Even pork has some gross passages, even lobster, it's all cultural. Maybe my body's not perfect enough for him. I'm too thin, my chest's too narrow. And it could be too that my looks are really gone, I can't tell from the mirror. The gym doesn't help, all we do there is gossip and look at pricks.

I return with the food. Melon and prosciutto, so civilized. Three cheeses. Grapes, salads, red wine, chicken, an illusion of abundance. If this were only for me it would all rot in the refrigerator. Victor's finished the floors, he's drinking a beer and reading a porn magazine, an old one I bought last year. It shows teenage threesomes, all nineteen or twenty. A tall, cute one with a Prince Valiant haircut fucks a not-so-good-looking one who's spread out on a kitchen table, while another cute one with curly hair, kneeling on the table, prods his dick into the throat of the one getting fucked. These boys are continually recycled in other magazines under different names: Chuck, Dave, Tony, Peter. Chuck fucks Tony's ass on the pile carpet, two pages later Tony kneels over Chuck and rams his prick into Chuck's mouth on the bed. In another magazine Chuck's name is Billy and he takes it up the can from Peter. Peter, it says, has ten inches of thick throbbing man meat. He sits on Billy's face and Billy's tongue goes into Peter's anus. Next Peter has two fingers jammed into Dave's joy chute. Tony's name is Jason. Jason's enormous wet prick slides into Bobby's greased hungry hole. Fuck me, fuck me, Bobby squeals, pushing his eager rosebud down as far as it will go on Jason's pulsating pleasure prong. Tim shoves his succulent pole down Billy's deep throat. Peter takes all twelve inches of Joe's delicious beef stick. Dennis spurts his salty cream into the crack of Pedro's hairy butt. Jim's man juice spurts into Chuck's suck tube. Victor closes the magazine. He's sprawled out expansively on the floor in the front room, his paint-splattered work boots crossed at the ankles, as if he plans on sticking around. The apartment still looks cluttered, but clean, as if the person living in it has a relaxed but secure grip on things.

I lay out the beginnings of dinner on the blue metal desk that functions as a kitchen sideboard. This desk is the bane of my kitchen, as the built-in shelving is the bane of my study, the flimsy fiberboard closet and yellow foam chair the banes of the living room/bedroom area. Each room has its special bane, mainly residue from the Arabic languages expert. Disposal of the blue desk is a perennial topic of speculation. Victor says the desk could be folded up or taken apart by its internal hinges, if the hinges haven't rusted, but the hinges have rusted, and therefore to remove the desk I would have to hire large, strong people with equipment for getting it down the stairwell, this always seems an absurd extravagance even when I have money, and when I don't have money it becomes an urgent impossibility. I must have considered a million times, at the strangest imaginable moments, getting rid of the blue desk, it has often seemed, in fact, that getting rid of the blue desk would dislodge a staggering freight of recurring problems, liberate my mind, and allow me to really live. And yet, here it is, as always, the blue desk, symbol of everything oppressive and stultifying attached to this apartment. I tell myself I *cannot afford* to dwell, just now, on the implications of the blue desk, removing the puckered, yellowish chicken from its plastic wrapper. I know I could easily, easily become paralyzed, if I think too long not only about the blue desk in the kitchen, but about all the related, unsatisfactory things which make me less than perfect, the things Gregory will instantly notice. The childish objects I save and leave out in the open, for lack of more precious objects. This general look of disorientation, the visible evidence of mental asymmetry.

Victor came into the kitchen. Do I look all right, I asked. Oh, he said, you look fine. Chicken. Yes, I said, chicken, I thought this chicken, plus rice, with some vegetables. Good idea, Victor said. Yes, I said, but I seem to have forgotten how to fix chicken. Chicken's simple, Victor said. I know, I said, I've cooked chicken a million times. Nervous? he asked. Yes, I said, although God knows why. Well, Victor said. Chicken. Chicken's easy. You take the chicken, he said, and run it under the cold water. Victor snatched the chicken from the blue desk and bathed it under the tap. There, he said, popping off paper towels from the roll, laying out the chicken. Now, we'll salt the cavity. Salt the cavity, I repeated, fumbling on the shelf for salt. Got the stuffing? Victor inquired. I indicated a bunch of celery and a net bag of onions. Victor washed the vegetables and commenced chopping them into bright mounds. I felt helplessness washing over me, helplessness and relief, Victor was taking control of the chicken problem.

I opened a beer and sat on the rim of the tub, watching as Victor kneaded the choppings into a mash of damp bread, chattering the whole time about the placid spirituality of his karate training and the locker room at the Twenty-third Street Y. Rousing escapades flourished at Victor's Y, in contrast to the furtive cruising that went on at my health club. Victor was always vocal and explicit about the day's libidinal perks. Richard did things without talking about them, Victor talked about things without doing them, and I didn't do anything and didn't talk about it.

Victor gnawed his lips contentedly and made a display of practiced motions around the cored, sanitized corpse of the chicken. He derived a certain pleasure from making himself useful, a pleasure that instilled indolence in everyone around him. As usual, I thought, Victor hasn't the slightest disabling dread of real life and the little physical chores that go with it. Victor can clean and dust and soap things down and mop and then stuff a chicken without falling apart. I thought: This must have something to do with karate discipline. And lately he's been blabbing about "creative visualization," perhaps if I could creatively visualize I would take control, snip off these loose ends, these threads of distraction. I thought: I don't really know anything or how to do anything, my memory's lousy, all these books I read don't make me erudite or learned, knowledge simply passes through me like this beer, nothing sticks, I don't make anything out of it. And now I've even forgotten how to cook, I'm afraid of everything and I'm particularly afraid of Gregory. He idolizes me, but he also looks down on me because I'm not twenty-four.

I felt a rush of tenderness for Victor, tenderness and schizophrenia. Victor did not occupy the world of my other friends. He saw himself, in some convoluted sense, economically or politically estranged from the groups of people Richard and I knew. A few years earlier I had had more friends like Victor, people who lived in the neighborhood and thought of themselves as a permanent core of dedicated bohemians, people who resented the success of others and believed that their own artistic purity kept them out of the larger picture. They were, I often thought, permanently damaged by the sense of their own inferiority, unable to compete with "real" artists, "real" writers. Among Victor's friends, I was considered part of the big oppressive culture that kept them ruminating in their rent-controlled ratholes. I was held to be a traitor to the pure values that ensured failure. Victor's friends felt embattled. They pretended to be philosophical and indifferent to the rewards other people extracted from the city. In reality, they drank too much all the time and smoked too much dope and never attempted anything except little sycophantic exercises in drama or poetry or music which they staged for each other in local "spaces."

Victor asseverated his loyalty so often that I knew he betrayed me all the time, not maliciously, but from habit. I sometimes caught a look at Victor's darker side, just a peep through the keyhole. Somewhere in the back of my mind, I knew that Victor's excessive devotion concealed a constantly tabulated score of grievances. He reveled in discovering my little character flaws and moral lapses. He did not really wish to jam bread and vegetable mush up the anus of a chicken, but doing this for me added to my staggering debt. And one day Victor would present the bill for all his kindness.

That, I thought, is how people really are. Unless they see themselves as equal to each other, there is always some deranged form of accounting going on in one or the other's head, and we live in a system where no one is equal to anyone, all are exploited by everyone, no one gives anybody anything and everyone owes everyone everything, the only equality available is equality in misery, and even the miserable ones argue about who is more miserable than whom. But that is another story. This one continued with Gregory's arrival, just as Victor left. I embraced Gregory, hurried through the introductions, and sent Victor on his way, wondering why Gregory had turned up early.

When he's conscientious, it usually spells trouble. If he's on time, it means he's not staying long. The polite phone call presages a cancellation. But no, he's actually planning to eat dinner with me. I nail this down as soon as Victor's out of hearing range. Gregory looks exuberantly healthy: rosy cheeks, clear eyes, the customary all-black outfit that matches his hair, the embroidered vest. Chatty. He's spent the day at labs, getting test prints. His work, he says, is developing in leaps and bounds. When I get these two new pictures, he says, I'm giving them to you.

A new theme surfaces. He owes me everything. My encouragement has given him the self-assurance he needs to forge ahead. His exhibition will be dedicated to me, by name. As I picture some egregiously corny press release bearing this dedication, Gregory pelts me with flattery about my magazine column, which stiffens my mouth, makes me hold my breath until it's over, glazes me with embarrassment—I hate compliments, and even Gregory's praise sounds grossly overdone, calculatingly therapeutic, phony. I know what I'm worth, I don't need to hear about it.

He looks over the apartment, especially the books ("Gee, you've really got everything here") impressed (I think) by the austerity of my private mess. No TV, the cheapest kind of tape player for music, a shortage of all the typical comforts. Actually, I don't know what he's noticing, though it all appears to fit some picture he's gleaned from our conversations, since he acts as if he's at home. He follows my routine in the kitchen. Just before dinner's ready, I ask him to settle down in the living room and let me serve him. Then comes a moment of felicity: not quite anticipation, but an affectionate pretense of it.

Nothing holds, though. He refuses wine but encourages me to go ahead. His expression implies that too many drinks on my part will spoil the evening for him. I've never been drunk around Gregory, but I feel uncomfortably defiant as I pour a glass, and inhibited while drinking it. He consumes a very full plate of chicken and most of the salad, whisks out of the room for seconds which he eats with fastidious, piglike concentration, as if he were alone. I've laid the plates out on the floor, we sit on cushions facing each other. His feeding pleasure should gratify me, but as I watch big forkfuls of meat pass into his mouth and observe his lusty chewing, his sensuality seems gross, like the lewd exposure of a half-pumped erection. He eats the way other people masturbate, with a dreamy detachment from his surroundings. He sits cross-legged, bowed forward slightly. I look at the crest of his hairline and down the lithe slope of his nose, ponder the grip of his thick, spatulate fingers on my dime store utensils, and notice a light speckling of dandruff on the shoulders of his vest. His slender frame looks vulnerable as an eggshell, but there is something fierce and stolid in his body's self-protective signals. The way Gregory polices the space around him repels the thought of touching him. I want to shatter this barrier but I realize that any movement will freeze before contact. He scares me. He knows how to hurt me. His eating is carnal, yet it belongs to a special order of narcissistic display, like the gigolo costumes he wears at work. These shows of physicality suck attraction from the atmosphere. The stirring of desire, anybody's desire, confirms Gregory's existence. Thwarting desire softens the awful powerlessness he complains about in so many different ways.

He gnaws a final chicken bone, slumps back against the base of the yellow foam chair, burps. His lips curl. He draws a cigarette from his shirt pocket and says, You know something, I went in the bar last night, Victor was there talking to some friends of yours. Oh, I say, you know Victor. By sight, he says, but of course he didn't know who I was. I've seen you with him, Gregory says, and then he says, I heard Victor telling them he had to get up early and help you clean your house because you had these very important people coming for dinner and your place has been a dump for months. . . .

I laugh, but I feel my face turning red. Gregory enjoys this moment: he likes letting me know I can't conceal anything from him, can't pretend to be different than what I am. His amusement is gentle, but unnerving. It's so easy for him to destroy my defenses, yet his are impenetrable. I realize now that he showed up early to catch me fretting over dinner, unprepared and nervous. This is how he likes to see me. Psychologically off-guard, distracted, embarrassed by the obviousness of my desire. Powerless. He enjoys deflecting my efforts to contrive "perfect moments," he wants to show me he knows how my mind works, that he's not taken in by my subterfuge. Sometimes I think he's trying to discourage my wishes with elaborate tact, hoping I will accept him as a friend and nothing more. Maybe he's afraid to let me down too bluntly. But when I act cool and treat him as less than my most intimate friend, Gregory burrows under my skin until his attention reaches my crotch. He knows my dick is hard every minute he's around.

He's brought some tapes for me, Egyptian music he says he bought in Cairo. Chanting, flutes, tambourines. With a faraway, musing air he reminisces about camel rides in the desert, the effusive friendliness of Arabs, burnouses and casbahs. He tells of the oblivious infatuation of his travel sponsor, a "fat old queen" who he says descended on him like a bird of prey right after Gregory graduated from high school, plying him with gold watches and opal rings and designer clothes. "I didn't know any better then," Gregory qualifies. The fat old queen whisked him off to London, then Cairo. Just those places, no other ones. Doesn't sound like much of a world tour. This long-ago sugar daddy sounds plausible enough, but I don't believe Gregory has ever been to Egypt, or to London, for that matter. His memories sound a little too generic. Maybe he's inventing them because I've told him a fair amount about my own travels, and Gregory can't stand any experiential differences between us unless they support the idea that he's seen and felt more than I have. A few days ago when we talked about politics, Gregory suddenly revealed that President Reagan's son was an old school pal of his, and that he'd traveled with him to California one summer and visited the Reagan ranch, had dinner with the First Couple, etc., etc. At first, Gregory's description sounded just dull enough to be true. But as it developed, I recognized the bravura, hurried style of Gregory's improvisations. When Gregory invents, he patters, giving his listener no room for questions.

When I don't believe what he says, I work my face into what I hope is a neutral, credulous expression. His lies make me embarrassed for him. As he tells the fat old queen saga, I find myself translating it into more believable terms. I can imagine Gregory ten years ago, even more beautiful than he is now, like a smooth doll unmarked by experience. Not that he's much marked now, but his eyes look as if he'd seen a lot of things he shouldn't have.

An older man came along, from where he doesn't say. But I picture this older man as not all that much older. Gregory meets this guy in a gay bar in New Haven or Hartford, and the guy, who may or may not be fat, installs Gregory in a brownstone on Gramercy Park. (He pointed out one of those houses once, as a place he used to live. I've forgotten what else he told me. With him I'm a poor listener, always waiting for what I want to hear and not hearing what he tells me.) Dresses him in elegance and for a while gives him the tasteful life lived by a certain dated kind of respectable faggot. This is a period of rampant sexual consumerism. The old offer the young their money, use them for a season, discard them for fresh meat.

Gregory soon becomes bored, but he's afraid to shift for himself, without the fag's money. He finds himself torn between friends his own age who are less uptight, and the townhouse and this man. Eventually the lover gets bored, too, first of all with Gregory's petulance, then angered by Gregory's physical indifference to him, and one night, a horrendous fight occurs, Gregory finds himself in the street. He drifts to the nearest meat bar, one the lover won't look for him in. He finds a companion for the night, works his way into this new person's life until he finds a job and a place of his own. Maybe this sequence loops over and over until he goes home and enrolls in college. Yale, he says. After two semesters, he craves the anarchy of the city. Nothing really terrible can happen to him, not with that face. If Gregory stands on a corner for ten minutes, something promising will land at his feet.

I knit this background from the odds and ends he's dropped since I met him. His flights of exoticism may be real, for all I know, but they don't really matter. The point of what he tells me is that his life has been disjointed and weird and he isn't too proud of it, but now he's trying to be good. He relates his past transgressions to show how deeply he's changed. His relationship with me, he says, is his first real step towards responsibility, balance, mature caring. His speeches on this theme are frequent and embarrassingly histrionic. When he goes on about "us," about this unique bond between "us," I feel he's jumping a chasm whose true measure is unknown to him, and that he's putting words on things that can only be real if they exist in silence. Where we actually live from day to day, in the shared fuzz of telephone intimacy, Gregory constantly redrafts the terms of this "us," but abstractly, he considers us glued together for life in a pact of behavioral rectitude, exemplary moral fastidiousness, a *correct* homosexual couple. We simply haven't evolved into our future state of happiness, where the physical stuff will flow naturally from everything else. For

Gregory there's no disparity between his brave declarations of love and his abrupt displays of frigid indifference.

We try going out to a movie. Gregory insists on *Desperately Seeking Susan*; I suggest *The Purple Rose of Cairo*. I thought you hated Madonna, I protest. Yeah, but you said you hate Woody Allen, he counters acidly, pulling on his leather jacket, his face inexplicably dejected and sealed as if he regrets having wasted time with me.

You don't have to get pissed about it, I say.

I'm just annoyed, he says through his teeth, moving quickly for the door.

For Christ's sake, I tell him, following, do we always have to leave things in some weird place? You know I'm going to think about you all night, wondering if everything's all right between us, can't you just talk to me in a normal way? Look at me, I told myself, in wonder: I'm following right behind him like a dog.

How can it ever be all right, Gregory whines, when you want too much too fast and you don't give me any room to breathe?

What about you, I say.

I want everything, he says.

8

"Pain and fever" (my notes) "the dual monarchy." A picture from my front windows, that spring, of the street where it converges with the corner of Second Avenue. The liquor store with blocky neon lettering, the metastasizing Korean vegetable empire under its parti-colored awning, the greasorama BBQ chicken & steak grille with grass-haired punks ranged outside at a bank of world conquest video games. Gurgling noises from excited microchips, the sizzling of suspicious meat. The odor of rancid carcinogens mixing with the perfume of irradiated grapefruit.

"M., vainly attempting to rescue me from the horrors of infatuation, has a searching talk with Bruno about Gregory's background. Is he sincere? A heartbreaker? Taking me for a ride? To worsen things, M. tells Bruno I'm so obsessed with Gregory that I'll kill myself if he leaves me. He further yacks that Gregory's the only real boyfriend I've had in years. Bruno, with characteristic insensitivity, reports the whole thing to Gregory, who storms into my flat while I'm writing, letting himself in with the set of keys I've made for him (a gesture which places my privacy at the mercy of his whims)."

Mid-spring, days of grossly fluctuating temperatures. From balmy to mild to ugly gray and clammy, the weather of hopelessness. The final grains of winter have dissolved. On Second

Avenue, a sprawling Neapolitan bazaar clogs the sidewalk. Wasted types slump against cars and squat over blankets covered with disintegrating clothes, trinkets, books, stereo components, neatly fanned skin magazines, the contents of their apartments and, no doubt, of other people's apartments. Junkie couples with livid arms, pederasts with sagging stomachs, leftover hippies coated with filth. After 6 P.M., the gypsy encampment swells into a major obstruction.

"Gregory is indignant, as only Gregory can be. Hurt beyond belief. Betrayed. Angry. Freaked out. *Your friend M.*, he sobs tearlessly. *And Bruno, all these sick faggots*, he laments, and suddenly we're back in high school together. *They're trying to break us up, they can't stand the fact that we love each other*. Actually, I'm touched by M.'s solicitude, even though it pisses me off. This infuriates Gregory further. *It's nothing to smile about*, he instructs me."

I've settled into a productive attitude, behind my typewriter, six floors above the disintegrating neighborhood. The streets have become esoteric. Lurching beggars proliferate, like waltzing mice liberated from a vivisection lab, demanding change, cigarettes, attention. And their eyes and voices are becoming wilder. I can't look at them without seeing murder trembling in their grimy hands. At night, my block swarms with ultra-thin chicks in metallic halter tops and satin hot pants, their customers circling in slow-motion cars. Last year's dusky storefronts are blazing neon oases of sushi chefs and radical hairdressers.

The very young dress all in black, which makes them look old and tiresome and ugly. Gregory has pioneered this look, but carries it off with startling panache. Men follow him in the streets, he says. Sometimes he turns up at my door in a panting sweat. His forehead glistens, the forked, gray-blue vein near his right temple pulses strangely. His days are chronic, infectious dramas. Bruno has given him a one-day-a-week job sitting in the gallery. Another day less for me. He's meeting smart young artists, he's in a fever of creativity. The restaurant job is a bad joke to him now, because any day, he'll kiss it goodbye. He pockets ever huger percentages of the nightly checks, blowing the money on lab work. He has three or four pieces already mounted.

The late seasonal change has jolted reality into giddy motion. The phone rings off the hook, strange calls come from strangers. I change the number and enjoy relative quiet for a week, the new number leaks out, I change it again. With Gregory everything's touch and go, mostly go. We scrabble around in the geography of circumspection, walking on the eggs of each other's neuroses. I file my weekly column at the magazine, slip my weekly check into the checking account.

Despite the grand larceny Gregory commits at work, he's broke. His photos soak up every penny. He neglects his bills. He's developed a specially plangent, acutely modulated, nervous whine for times he needs to borrow money. At first it's $10, then $20 as a routine thing. Soon it's $30, $40, $50 at a go. M. is horrified. For Christ's sake, don't give him money, it's the quickest way to poison a relationship. But it's only *money*, I protest. All I'd spend it on is books, and I've already got enough books to read for the rest of my life. So, M. says promptingly, buy yourself an air-conditioner for the summer. Take a vacation. Invest in a new wardrobe. It's your money, you're working hard for it. And listen, M. says, his voice dropping down to flat, serious straight talk, you know you're just like me, you go out of your brain over these fucking *guys*, man, and don't tell me he's different, because I know he's different, he's nice, he makes nice all the time, he's not a creep and he really loves you, and all that, but your impulse, when somebody returns your affection even slightly, is you want to give the guy everything you have, make his life over, make him feel like he's wonderful and accomplished and equal to you, which is really beautiful, but let me tell you, M. says, if you give somebody all your love, and all your money, and try to put him up where you are socially, or careerwise, and he's not there on his own power, no matter how he justifies what he takes from you, somewhere in the back of his mind he knows he's exploiting you and he doesn't deserve it and ultimately he'll end up feeling like a piece of shit anyway, and if *he* feels like a piece of shit, M. goes on liltingly, you know goddamned well what he's gotta make *you* feel like for him to feel *equal*.

What do you mean "up where I am," I plead indignantly, what, I can't have a boyfriend because a few people know who I am?

In his head, that's up where you are, M. says. People read that magazine, he says. I hear your name all over the place lately. Don't think he doesn't feel like a trick.

I know, I know, I know, I chant, I try not to offer him money when he starts in, but then I feel like I'm being hard with him and in a way reminding him what a comparatively unfavorable position he's in, since I just sit here spinning things out of myself, I don't have to leave the house, whereas he's got to stuff himself into uniform and work on his feet for twelve hours every day.

He isn't the first pretty boy who had to work, M. retorts.

The high temperature has flushed M. from his studio. He's done a little walking tour of the East Village and ended up at my place, his fifth or sixth visit in as many years. M. marvels at the light, since there's no space. This apartment is, in fact, blessed with an unusual number of windows. At this time of year the bushy-headed trees soften the neighboring architecture. We could be in Paris, M. declares, as visitors often do, indicating the mansard roof and porthole windows of a chunky three-story building across the street. Like Libby and Jane, M. enumerates the advantages of my place on these rare visits, as if proving the folly of my malcontent.

M. is short and nervous and thinks his hair is going back, which it is. His face is moony and saturnine. When he's excited his voice swells and turns sinusy, ironic, a Jewish mother's voice. Behind his abrasively practical view of things, M. has a marshmallow heart that any perfectly formed young man can reduce to cinders. When he's infatuated he can't work, or thinks he can't, M. actually works more when he's in love but believes he's getting nowhere. This year his paintings are getting lots of attention. But M.'s new success hasn't made a dent in his suicidal depression, any more than the money he was born with. Five years ago, on one of the very rare occasions when things got insupportably bleak, I made the mistake of phoning him. *I feel my life isn't worth going on with*, I said, with realism. *You're right*, M. replied, *and neither is mine*. Perhaps calling him then wasn't such a mistake, everything considered. At any rate, just now M. has no companion and no fleshy fantasies, so his work goes well, and he finds time to fret over my affairs.

I steered Gregory around to a tolerant view of M., by forcing them into conversation at an opening. Gregory succumbed to M.'s standard, flatteringly seductive manner, mistaking an homage to sex appeal as a genuine interest in Gregory's personality. As a matter of fact, M. is indifferent to Gregory's existence, since Gregory is not available.

Memory places M. at the front window, occupying space in a stoutish way; memory paints in the avid flush of a tourist in an unexpected country. Despite the brevity of his visit, some months later, on my birthday, M. gives me a little gouache painting of a patch of brickwork above the yellow chair. We each have our way of being here and marking the time as it passes. Not long after this, M. and Jane throw a dinner party in honor of my new job, for a few close friends; an hour before I leave the house, Gregory calls to say he can't make it, that Philippe has suddenly demanded his presence at the restaurant. I mark his absence throughout the evening, blankly register the praise of friends, numb out when I should feel generous and happy. Somewhere between the entree and the Remy I phone the restaurant, and learn from a husky woman's voice that Gregory is not, in fact, working. As this information sinks in, I realize that Gregory intends for me to find this out, that he knew I'd call to make him part of this moment.

One night, after taking a Valium, I ask Gregory why he needs to hurt me. He says it isn't him, but Bob. Bob? Yes, Bob, he insists. Bob "takes over" when Gregory feels threatened. Bob unplugs Gregory's phone, cancels Gregory's dates. Bob hates Gregory and wants to ruin his happiness with Anna. Who is Anna, I ask him. That's you, he says, Sweet Anna, when you're sweet and nice with me, but when you're upset because of Bob, you change into Ruth. Ruth? Ruth's the one who protects you from getting too close to people, Gregory informs me. Bob protects Gregory even when he doesn't have to, he thinks if Gregory gets serious about another person, even Anna, he'll suffer so much it will kill him. And Ruth's afraid Anna will give herself body and soul to some worthless creep. Ruth is beginning to trust me, finally, Gregory says, so she doesn't threaten to destroy our relationship any more, but she still insults me, to test my love for Anna.

So Gregory and Bob and Ruth and Anna, and, I suppose, I, are locked into this thing together, apparently. Do others live like this? The discovery of these extra people defuses some of our antagonisms for a while: when an argument gets tripped off by an edgy tone of voice, Gregory says, Is that you, Ruth? Mind putting Anna back on the line? And I find I can coax Gregory out of nasty sulking by asking Bob what he's done with Gregory. The game runs its course in a few weeks, but for a time it plays out at absurd length whenever we talk.

And then other games, fictions woven between us; one of us holding the yam, the other knitting. First Gregory assumes a Southern accent. Soon he's doing it all the time, without much dramatic skill. From this artificial voice comes all the tender language I want to hear, the gurgled intimacies, the brazen sex talk, the things he can't or won't say when he's himself. In his own voice he's mercurial, drifting from enthusiasm to irritability without any logical transitions. In character, Gregory's face colors up with reckless optimism. He flies into the apartment, beaming with upbeat news: he's met X, X looked at his slides, said nice things about his work. Y talked to him, Y has befriended him, Y is an important artist. People around him are perking up, paying attention to him.

Against this pile of hopeful developments, the weight of his—what is it, exactly? An infernal dissatisfaction that contaminates everything. An expectation of disaster. Fear of the sabotage his own mind can easily wreak upon his plans, without warning. Trivial incidents oppress Gregory with obscene power. *As long as I've got you*, he moans, in his assumed voice, as if we were clinging together amid debris. But he doesn't have me, declines any opportunity to have me. When he plants kisses up and down my neck, I wonder who exactly is the "you," here. He bursts in one afternoon, croons that he's met Anna's sister, and presents me with a Xeroxed photograph on green paper, from where I can't imagine: a woman in a loud sixties dress, nursing a drink at a cocktail party. Her face matches mine in three-quarter profile. Who is this? Gregory smiles coyly, then rattles on about something else: Pugg wants to meet me. Pugg read a story of mine, he thinks it's a classic. Pugg told me, Gregory says, This story's a classic. I liked it last week, and I like it this week. Pugg has been floating around in the white space of our relationship long enough for me to wonder about him. From what Gregory tells me, they're like kids together, schoolmates or something. Pugg, for that matter, is a kid, twenty or twenty-one. I'm reluctant to meet him, worried that our age difference will make me seem old and out of it.

Pugg turns out to be a tall, broad-beamed, quiet boy with a shaved head and nervous features. His brown eyes flash away when you look directly at him. His mouth has a gliding, reptilian thinness. His voice, soft and uninflected, provides no clue to his personality. He's abstemious, guarded, like Gregory an ardent, flagrant narcissist. Every time I catch his gaze, he tilts his head as if peering into a favorite mirror. We're introduced at so-called brunch, in a dreary Art Deco joint where the glare of dead Sunday afternoon light filters through inch-thin hyacinth blinds. Gregory talks and talks, telegraphing their private jokes and observations. He knocks himself out to sound clever, and at one moment when he actually does, I touch his arm affectionately, then catch Pugg's eyes indignantly widening as they fasten on the point of contact. From this look, I understand that he and Gregory have just woken up in the same bed. Gregory immediately shifts the force of his charm from Pugg to me, talks in our private lingo, pushes Pugg into the wings of the conversation. He doesn't miss a ripple of tension. By the time we finish eating, I'm no longer sure what Pugg's look signified.

Pugg desires him. But does Pugg possess him? What kind of name is Pugg, anyway? They've slept together, I can tell, but maybe not so recently. Later, the three of us walk around the maze of Gregory's neighborhood. We poke into shops, examine clothes hanging off awnings on Orchard Street. The two of them seem very bonded, at least on the level of shopping. The lens of the afternoon keeps shifting. At certain moments I feel I'm the object of their interest, an adult whose behavior they're curious about. At other times Gregory's my lover. Then again, he's Pugg's. Gregory is threading his way to work. When we leave the Lower East Side, the walk becomes a silent tug of war between me and Pugg. I wait for him to detach himself; he waits for me to leave them alone. I'm tenacious. Pugg pretends obliviousness. When we reach West Broadway, Pugg finally relinquishes his hold. Before he gives up, though, Gregory goes into a rap about sex. A familiar theme lately. He feels clever articulating it. Now, he says, because of AIDS, he's not having sex with anybody until they find a cure. The only safe sex, he says, is if one person jerks off at one end of a room and someone else jerks off at the other, both trying to hit the same spot in the middle of the floor. I hate the smug, funny delivery of his little speech. It's as if the disease gratified his sense of justice. As he rattles on, Pugg's face parades an odd morphology of appraisal. Hard to tell if Gregory's letting him know he isn't sleeping with me, or letting me know he isn't sleeping with Pugg, or letting Pugg know he's kept me in the dark about the fact that he sleeps with Pugg.

Then Pugg skulks off in the direction of Washington Square. Gregory asks me what I think of his wonderful friend. He's charming, I lie, I guess the two of you are pretty close. You see how beautiful he is, Gregory says, catching my drift. Now he lets out a petulant sigh, his "I'm tired of explaining things but since I care for you I will" sigh: The first time we saw each other, Gregory confides, we wanted to rip each other's clothes off and fuck, but we didn't, he claims, we decided it was better to be friends. And isn't it, he insists, when you consider how fast the physical thing gets used up? Couldn't *we* be friends like that?

Personally, I don't find Pugg even remotely attractive. His face is so evasive and creepy. Everything about him is alien and slightly repulsive. If that's what Gregory's drawn to, he's more perverse than I imagined.

If you think I'm always fantasizing about having sex with you, you're wrong, I tell him, lying. But I'm sick of hearing how awful and disgusting sex is, Gregory, you made your point a long time ago.

It's the same as death, he says, the way things are now.

No, I say, it isn't, there's this disease, and it happens to get passed around through sex, that doesn't mean people who've had sex with each other deserve to get sick, and besides, Gregory, you slept around as much as anybody else a long while after this thing got started, don't pretend otherwise, maybe you're afraid of getting it from me, but I'm a lot more worried about getting it from you.

And it's true, though I suspect I'd forget about my own health if Gregory wanted to sleep with me. Some of Gregory's past lives have recently surfaced from other sources, including a suite of provocative photographs taken years ago at the Everhard Baths: these pictures, in the collection of a local jewelry designer, have fueled my jealousy of everyone who ever had him. And it's exasperating to consider how many people that includes.

Believe me, he's saying, you've got nothing to worry about, because I'm not taking any chances.

That's your prerogative, I say, but it's one thing to be phobic about it, and another thing to judge everybody else.

People are killing each other, Gregory replies, climbing on his mental soapbox, because they can't control themselves. I don't think it's wrong to pass judgment on that. Yes, I tell him, it is. I happen to think, he continues, that it's immoral to risk another person's life for the sake of your own uncontrollable libido. These queens, he says, I see them all over the streets, all they've got on their brains, apparently, is getting their mouths around some dick, it's like they want to die and take other people with them.

Oh, please, I say, disgusted.

Gregory makes a face. Look, he says, now grave and reasonable, these are the times we're living in, we've got to adjust, and that's it.

He keeps it up until we reach the restaurant. No one is inside except the cleaning lady. Gregory taps on the plate glass with his bunch of house keys. She shuffles to the door, a bosomy old party with a mustache, her mouth creasing into Slavic delight. We step into the entryway near the bar. I have a strong urge to slap him around. I want to beat him into submission.

The cleaning woman gives him an adoring look. The restaurant smells of garlic, stale smoke, and cognac. Ammonia wafts off the shining wood floors. Round tables crowd the narrow aisle between the bar and the dining room, where the walls carry large tin advertising signs for French products. This place looks like a struck stage for a play that's been running many years past vitality; I can remember when it was popular for two or three seasons. 1978, 1979. Crazy how long ago that is.

I watch Gregory as if through soundproof thicknesses of distorting glass. He wraps me in his arms and squeezes, an unexpected present. Darling, he whispers, in his Southern accent. He drawls something about dropping by later for a drink, as if he wants me to. Call first, he says. If things are slow here, you could come over. He talks as if it were usual for me to visit him at work.

I can't resist the invitation, though I sense it's a trap, another way of measuring my enslavement. He'll know I waited all night for the fun of traveling twenty blocks just to talk to him for ten minutes. Anyway, when I call, he tells me the restaurant's a madhouse, and not to come. If I could just seem for a few days not to care, one way or the other—this is my fantasy, that the ratio of need would reverse itself. But I know better. *I don't need you*, he sometimes says, *that need stuff is from a movie. I can love you exactly as much as I do now without ever seeing you again.* And *If you really have to get fucked, just go out and find somebody who'll fuck you.* The bathhouse photographs make his coldness seem doubly insulting: if he gave himself so freely and indiscriminately before, why can't he give me what everyone else has had?

I can't sleep. I decide to "leave him." Even this dire part of the lover's vocabulary sounds absurd in this situation. You can't leave someone unless you're living with him. If I break this off I'll go crazy, but if I wait, it will kill me. I'm living two distinct lives with Gregory. In one of them, things really happen as they do, I thrash the whole time against the wall of my longings. But the other life proceeds on dreams that can never materialize, since Gregory's strength consists of keeping them alive and slightly out of reach. This fantasy life has warped and buckled like a length of cardboard in a bathtub. I no longer picture happy endings, I know the twists and hairy turns aren't really part of some baroque courting ritual. All this madness is what I am going to have at the end, the same as at the beginning. We are traveling exactly nowhere. Away from the purring spell of his voice and the inexhaustible allure of his body, I feel madness brushing against my skin. My solitude has the fatal ugliness of wanting.

9

On Monday nights, fear puts me into a state of shock, although my editor assures me that whatever I feed into the magazine computer Tuesday morning will be, at worst, "enough to work with. " Gregory stages our worst arguments on Monday evenings, a fact he seems truly unconscious about. He knows his only rival is my job, and if he could amputate my legs to prevent me from walking to the typewriter, he would. The job is my only remaining source of self-respect. Gregory has already taught me that my face is plain and my body doesn't look wonderful and nobody else wants me. He also skewers any flaws in my thinking he can find. The only thing I can do that he can't comes from working. And so, on Mondays, he calls up and says, *This guy's been after me at work, he buys a drink and then tells me how he wants to get it on with me, he says he wants to get my meat hard. He says it like a joke, but you can tell he means it.*

Everything he tells me on Monday night is about his meat, his prick, his dong, his dick: *Guys used to tell me, You're crazy but you've got a fantastic cock. This queen used to pay me $100 to beat off while she dressed up like Marlene Dietrich, it actually got me turned on. I'd squirt and she'd rub the come all over her dress.* And sometimes Gloria drifted into the narrative, like an errant coal barge: *I'd wake up and she'd be licking my balls, or sucking on my toes, or have her* *tongue halfway up my asshole, and I'd tell her, Gloria, why don't you just fix yourself a sandwich or something . . .*

I thought: Oh, please, go cram it. The verbal invocation of his penis was foreplay to darker themes. He'd gone into the neighborhood gay bar after work *and this guy I used to shoot up with, he said you used to be in love with him years ago and told me you'd write him these desperate letters.* Gregory conjured a smoke-filled, gibbering underworld of low types eager for gossip and full of stories about me. It's funny, I told him, how in a world where there are no brains there can be so many long memories. Why are you going in there unless you're trying to score? *Are you so insanely jealous that everything I do has to be about sex? Can't you imagine I might want to relax a little bit after fourteen straight hours of hell?*

Meanwhile, after a month on the job, I feel a constant pressure in my head, paranoia in the street, a kind of constant embarrassment. People recognize me wherever I go. I've begun to feel like I'm walking out on stage whenever I leave the house. When I read over what I've written in the magazine, I pretend I'm specific other people reading it and imagine their reactions. And every week, the moment rolls around when I must *perform*, make my brain do something fast, develop an idea into 1500 tortuous words that will have some sort of effect on the public.

The deadline terror feels like something worse, so I make an appointment with M.'s new doctor. I notice blood, sometimes, on the toilet paper. Bright red, which usually comes from hemorrhoids, if you have real internal bleeding it comes out brownish. But my mind jumps to stomach cancer, perforated ulcers, vast systemic maladies. Maria Lorca, a short brown-haired woman in her late twenties, projects thoughtful competence and a faintly terrorizing, ruminative manner. Her practice has clean lines and muted colors. Her voice lets the air out of the doctor-patient helplessness I've brought in with me. I complain of unbearable tension, debilitating sleeplessness, and morning shakes, hoping at least to wangle a Valium prescription.

Maria Lorca peers into my rectum with a proctoscope and declares it free of pathology. She palpates the flesh of my stomach, my back, my chest. She says: I can't feel any tumors in there. She says: Is it just your job bothering you? What's the rest of your life like?

I think: What is the rest of my life like? I have this boyfriend. At least he's sort of my boyfriend, but that isn't too clear. He used to be an addict. He kicked it, but the way he acts seems like he learned all this junkie behavior he can't get rid of. For instance he's always late. Not a few minutes late, but at least a half hour, sometimes so incredibly late I can't believe it's happening. He never understands why this upsets me. Sometimes he doesn't show up at all. Or he calls, insists on seeing me, tells me it's urgent, so I get all prepared, interrupt whatever I'm doing, if I'm working I stop dead, an hour goes by, he calls and says he's been delayed, but now he's coming right over, another hour passes, then another call, at this point I say, If you don't plan on coming, I'd like to go out. He gets pathetic then and says, Of course, if you've got something more important to do. And I say, There's nothing more important than you, but you can't eat up all my time like this. I'll be there in ten minutes, he says. So I get on the phone and call up a friend, to make the ten minutes go by without going nuts, I'm talking to this person, I even say, I called because he's on his way over and I don't want to feel like an idiot, frozen in anticipation. So we talk. But I can't concentrate because I'm expecting to hear his key in the door. I even take the phone to the window and stick my head out, if I think I see him coming my blood pressure drops about twenty points, but no, it's never him, then I walk away from the window, thinking if I don't look out, that will make him get there faster, and when I think, Well, he'll be here any second, I get off the phone, more time passes, I start freaking out, I call someone else, this time I say, That little bastard has done it again. I say I'm at the end of my rope, he's been doing this to me since I met him, I know I'm debasing myself putting up with it. A few times when he phoned, I waited the usual time, more like an hour, then I went out. The whole time I was away I thought about him, wondering what his reaction was when he found out I'd left. So I go home, expecting to find calls from him on the machine, or a note, but surprise, he didn't call, not even to say he'd be late. Then I can't reach him the next day, or the day after. When I finally hear from him he tells me he went off with some friends that night, not because I wasn't home, but because between the time he called and the time he said he'd come, someone else called him and asked him out so he just went without thinking anything about it.

I'm having a relationship that's a little bumpy, I tell Maria Lorca. Suddenly I tell her: I don't know if this person is a junkie or not.

I don't know why it comes to this definite point just now, when it's never framed itself that way before. Maria Lorca looks alarmed, wary.

I think you had better nail that down, she says. We're hearing now that 60 percent of the addicts in New York are seropositive.

I've been wondering about that.

Well, you should be, if you're having sex with this person.

The fact that I'm not, after all this time, having sex with Gregory is a secret I dissemble without actually lying about it. Everyone assumes that I am. I let them think so: I don't want to feel like a sexual failure. I cling to the belief that Gregory will want me someday. Only M., because he hints as much, has guessed the real state of things. M. has had the same frustrations, with guys who wanted to be "more than friends" but less than lovers, although M.'s a genius at getting what he wants. When M. asks me about it directly, I do lie: if I tell the truth, he'll think I'm a complete masochist. What if my friends get the idea that I'm too cranky and difficult to have a real relationship? I want this thing with Gregory to look normal, so the emotional fragility people see will seem justified by compensatory pleasures. I want them to think we work things out in bed. In the meantime, I wait for Gregory to fall in love with me. What else can you do in this life, except attempt miracles?

At least let me cook you dinner, I asked, I pleaded, I begged. So he started coming frequently. Even if I had a full day. I raced through my appointments so I'd have hours free for shopping. I never just bought dinner. I stuffed the refrigerator with ten kinds of vegetables and five kinds of meat and dozens of bottles of mineral water, soda, quarts of vodka for the freezer, several kinds of cheese, fruit, exotic condiments, anything to suggest an ample, nurturing environment. Like the suburb he grew up in.

I bought tapes of the same music he had at his place. If he mentioned a book, I immediately read it. I wanted to know everything in his head, except what he watched on television. Gregory said he learned a lot from TV about what people were turning into. I told him I could see what people were turning into by walking out the front door. But I considered buying a TV, thinking it would lure him over more often. At his place, Gregory had it on all the time.

Since he had worked in so many restaurants and people used to drive twenty miles to Helen's Truro Hash Palace for his celebrated omelettes, Gregory quickly usurped my nurturing role and insisted on cooking every night. It took, he said, too much time from my work. His palate favored bland heaps of tofu and overcooked fish, which I couldn't get down without effort. I pushed food around on my plate while he sucked it in in bulk without ever gaining a pound.

We talked. We ate. He usually stayed until eleven or twelve, on festive occasions until one or two. Every time he left, he went with inflexible abruptness. He would be stretched out on the floor with his shoes off, and a second later was standing at the door, delivering my ration of farewell kisses.

We developed certain fantasies. We talked as if we were writing a play, improvising in regional dialects. For a long time we never spoke in our real voices: always an accent, a fictitious character, safely distanced from ourselves. We analyzed friends, identified adversaries. Gregory's problems with Bruno were a running theme. Now that Gloria no longer materialized regularly, Bruno had become his chief impediment in life. Bruno asked him to do things that were inconvenient. Bruno found ways to damage his ego, bringing up Gregory's past fecklessness, casting doubts on Gregory's artistic abilities. Then there was Philippe, whose gargantuan importunities grew ever more unreasonable and edgy with cocaine paranoia, and of course the nightly horror of porcine customers, drunks, and drug addicts whooping it up at the restaurant.

We were under the spell of suddenly tolerable weather and unchanging dissatisfactions. Sometimes, on my way out of the apartment, I misplaced my keys, and then my wallet, and then a dozen other things, until I felt angry enough to smash things. And then I forced myself to sit down, close my eyes, and breathe. I knew I was afraid of one more thing happening, afraid of the slightest event.

The only person Gregory feels "really close to, " besides me, is Pugg. Puggy. I bump into Pugg at a TriBeCa loft party. We're standing at a table festooned with artfully sliced raw vegetables and a vast bowl of mint green dip. There are too many loud, desperate people in this place, despite its cavernous size. Pugg questions me, about neutral things, through the crossfire of several conversations. Everything about Pugg conveys neutrality, reserve. A preoccupation with looking out for number one, not giving away anything himself. A prig, I conclude, but not a particularly bright prig.

He's studying video art at the SVA, not that I'm curious. While we talk he cruises every man in the area. The way Pugg opens and closes his mouth suggests that he performs this activity for hours every day in the bathroom mirror. Why do I hate him? He's not exactly formidable. Since he doesn't mention Gregory, I assume Gregory's connection with me is a problem. Stupidly, I quiz him. Has he seen Gregory? I haven't, I assure him. Not for days. Does he happen to know what Gregory's up to? I even become confidential, spurred by several gin and tonics: Gregory's so weird, isn't he? I see him every day for a week, and then he just vanishes. What the fuck is wrong with him?

Well, retorts Pugg through clenched teeth, but with an air of satisfaction, that's Gregory.

I think: Pugg lacks charm, and grace, and personality, but he has something far more valuable in Gregory's eyes. He's seven years younger than Gregory and fourteen years younger than me. And his mental age is even younger.

A few nights later, still missing Gregory, I wake M. out of his nap and send him into the chill evening, to walk his dog seven blocks past their usual route; I ask him to "casually" drop by Gregory's restaurant to see if he's on duty. M. phones back two hours later. He's had "a nice chat" with Gregory. Gregory talked about his new work. He said he's "getting into pornography." And, M. adds brightly, his face lit up when I mentioned you. He adores you, M. says. He thinks you're the most fabulous person he's ever met.

Gregory calls the following morning and asks, slyly: *Were you checking up on me, making M. come into the restaurant?*

Gregory takes me for a drink, to a new bar on Avenue A. A bar full of dusky alcoves, twenties torch music, lacquered tables that belong in a Victorian sitting room. The kind of place that will be fun for two weeks, until it degenerates into a scene. We hold hands on a grimy sofa. He nuzzles my neck, his palm sweating in mine.

I don't want to drink my rum and Coke. He sips a Remy Martin. I know he'll only drink one, but I'll keep going and get sloppy. I squeeze his hand. I kiss the shoulder of his vest. His face looks translucent. He's pleased. He knows the guy who owns this place. A skinny dude with a blond crew-cut, who pops out of the office every few minutes to chat. Gregory knows a lot of young, skinny, tall blond boys with crewcuts. This one looks about nineteen. He wears a diamond stud in one ear. He's offered Gregory a job. He's nice, Gregory tells me, even if he isn't very bright.

These joints resemble one another so closely the street could be one continuous sushi bar. At home, Gregory picks apart the steady remaking of the East Village, the pointless visual shock effects worn by the teenagers, the uniform restaurant decors, theme boutiques, ghastly art galleries. But in these places Gregory seems utterly relaxed and in his element. Heads swivel like radar sensors picking up his vibrations. We walk into certain rooms where I feel the atmosphere ripple as if he'd slept with everyone in the vicinity. Rooms are fatal, every last one of them.

In April Gregory gave me two pictures that later acquired a brief notoriety when Bruno included them in his slide presentations on a college tour. In April Sarah arrived from Italy, like an emissary from another world. At the end of April everything changed unexpectedly, and yet nothing changed.

Fog rolled into the city at night, thick muffling fog so uncharacteristic of New York that a general disorientation of things made the neighborhood interesting again. Flights out of Kennedy and LaGuardia were grounded throughout an entire weekend. The fog erased the World Trade Center from my front windows and even steamed up the view of Second Avenue. The sidewalks sparkled like veins of obsidian. The bazaar spilling down Second Avenue and across St. Marks Place looked for once as if it belonged there.

The fog gave the nights added menace and allure. Random encounters in the streets had a film noir narrative attached. It was as if a culminating murder were about to happen. During lightning storms in my childhood, the power would blow and my mother, no friend of storms, filled the house with candles; the fog exuded that fear-quick alertness and promised dark adventures. Even though I was obsessed with Gregory, I lost all thought of him during the foggy nights. He was working double shifts and seemed safely iced. We froze in a holding pattern. For a few nights, I felt a strange peace after his late evening call, glad to have him out of the way.

I visited Bruno after seeing Maria Lorca and asked him if he would spend a little time with Gregory, watch his behavior, see if he thought Gregory might be shooting junk. Bruno was incredulous. I could see his indifference slipping. Bruno had a lazy, laid-back mask that covered a fierce ambition. He never displayed "difficult" feelings and tried to seem amiable all the time. It was no good pushing him into an expression of concern; Gregory had diddled around with his emotions and Bruno wanted to appear above all that. So I presented it as a test of Bruno's powers of observation and knowledge of human character. This appealed to his conspiratorial side.

I knew nothing about heroin. I had heard all the truisms. The drug is stronger than the addict. The addict doesn't know what he's doing half the time. You might as well forget any sort of friendship with an addict, because an addict will sell his mother's wedding ring for a fix.

Yet there were many people who found heroin addiction glamorous. The idea of being beautiful and damned was a perennial youthful myth in the downtown area. People went on smack when they had money and stayed on smack after all the money got used up and then started ripping off their friends and families and usually became incredibly sick and horrible-looking and got these strange diseases like lupus or hepatitis B and now, according to Maria Lorca, half the addicts in New York have HIV infection from needle-sharing, and of course the terrible thing is, the addict knows all this but can't do anything about it because it's the drug that makes the decisions. And if this is the case, I thought, what then?

Bruno, for all his infatuation, knew nothing about Gregory, and even less about heroin. He simply asked Gregory point blank if he happened to be shooting smack. *He acted completely surprised like it was the last thing in the world on his mind*, Bruno reported.

The boulder of Gregory's depression levitated slightly. He still waxed bitter about his job, but devoted less energy to tearing apart each evening's humiliations. He began sounding almost good-humored much of the time, judging from his epic morning phone calls. He had turned invisible again: seeing anyone was just too much for him. But hearing from people gave him some little pleasure. I didn't make an issue of this, which irritated him.

We could see each other tomorrow, he suggested.

Work tomorrow, I said.

Wednesday?

Can't. Meeting somebody for lunch.

(I liked the "somebody." I always told who, and he never did.)

Dinner, then.

Dinner plans, too.

It was folly to put him off. He readily found a way to re-engage me. He stopped calling. A day went by. A fresh contest of wills had begun. A depressing prospect. I hadn't the slightest hope of winning.

Long, brittle silence. My walks gravitated to the streets he favored, the places he ate lunch, anywhere he normally spent time. I thought, it's like smoking: you tell yourself it's finished, you will not under any circumstances light a cigarette, you go for hours fighting it off, the phone rings, someone's talking to you, halfway through the conversation you notice you've got this cigarette in your mouth. I decide this time I'll let it go, I don't need his company. Settle down to work, get my papers arranged next to the typewriter, train my thoughts on all the projects I've shoved aside, and suddenly I'm circling the neighborhood, pretending to shop for food. Or rushing home so I'll be there if he calls. If I knew he was thinking about me, suffering from my silence, I could go out and enjoy myself But he's not put together that way. He knows I'm crawling out of my skin.

Jane said: So call him up. Big deal.

I said: I can't possibly do that.

What, she said, too humiliating, after all this?

Jane, I said, you don't understand, Gregory *loves* me, we really do have this deep understanding, but he's sensitive, if he thinks he's not getting enough attention or affection, I mean from his point of view he can't really humiliate me anyway, unless I agree to be humiliated.

Jane said, You mean this is just provisional humiliation?

He just wants to know that he's wanted, I said.

Him and a million others, she said. Are you supposed to go over there and disembowel yourself on his stoop? Hey, that might make him happy. Maybe he could make an artwork about it or something.

Well, I said, he probably would.

Creative type, Jane said.

An English writer asks me out for lunch. I've never met him. He wants to discuss "postmodernism" and feels that my work is "postmodern." We meet in a cafe near my house. I can tell I'm one of several people on a list. He only has a sketchy idea of my work. He's a man of medium height with sharp features, about forty-five but looks younger, his hair's dyed bright blond and clipped in a shag. He has a journalist's way of asking questions and then rephrasing the answers, adapting the other person's vocabulary.

A few minutes into this lunch, Gregory walks in. He sees me, comes over to the table. He says, I won't bother you now but I hope we can talk soon. Then he takes a table near the back and orders lunch. I can't continue my conversation. I see him looking miserable while he spoons soup into his mouth. I excuse myself rudely. I plant myself down at Gregory's table and start to demand an explanation. He cuts me off. He's almost sobbing. He says he didn't know I'd be in here, he says, I swear I didn't follow you.

The idea that Gregory would feel insecure enough to follow me around is ludicrous but comes as an enjoyable surprise. He asks why I haven't called him. I know it's none of my business, he says. But are you seeing someone else? I know this is all a big act, he knows perfectly well I'm not seeing anybody and that I've been waiting for him to call for several days. His pretense that I'm important enough to cause him all this anxiety charms away all my defenses and I fall instantly under the spell of total slavery.

Paul dies, owing to "complications." Someone calls and lets me know. The parents came and took the body back to Pittsburgh. I draw an emotional blank. Somehow as soon as someone gets sick from this you begin to insulate yourself. If you see them it's as if they've returned from the dead for a moment or two. I walk through the apartment without seeing my messy piles of clothing, my books, my sea of papers. There should be special messengers who come and tell you these things in person, a pair of eyes to look into at least. Every death in my life has announced itself over the phone. It's a dream. You believe it but there's nothing there.

Later that day, Gregory calls. I decide not to tell him anything. We talk, as usual, about "our relationship."

You keep trying to seduce me, he accuses. I won't deal with that, I can give you what I can give you and no more than that until I'm ready. But you have to believe that I do love you, any time you need me to come and put my arms around you and hold you, he says, I'll be there.

Well, I tell him, look here, Gregory, it so happens that I do need you. I'm in a bad state of mind.

I can't right now, he says, I'm doing some paste-ups.

Sarah had arrived from Rome. I spent the morning thinking things over. I'm too far gone to cut my losses, I realized. We're here on this planet, all these people. Endless people. We all have this stuff in our heads that sounds like gibberish. It seems I am digging out a life for myself, but the things I used to want have changed.

There had been a long time when I thought I would stay in New York just long enough to leave my mark, get the money problem permanently fixed, move on. And years of shopping around for another place to be. I had been spending every summer at Sarah's house in Italy, a ship on an ocean of land. It was a cross-shaped former monastery that Sarah and her mother had bought in the sixties. Dozens of cats roamed the house and the property, sheep cropped the surrounding hills, islands of forest hid the place from its neighbors. We had a farm-size vegetable garden there. For a few pennies we got eggs and meat from the local farmers. Weeks went by when we never spent money on anything.

I had a suite of rooms on the north side of the house where I holed up for days without seeing anyone. At night we drank the local wine and jabbered until four or five in the morning. There was Sarah and her boyfriend Jacques and her mother Ursula. Ursula was eighty-three and had a lover, fifty. Nights were blacker than velvet. From the fields you saw a sky crowded with stars. The world was far away.

When I left in September it always seemed unthinkable that I was going back to the squirrel cage on Tenth Street. I stopped in Munich for a week to see Rainer, who kept up with things in the world. He lived in a large, impersonal flat overlooking the English Garden. There was nude swimming in the river and a wine garden spread out at the base of a pagoda. Sometimes Willie was in residence, but less and less over the years. He had started a going business in Australia. Rainer spent a lot of time on flights. He'd put together many little films and after the film in Colombia we talked about developing a project but since Willie's death Rainer didn't talk about projects any more.

I had had this second life, a seasonal escape from New York. It turned down the volume on my ambitions. Perhaps I could get through without wanting too much after all. It had seemed, for many years, that Sarah had left off wanting things. In the sixties she had a short, fairly spectacular career in films, retired at her peak, and now spent most of her time painting. Jacques directed movies, the kind of light sex comedies that typically feature Monica Vitti. Sarah sometimes played small parts in his films, for the money. I met them when Jacques hired me for a part, he'd seen a short independent film where I'd played a hotel clerk. Six weeks in Berlin, in the crushing melancholy of a Berlin autumn. The film played festivals and art houses in Europe for a while and then disappeared. The following year Sarah showed up in New York, looking for a gallery to show in. We slogged around for a month with her portfolio and finally settled on a cavernous, unfavorably situated venue in northern TriBeCa owned by a pleasant, enthusiastic amateur named Doris.

Sarah began coming to the city every four or five months. She stayed with a former brother-in-law, Cyril. Cyril was a nervous, balding lighting designer who had turned gay in his forties and now lived in an all-white triplex on Grove Street. Cyril's crowd was a fashion crowd. Bracelets and shoes. Sarah, with her show biz history, moved in the fashion world more easily than in the art world. Her stock was higher there. This had an unfortunate effect on Doris's marketing efforts. She couldn't decide whether to promote Sarah as a serious painter or capitalize on the scads of free publicity available to Sarah as a former movie star. Sarah was no help in this matter. She wanted to be taken seriously in the supposedly high-minded art world, where she really wasn't known. But during her years of fame she became addicted to the idolatry of others. She ridiculed the glamorous people behind their backs, but found it impossible to let go of a scrap of old glory. She was expecting much too much from a first show of paintings in the city, I thought.

The day she arrived, I phoned Cyril's place. He said they were at lunch with Doris. I left for the gallery in a state of indecision: what if Gregory called. Too bad for him, I thought. I have a life, too. It's one of the first full days of spring, the mailbox is full of junk mail. I walk to Third Avenue, brushing aside ghosts of the brain. My street is crawling with memories. Sometimes, turning a corner, I expect to see Paul or Michael or some other dead person going about his business. The cab driver is a young black with Rasta hair and deep bedroom eyes and all the way down to SoHo I imagine undressing him on a king-size bed. His knees are planted on the mattress beside my shoulders. He guides his long, ebony member between my parted lips. His eyes find me in the rearview mirror at five-second intervals. I fix my face in a mask of fascination, wondering if he'll speak, and, if he does, whether the conversation will lead anywhere. Finally he says the traffic's bad. I can see that. Now he's going to tell me why the traffic's bad. Crazy out of town drivers, or else the tunnel's closed, or Fifth Avenue's blocked off for a parade or a demonstration or a motorcade.

I see Jacques and Sarah and Doris crossing lower Broadway. I jump out of the taxi. Sarah throws her arms around me. She's jet lagged. We're still putting up the paintings, she says. The paintings were at the framer's until a half hour ago. Doris is dwarfed by the two of them, who look like thoroughbred horses. Doris looks excited. Doris babbles. Jacques rolls his eyes warily and shrugs. We walk. I'm aware of all we've ever said. I'm especially aware that for years I've bemoaned my bad lot here in New York and told my European friends that someday in the near future I'll leave. We've laughed at the absurdity of life here, the crassness of everything. I've always been the rare "good American," a person of unusual refinement, someone appalled by this culture of spectacle and commerce. As we walk all the jokes we've made at the expense of my environment crop up again in abbreviated phrases, tag lines, bits of old jazz. And I suddenly feel this awful distance between our summers in the country and the way I am now, peering into a beautifully decorated room that now has the proportions of a doll's house. The three of us are never going to live happily ever after in the monastery. At first, I'd even pictured bringing Gregory to the enchanted forest: somehow we'd all get by on our vegetables and penny eggs in blissful retirement from everything and everyone. At this moment I understand that I could never live like that, and in fact have probably even spent my last summer in Tuscany.

In the gallery, two men in white overalls lug the pictures out of the office into the hangar-like white space. They hold them up here, move them there, Sarah stands in the center of the room directing traffic. Jacques, perched on the front desk near the door, untwists the wire ribbing around a champagne cork. Pop, fizz. I'd rather not get drunk this afternoon. Alcohol is softening my brain. What's especially dangerous is Monday night, when Gregory calls up and talks about his cock; I know I've got to get my copy into the magazine computer before two the next afternoon, but what I want more than anything are several shots of vodka, one right after the other, and then the nights popped. Sometimes I can work myself into a rage and call him back, but the little prick always unplugs his phone before going to sleep. God forbid anybody should need him for anything.

Jacques has floppy brown hair and deep soulful brown eyes, big exaggerated features, big nose, he laughs easily like Sarah does. Hanging the paintings takes concentration, but after a while the serious way we're shifting them around turns into a joke. It takes two hours to get them on the walls. The champagne's long gone. Jacques says, Let's get out of here and get a drink.

I suggest that we visit Gregory, who's at work just around the corner. Sarah is eager to meet him. In my letters I've made a literary picture of him, with large areas left blank. "He's not like the others," I've assured her, since Sarah has met one or two of the others. There was, for example, a perfect imbecile who made paintings of natural disasters. I fell for the creep in a big way, just long enough to ruin a whole spring. But that was different. I want Sarah and Gregory to like each other. I think that Sarah, a great beauty and famous for it, too, will see him more clearly than I do. They are both cursed with beauty, and Sarah has managed to live a real life. Gregory's stuck inside his face, he can't get out of it.

We leave the gallery laughing. Isn't it a relief that we're all still alive? SoHo looks sleepy. The sun's shining. The buildings absorb a hyperborean light that flattens against the street like a patina of dust, turning the black pavement blue. I decide I'm not going to die, the things I'm afraid of are not going to get me. I'm going to grow old with equanimity and physical grace.

The empty restaurant. They open at four, but nobody goes there before seven. Gregory's standing with his back to the door, in the passage between the bar and the dining room where the industrial-looking espresso machine faces the toilets. He's talking to Sammy, the new bar manager. They don't react to our entrance. It's as if they don't hear us. I leave Sarah and Jacques at the bar and walk up behind him.

I say his name softly, still wrapped in the airy feeling that everything is going to work out fine.

A reaction. His strangest to date. The blood drains from my head. Someone has chopped an important section of the film. Gregory doesn't turn around. His back goes up as if he's been struck with a bat. Sammy spins around and walks out of the room as if on cue. And now Gregory turns, slowly, like a wax dummy on a carousel. I see the face twisted by an uncontrollable force, a paper face someone has crushed and smoothed out again, the eyes black and blazing.

I brought them to meet you, I whisper, waving towards Jacques and Sarah. I see he's about to scream, he's going to push me down the corridor and throw me through the front window. He marches past me, I see Sarah and Jacques freezing in bewilderment, their faces clouding up, Gregory starts shrinking as he gets close to them. The air turns silver and grainy and the walls of the room shine like sheets of mercury. I'm watching him evaporate. Looking down a long bleak funnel at a throbbing blotch of insanity. His body stiffens while he shrinks, he's suddenly three feet high and completely emaciated. The floor stretches and sags, a ribbon of varnished pine chugging like a treadmill. He's gotten away from me, and now he's going to explode into a million pieces. I follow him, feeling like an oversized nurse in a mental hospital tagging behind a psychotic dwarf. When he reaches the bar he's the size of a dashboard Jesus, his mouth erupts in a horrible grin, full of teeth that splay loose from his gums and shatter on the shiny floor, teeth the size of nail heads. Jacques attempts a smile. The figurine's lips spread out across a tiny face in agonized congeniality, now it expands as it breathes, the limbs blow up enough to fill out the clothing, Gregory's wrists reappear in their frayed white cuffs and his neck puffs out and fills his collar. He is almost himself by the time he speaks. Bits of him return in hazy leaps of some chemical reaction.

He catches my eye and smiles again. I smile back grimly. He drapes his face in a transparent, friendly look. This, he announces, is a bad moment. There is an elephantine silence in which I appreciate Gregory's gift for understatement. I tell him we'll leave. But he insists that we stay. He glides away into the restaurant's hidden heart. Jacques smiles again, shrugging off the situation. Sarah says, Something's wrong, we ought to leave. I tell them I've never seen him like this. Not like this. And I'm thinking that I've now seen him for the first time: almost mute with loathing and disgust. It's far too late for this realization. I am part of this monster heart and soul.

He returns, magically composed, high-spirited, happy. He pours three goblets of Remy Martin. He asks Sarah about her show, her flight, her living arrangements. He listens raptly as Jacques talks about himself. Gregory tells a little of his work routine, smiles and sparkles like someone enduring the brief interrogation of a television camera. Now it's his clothes talking. I imagine cracks and lesions appearing all over his skin, the roof of his skull popping open, snakes crawling out of his pockets. And finally this unendurable congeniality burns itself out as we leave, I picture a theatrical puff of smoke behind my back as we regain the sidewalk.

Jacques diplomatically observes that Gregory seems "anxious." Sarah is less muddled. That look he gave you, she says. That was *scary*.

He later felt that he had to apologize: had to, according to some private system of accounting. His equilibrium had been pointlessly disrupted by the demon. He had revealed too much, for no reason. Perhaps no one has a personality when he's alone, and some people cease to exist. Gregory had another person he became when he was out of sight, not necessarily one of the fictional selves who took credit for his dark moods, but someone else altogether. I was not supposed to encounter that person, and when I did the fragile cords of Gregory's confidence ripped apart, the picture on the screen began an interminable vertical roll. In the course of a bitter argument he ended a string of accusations with the breathless announcement that I "wasn't capable of love," that I "didn't know the meaning of the word. " And in the next moment he retracted this with a high-pitched giggle, maniacally spluttering that he guessed he'd gone a little too far, that of course he didn't mean what he was saying. It was as though he had been talking to himself, rehearsing things before a mirror, and then realized someone else happened to be in the room.

No one who answered the restaurant pay phone ever expressed complete certainty as to whether or not he was there. They covered the receiver and consulted other voices in the furry auditory background. He was often said to be running an errand, coming back later, to have already left for the night. In April, they started blatantly screening his calls, which told me when he didn't want to talk to me. Since he often did come to the phone, I realized there were other people he didn't want to hear from.

I told Bruno: *His whole body just went rigid and when he turned around he looked like he was going to murder me.* What goes on in that apartment when he's got the phone unplugged? Nothing, Bruno said, yawning. He's staring into space doing nothing. Or jerking off. One of the two.

There was a problem about going out together. Declining certain invitations he said, *I want our relationship to be private.* Declining others, he said *I don't want people to see us together and make all kinds of false assumptions.* Declining still others, he said he couldn't handle large groups of people.

We meet Libby and Jane in the cement stairwell of a SoHo building, at an afternoon opening. Uncharacteristically, Gregory has volunteered to go with me. Libby finds us on the stairs. She's wearing a Barbara Kruger T-shirt that says, I CAN'T LOOK AT YOU AND BREATHE AT THE SAME TIME. Libby looks amused and depressed, or amused at her depression, or depressed by her amusement. Her hair is an ungovernable woolly cloud. I introduce Gregory. I pray that Libby won't tell him she's heard a lot about him. Gregory tells her he liked her book. She's published several, so she asks which one. He tells her. Jane comes out into the stairwell, looking like a large, restless cat in a state of murderous boredom. Gregory is dazzled. He idolizes Jane. He wants his work to be just like hers.

Later, at midnight, Libby calls and says: My god, watch out. He's beautiful. That face.

A half hour later Jane calls and says: So, he's got a problem with his job? What's the matter, *GQ* isn't hiring?

Gregory brought me two of his pictures, mounted on wood. He laughed defensively, removing the bubble wrap. I don't know what you're going to think, he said. But I want you to tell me if you don't think they're any good. Or if they're just all right. The one thing I don't want to do is delude myself.

But Gregory, I said, while he hid the unwrapped pictures from sight, don't make me the judge, because I can't be, I mean, please, don't ask me to tell you or explain why I like them if I like them, or appraise them. I'm not good at coming up with things verbally, just like that.

But your opinion is important to me, he said.

See, I don't want my opinion to influence what you do. It's too big a responsibility. You should do what you want. Follow your instincts.

What if my instincts are fucked up and adolescent?

So, I said, whose aren't? You have to go with what you have, really.

A further display of reluctance. Finally he propped them side by side on the edge of the bookshelf above the desk. They were eight and one-half by twelve inch horizontals. One was a rich black and white, the other had a silvery bluish tint. The surfaces glistened like frosted glass.

In one picture a boy with a crewcut and severe, womanish features stood with his eyes looking down, in the extreme right foreground, while behind him a slightly blurry, squat figure in a vaguely military outfit glowered at him, pointing a square-format camera at his back. The mise-en-scene had an Alpine atmosphere, craggy peaks and snow. The other showed an interior, something like a boarding house room in a Weimar-period Fritz Lang movie. This time the right foreground was filled with the fuzzy, naked rear end of a young man, the frame cropping off his head and his legs below the knees. In the background, in sharp focus, a middle-aged man wearing a dark suit stood in the open doorway of the room, one hand clutching an indistinct figure drawing.

Gregory eyed me as I looked at them. They seemed so clearly to be icons of my worst fears about our relationship: that I was old and unattractive and dominant, exploiting a younger man's confusion.

Tell me, he said.

Well, I said. What can I say.

You think they're terrible.

No, not at all. They're just . . . you know, depressing. I mean they are about you and me, aren't they.

Gregory put on his shocked, outraged look, like a Kabuki mask.

That's not the idea *at all*, he insisted, indignantly. Don't you realize, he went on, pointing at the pictures, switching to a tone of maniacal reasonableness, Don't you understand, if I make a picture like this, *who it is I identify with?* Isn't it obvious?

He meant the older, unattractive figures, but I didn't see where that was obvious at all. And then, looking at the bluish one with the mountain background, I noticed the strong resemblance between the youth in the picture and Pugg.

Gregory sighed. I feel, he said, like I'm about sixty years old.

Lucky for you, I laughed, secretly infuriated by the thought that Gregory was in love with Pugg, you're only twenty-seven.

Gregory's voice tightened. The last thing I expected when I came over here, he said, was *ridicule*. He spat the word out with ugly finality.

I touched his shoulder. He twitched my hand away. I could see him racing for the basement door of his dark mind. If he numbs out on me, I thought, this time I will actually slap him around.

Gregory, I said, *don't*, please? For once will you just stay right here on the set instead of running away? I was making a joke, Gregory. A harmless little joke. I wasn't *ridiculing* you, I'm not trying to *destroy* you, you take everything too seriously, you let everything disturb you, when I say something light and silly you get offended and act like I've committed a capital crime, and then you disappear for days and days and I flip out wondering if you're still alive, and end up thinking it's better if you really have committed suicide because if you haven't I should hate you.

He looked at the floor and pouted.

Look, I said, very gently. If we can only be miserable together I'd rather see you happy with someone else. If you want to be with Pugg then go be with him.

I instantly wondered if it were true, that I'd rather see him happy, or if this was an unfortunate rhetorical flourish. Now what, I thought, if he suddenly says he's seeing someone else.

Pugg doesn't want me, he whispered.

He had sat down in the metal semi-reclining chair one of my decor-minded friends had outlived. It consumed an unreasonable amount of space in the study, which was already jammed with wall-high bookshelves, the desk, a plain wooden bench piled with back issues of *The New York Review of Books*, and the wheeled office chair. The tiny figure of Gregory—slunk in inexplicable anger, smoldering in that ridiculous chair, on an afternoon when sunlight blazed through the apartment and a pleasant, fitful breeze kept dislodging all the papers on the desk—looked so incongruous and idiotic that I feigned a coughing spell to avoid laughing. And then I burst out laughing anyway. Gregory's head came up and his face shifted from tragedy to bewilderment.

I could see he thought I'd finally snapped and gone loony. His interest in the situation revived.

It's a mistake, someone said, to swim in the ocean if you happen to be menstruating. Too true, too true.

When a whole day and night went by without calamity or fugue, I heard myself thinking: It's at this moment in a novel that the protagonist is brained by an unknown assailant, found dead in the trunk of a stolen car, or learns of his fatal illness from the family doctor. And of course it was the irregular, blissful evening when we left each other's nerves intact that raised, in its immediate wake, the most noisome fears, the specter of random violence and accidental death. We functioned so habitually on pain and anxiety that their occasional absence automatically foretokened doom, the intrusion of the world's casually distributed misery into our privately cultivated torture garden.

I wanted the line free, in case he called. When people kept me on the phone, I knew he was trying to reach me from the corner, to ask me to dinner, a movie, to hear some live music somewhere: Let's breathe for a change, he would say, enough of this claustrophobia. It never happened like that, never once. Even if we went somewhere we dragged along a ten-ton weight of exiguous distress. Nothing was ever right, not entirely, and even if it was, you felt it could go wildly wrong in a split second, for no apparent reason.

Two hundred people swarmed through Cyril's townhouse for Sarah's pre-opening party. Doris had fulfilled the questionable inspiration of having two openings, on consecutive evenings: the first for "VIPs, " the second for "the art world. " The people who turned up at Cyril's after the VIP opening were not, on the whole, art people. There were fashion people. There were jewelry people. There were, mixed in, entertainment people.

There were tall, equine women in Halstons and Chanels and Lagerfelds who used expressions like *shockhorror* and *mega-brill.* There were marketing people from Laura Ashley and ad people from *Vogue* who assured one another that they wouldn't be trapped into using the C-word, or the M-word, or the E-word. They were perfectly nice, mediocre, irrelevant people for whom Doris had passed over the entire art community. Sarah held court in a third-floor bedroom, where breezy international types repaired to adjust their mirror images and toot a few lines.

Victor had accompanied me, since Gregory had refused to. Victor's discomfort was more or less total. Worse, he'd dressed horribly, in what looked like the Sunday clothes of a trucker. Jeans and a sweatshirt would have been fine, but Victor had struck a fashion note of proletarian obtusity as if intending his clothes to convey his loathing of luxury and graciousness. Yet his natural sweetness defeated him. He assumed the job of fetching drinks for people, up and down the narrow staircase, and otherwise stood around with the chandelier glazing his eyeglasses, smiling miserably at the glamor hounds who circulated through the house.

I couldn't work up to any embarrassment about Victor's awkwardness, though he clung to me like a puppy, since I didn't much care about the people he felt awkward around. Sarah, I considered, had really fucked up by letting Doris invite this glittery flotsam. Not one person there would buy a single painting or encourage anyone else to. Even so, watching Victor haplessly shifting his weight from leg to leg as he stared into space, I wanted to grab his hair and scream at him: *For Christ's sake, can't you hold your own, just once?*

The whole affair passed in a merciful blur. I would wake late the next day, hung over, dreading the second opening ahead, my mouth tasting foul from the spiced wine cooler Cyril had served, two packs of Marlboro, and the five beers I'd drunk with Victor at the corner saloon, where we'd sat until closing, dissecting Cyril's guests. This midnight-to-four postmortem with Victor was becoming a regular feature of any complicated evening. Victor had some temporary stage design job uptown at night. He usually looked for me in the bar on his way home. Victor had such a protective attitude that more than once, in the throes of liquor, I thought about taking him home. He was sexy if you didn't know him, or if you just thought about him physically. I didn't fully imagine what having sex with him would be like, and it never happened, in any case. It was a bit awkward that Richard had begun sending off sexual vibes at the gym, where we viewed each other naked three mornings a week, did aerobics and free weights together, and joked all the time about getting it on with each other. When I was with Victor, Richard often entered the back of my mind. I thought if Victor split up with Richard, Richard would immediately come on to me in a serious way. But he would have to feel it was final, his breaking up with Victor. And it would also signify the end of Victor's friendship with me, because he would always be in love with Richard no matter what. Some people are like that. Even after there's nothing left between themselves and someone else, they persist in being in love with that person to the point of mania.

Whatever Victor and I raked over during that first happy flush of alcohol was simply a prologue to the somber topic of Gregory. I still tried puzzling out whether or not Gregory was on smack. I described our arguments and his mood swings and flaky habits, reconstructing conversations in precise detail, thinking Victor could see something I couldn't, since he wasn't involved. I had a definite picture of how a junkie talked and what a junkie looked like: a sort of boneless, vague, implacable person, incapable of prolonged lucidity, furtive about everything. Gregory didn't exactly coincide with this picture. He just seemed impossibly unhappy. Sometimes I felt certain he had started shooting drugs again or maybe hadn't ever stopped, but then he'd say something, or do something, that made him enigmatic in a different way. I couldn't draw a conclusion. I began to think that was all I really wanted, to know how things actually stood. Victor said he had the impression that the key to the whole thing was: whatever I wanted was exactly what wasn't going to happen. If I wanted to know just one simple fact, I would find out everything except that single piece of information. That's why, he said, you should cultivate a Zen attitude.

Gregory turned up an hour and a half late for Sarah's second opening, so close to the end I'd given up hope, and I'd told Jacques, He's always like this, I never know, no matter what he promises, and he knows it's important to me—and Jacques laughed and barked, Have another drink. The over-lit gallery and the pictures and the people sagged like weathered flesh. I was watching the damaged frames of a lousy movie. People in thick, smoky, boozy clusters. Lots of toothy smiles, lipstick, fur, the erratic progress of people moving through a room in order to avoid certain people and be seen by other people. I circled about feeling mortified and fragile, meeting up with Jacques every few minutes. Well, he said, if he doesn't come, it isn't the end of the world. But it was, because he'd promised, this once, to do just this one little thing for me. By the time he showed up I'd gone into my own fugue.

Libby always told me stories. Jane recounted her day and horrible things she'd seen on the television news. M. had things to say about food, foul behavior witnessed at dinner parties, and the location of various attractive men in the city. Richard described the state of his friendships, itemized his clothing purchases, and needled me about things I'd written or said, for no good reason I could think of. Richard cultivated frivolous and embittered people who wanted to be famous. Most of his friends had missed the boat for reasons that were obvious to me but completely opaque to him. One had been a child prodigy as a violinist, and had become a failed writer with a profitable sideline in ceramics. Another one did subtle copies of other people's paintings. They all clung to Richard like barnacles. Whenever I went to his loft they were hanging out, bopping around to salsa music. They were often stoned and tended to break things. Richard was incapable of sustained anger. He wanted desperately to be liked by everybody. Richard told me his version of his day at the gym, and then Victor gave me the annotated version in the evening. Victor was a better storyteller.

When Jacques saw us he shot me a big, gap-toothed grin. He turned away from Doris and clapped Gregory across the shoulders. *Here he is, the little bastard,* he cackled. Jacques was drunk. A look spread over Gregory's face, like the look he'd worn in the restaurant. Unspeakable pain, rage, embarrassment, humiliation: all that jazz.

Todd, Martha's friend, cursed me before he died, not so close to the end as to seem an obsessed malediction, but when he was failing, during the third attack of pneumocystis, at a time when his survival prospects were nil, and his last conversations were sure to be remembered. He said, I'm told, *I hope he gets it.* I had known him for fifteen years. Some people choose to die like pricks, taking their bitterness right into the grave with them. People are funny, Jane said. And then she said, Give me a dog any day.

At the tail end of the opening Doris asked Gregory to bring his slides to the gallery. It might have removed Gregory's suspicion that he was considered a "trick" by my friends, if Doris hadn't also cast a baldly appraising glance all over him and added, *I'm interested in anybody who wears an embroidered vest.*

Let's get out of here and go someplace, he murmured. We drifted out into a cool evening full of mist, through TriBeCa along West Broadway. As we approached Spring Street he said, as if suddenly remembering it, Jack owes me a hundred bucks. Jack was a tall guy with bad skin who tended bar at the restaurant.

We walked up Spring and went in there. It was jammed with coked-up Europeans simulating the atmosphere of an early Virna Lisi movie. The last place on earth I'd thought Gregory would go on a night off. We wedged ourselves into the alcove at the near end of the bar, Gregory ordered two Remys. The glasses appeared, Gregory said, Wait here a second, and darted off into the kitchen. Then Jack disappeared through the swinging doors on his side of the zinc. I stared into the Remy, feeling I'd suddenly lost control of the evening. Time dragged past while a Latin song drummed away on the high-distortion speakers. It was a song that had blared out of every bar and bodega in Cartagena when Rainer and I were filming there. The words translated into something like, *Mama, my sister's run off with a Negro.*

I remembered the choking humidity of the Arsenal Disco on the canal bank, with the fishnet ceiling studded with Christmas lights. A mestizo bartender I spent a day and night in bed with, a pile of finely crushed powder on the glass bureautop shrinking down into dandruff; and I thought of Willie, who had not been sick in Cartagena, playing "I Wonder Who's Kissing Her Now" on the Bechstein with missing keys in the house near the Plaza de Bolivar, Willie like a small, trimmer version of Adolphe Menjou. I had hunted through Carl Fischer for the score, the day before getting on the plane for Bogota, so that Willie could play the song in the movie. The man who sold me the sheet music wanted to go to Peru. *Mama, my sister's run off with a Negro.* Gregory reappears. Jack only has fifty dollars in the till. We'll have to wait until he makes up the rest of it. But why, Gregory. We don't need a hundred dollars just to go out. Oh, he says, he'll have it in no time. Just be patient. Have another Remy. *Mama, my sister's run off with a Negro.*

The amplifier over the bar telegraphs red dashes, oscillating in length to the volume. Gregory puts his fingertips on my face. Don't get excited, he says. But something else is going on. I'm thinking about Willie and Rainer and I hear Willie's voice singing, *I wonder who's looking into her eyes, breathing sighs, telling lies* . . . Jack motions at Gregory, some cases of wine are wheeled in on a dolly, Gregory snaps into the rigid motions of work, the crates and the dolly and Jack and Gregory disappear through the basement door, a long time passes, the speakers drizzle noise through the damp air. I drain my Remy and stare at a Laurie Anderson poster above the pay phone. I watch people I know walk by on Spring Street, one's an architect and one's a composer and the third one, I seem to recall, is under indictment for tax fraud and owns a huge discotheque in the West Forties. Then I see a group straggling home from Sarah's opening. There's the critic from *Newsweek* and a woman who writes children's books, finally I see a boy I once paid $54 to suck his dick, I've forgotten his name, but he went on to invent a duck-shaped lighting fixture that earned him half a million dollars. History waddles along as I wait, Jack returns to his post behind the bar, still no Gregory, Jack pours me another Remy as if he's been told to, I stare at the glass, I'm ready to burst into tears.

He comes back looking agitated. Let's go, he says. We walk outside, go up Spring, across Mercer. Where are we going, I ask him. He says: I've got to go home now. I tell him: But we're going out. He says: I can't do that, I've got to go home now. I've got to be alone. Now I really don't understand anything. But I'm fed up, I've swallowed enough nonsense. Suit yourself I tell him. He seems to be trembling. Don't say that to me, he says, don't ever say that to me. You don't understand anything, he says. We walk together up Houston. Near the corner of Elizabeth Street I stop walking and scream, What is *wrong*. I've got to be alone, he whines, without looking at me, his pace quickens, he moves faster. I stop. He keeps walking. As far as he's concerned I've disappeared. He doesn't look back. Finally I turn down Elizabeth, thinking he'll turn around and follow me. I sit down on a stoop and gaze into a fenced-off filling station at a pile of tires.

What did I do to deserve this? What's wrong with me? I cannot quite believe he's kept on walking and left me here, but in fact this is exactly what has happened. I know the trees on this street better than I know him. I walk home along Bowery. Just near the corner of Third Street the sidewalk swarms with derelicts, some of them collapsed in piles of garbage. They've taken over one corner of the big gas station across the street, the empire of smelly drunks and crack addicts fans out from the men's shelter on Third all across the Bowery and down the lower end of Second Avenue. The procession of bums tapers off at Phebe's on Bowery and Fourth. Then there's a brand new Japanese restaurant, with a bunch of yuppies chawing sashimi in the window. The mission church. A pizza joint. Cooper Union. The Optimo Cigar place the Koreans have taken over, that sells the good porn. And then the stretch between St. Marks and Tenth, where the old parking lots are being excavated and blasted to make way for hideous NYU dormitories. In another year there won't be any trace of the neighborhood left. The hookers have already moved from Third Avenue to Second and Eleventh Street.

Up the miserable stairs. I unlock my door and bolt for the refrigerator, find a beer, and sink down into the study reclining chair, next to the phone, and wonder if I'm strong enough not to call him. A stupid thing to wonder about. When I do it there's no answer. Maybe he's dead. Maybe he's overdosed. Maybe it's just his way of saying I'm the biggest fool he ever met.

10

In the dream time Maria Lorca told me: If you don't quit smoking, you're going to have some problems in about three years. It was a feature of the dream time that this kind of information got stored in the same place as unwanted invitations and requests for non-paying lecture gigs and the kinds of embarrassing things I some-times did when I got drunk, a place where irritations pooled in the short-term memory and trickled their way down to the dumping core. In the dream time Gregory told me: I've got these swollen glands in my armpits. I am not calling it the dream time for any poetic reason, the dream time is simply what it was.

I knew a man who'd made a film that happened to be playing at the Public Theater. The director led a prolific career in Europe but had had no success in America, and when I saw the ad I told Gregory, Can't we go see this together? Although he hardly ever agreed to do anything, when I pleaded Gregory put on an aston-ished, bruised air. Of course, why not? he said. Why not go to the Met on Thursday? Why not go dancing at the Pyramid? Why not have dinner out? And invariably, a day or an hour or minutes before the promised thing, the date, the "shared experience," some terrible, unprecedented psychological disaster made the whole thing impossible. Gregory cross-hatched my disappointment by telling me there was always another day. We had our whole lives to go to the movies. And in the dream time it did mysteriously seem that we had eons stretching out ahead of us, miles of time for all the things we never did.

But we did go to this particular movie, debating the whole way, right up to the ticket window, whether this was the right night to go out, whether Gregory would actually like the movie. If I don't like it, he cautioned, don't be offended if I walk out in the middle. The threat of disaster was always palpable. A boring movie would never simply bore. It would ruin an evening, and by implication help to ruin everything.

After ten minutes I knew I'd made a hideous mistake. In the film, a young auto mechanic fell deliriously in love with a much older woman, a pharmacist. She rejected him. He became deranged. He parked his car across from her drugstore and started living in the car, putting a carpet down on the street, decorating the car with vases full of flowers. I felt Gregory turning restive immediately, and when the car business started I remembered the story of his father. Gregory's mind blackened in the seat beside me. He endured every frame like a crown of thorns. When we got outside the theater I said, That was heavy. He stared at the facade of the Colonnades as if willing the neighborhood to explode. Looking away from me he said, in a soft voice, You knew, didn't you. You knew what this was about when you forced me to go, didn't you.

Gregory, I said, I had no idea what this film was about. Oh sure, he said. If you expect me to believe that, he said, I don't think we have anything left to say to each other. And he marched away from me down Lafayette Street. I watched his determined back getting smaller and smaller. There was no point in catching up with him or trying to put things right: he would already have

a specific place he'd decided to go, and once he'd decided something, nothing on earth could change his mind.

Libby, I said, whatever you're doing, I have to see you this instant
or I'm getting in a cab and checking into Bellevue.

I'm feeding the cats, she said. Where are you?

I'm at Indochine, I said. I'm in the pay phone at Indo-chine.

Give me ten minutes, she said. And keep in mind, you know,
that Indochine is a particularly unfortunate place to go crazy in.

I waited behind an immense tropical floral arrangement and
drank three vodka martinis. I realized that every relationship I'd been
in before had somehow prepared me for Gregory in a special, awful
way. I had always wanted someone to take control of me body and
soul, rule my life, fill my consciousness to the exclusion of everything
else. And at last someone had, a full-blown psychopath. I knew we
had reached the point at which Gregory could take it all away from
me: my money, my sanity, my status, my sense of humor.

Libby appeared in a Gaultier T-shirt and a pair of tight
bleach-splattered jeans, her Brillo hair tucked up inside a straw
hat. I stood up and waved at her and gave her a kiss.

I feel terrible, I said, because since I called you I've drunk
myself into a philosophical mood.

That's all right, she said, I actually need a drink.

I got her a drink. Libby is not a drinker. It makes her silly, and
later acrid. She doesn't smoke or drink coffee. She likes two cans
of Bud at the end of an evening. She said she had already had
them. She now had a gin martini.

What made you come here, she asked.

Well, I said, we were across the street.

I told her the plot of the movie. Libby said it sounded pretty
good. "Let It Bleed" was playing at insect volume. Libby hummed

fitfully and mimicked the loose body language we all had back in the sixties. Then she scanned my face for depression.

He went into this fugue about the movie, Libby paraphrased, piecing events together.

That's the trouble, I said. He goes into a fugue over a chipped nail.

I know you love this guy, she said, but I don't think he's wrapped too tight.

No, I said. I sensed the alarming transmutation of my misery into the material of a therapeutic narrative. A story that would circle and circle around itself until it all came out fine.

A lot of American men can't handle relationships, Libby averred. Especially at his age.

I think it's all finished anyway, I said. I mean I don't think I can stand much more of this, breaking down and blubbering about him every night of my life. How can he continually do these things and why do I let him? It's mind-boggling.

Libby reached for one of my cigarettes. She started to light it, caught herself, then laid it aside near her glass. She pressed her lips together.

He does adore you, she said. You look so happy when you're with him.

I'm so obsessed with him it's making me sick, I said. And it must be incredibly boring for you to hear every little twist and turn. It's so embarrassing to feel publicly vulnerable and kicked around . . .

Actually, you somehow manage to make it sound interesting. But I do worry about you lately. This should be a good time in your life, with all this recent success and attention, and instead Gregory's spoiling it all. He's probably getting back at you for the things that are working out for you.

He says he admires me, he's always praising my work and all that.

Well, Libby said, people are never all one way or another. One part of him does admire you and another part resents your independence and the freedom you have. When people recognize you in public he feels very small and minor next to you, probably. He's still young and confused.

He's not *that* young, I said.

Libby sighed. Is it possible, she wondered, that you could somehow put him out of your mind for a while?

She ordered another martini. Alcohol was making her giddy for a change.

I'd love to be able to forget about him, I said. If this is the way things are going to be.

If you could leave town for a few days, Libby suggested.

Oh Libby, I said, you know I just can't. I'd like to, but I can't.

Well, she said, there you are.

Right. There I am.

Did he think I had taken him to the movies to torture him, rub his nose in stories of mania and failure, shatter his fragile equilibrium? I doubted it. Nobody could possibly be that delicate, that vigilant about another person's motives. Gregory had simply found an opportunity to strike out at me. We broke off, with the usual suddenness. He didn't call. I thought it unfair that we hadn't broken off before, the night he kept walking on Houston Street. I had hounded him by telephone right after that, to forgive him.

The magazine writing became effortless. Since it couldn't bring him back to me, I attacked it with indifferent competence. I was too depressed to write with any grace. One bleak evening when fog had again crept into the city, I discovered six boxes of Captagon in a rusted drawer of the blue desk. This will get me through, I thought.

There are myriad ways not to think of someone. You can think about another person. You can read books which are not about love. Books about thermodynamics, or ecology. You can plunge into a whirl of partygoing and flirt with every available and unavailable person. You could also go to the movies, take walks through Central Park, carefully avoid any place or object or person that reminds you of him. You can overwork, lecture out of town, wear a Walkman and blast really coldhearted music into your ears. And while you do all these things, if you happen to have six boxes of it laying around, you can take speed.

I ate fast, on the run, to get it over with. Never anything like a meal. I doused my stomach with coffee while sucking in the first ten morning smokes. I swallowed the day's first Captagon with a double tablespoon of Pepto-Bismol and settled in behind the typewriter. I had decided to write a novel. I would make it up out of my imagination. I gave it an island setting, somewhere near Lipari. The hero would be a fifty-year-old man living on a trust fund. Bog, his name was.

The story of Bog and his adventures. Bog walks down to the port every day from his hilltop retreat. He lives here because it's cheap and within his income. In summertime the port was overrun with tourists, but much of the time only a few people live on the island, demoralized and out of contact with the world. Bog eats breakfast at the same cafe every day. Every afternoon he plays cards with two other fifty-year-old men. Bog eats lunch at the same taverna, dinner at the same outdoor restaurant, under a carpet of stars. He doesn't talk very much, but he's a good listener. No one knows much about him. He knows everything that goes on, all the marriages and deaths and feuds and infidelities, Bog listens, but he offers no advice. He has no conversation, no repartee, no aphorisms. He doesn't really exist, in a way, and yet he does, because there he is. I thought I would write the story of Bog's life, describing all the objects in his house, the awnings of the port cafes, the colors of the ships, the exact look of all the people: only sharp, objective physical details, no psychological explanations, just facts.

Bog carried me away from my problems, into a world of graphomania. I wrote all day without eating anything. Food became something I forced down to settle my stomach, something easy to chew and "nourishing": a few plums or a nectarine, a soft roll, a take-out cup of cole slaw. Yogurt, which I spooned down so fast it passed right through me. At night, I boiled a few handfuls of curlicue pasta and doused it with butter and a flaming chili and garlic sauce, the house brand of the Korean emporium. I believed the garlic would squeeze all the toxins out of my body through the skin, toxins having become my principal diet. Eating annoyed me. I wanted to get through it so I could smoke another cigarette.

I took little breaks to refresh my mind, to flip through an improving book, looking for a phrase or a paragraph to spur my thoughts. I ventured down to the sidewalk, getting dry heaves, gagging if I walked too fast. Ideas for this book, Bog's book, flooded through me like laser beams. Every building suggested a fresh detail. Every torn cloud in the sky opened vistas of descriptive possibilities. My mind seemed to expand at every corner. The whole thing typed itself out in my head. Intricate plot revisions worked themselves out with dreamlike ease. And at a certain moment during this pause from work, I'd find that I had walked fifty blocks, to Battery Park or Lincoln Center.

I wrote through the evenings and at midnight or one I called Libby, then Jane, or Jane, then Libby, and told them I was making fantastic progress. Any word from you know who, Jane asked, and I said, proudly, Who. Jane said, I guess you are making progress after all. Libby asked, Do you miss him a lot? Breathless from amphetamines, I declared that I wanted to put masochism out of my life, that I was getting a little old for that sort of thing, and I now had to get Serious about my Writing. Let's face it, I said. If we want to get anywhere we have to get tough with ourselves. All Gregory wants to do is generate endless dramas that have no conclusion and will ultimately drive me out of my mind. Of course, I said, it's painful that things turned out this way, but if I let it get to me I'll just become paralyzed. No, I said, that isn't my way. I'm stronger than he is. Which, I promised, he will find out to his own surprise.

Right after hanging up, I tapped my way down six flights and across Second to the Lebanese deli (which I preferred to the Korean one, because the horny Lebs flirted obscenely) for a six-pack. Quite often I drank the first six-pack and crawled out to buy a second one, this time at the Koreans' so the Lebs wouldn't know what a drunk I was. Eventually the beer brought a maudlin edge to the amphetamines, and at four in the morning I would read through my Bog manuscript, becoming tearfully moved by the beauty of my own prose, meanwhile playing the Callas *Tosca* at volumes that crept ever higher the drunker I got, creating an acoustical nightmare for my neighbors along the airshaft.

Despite the alcohol, my literary circus resumed at nine or ten the following morning, since Captagon has its own quirky bio-clock. I woke in a world-annihilating despair, staggered to the coffeepot, considered suicide, waited for the speed to kick in. I watched myself turning cadaverous in the toothpaste-speckled mirror over the kitchen sink. Am I letting this happen to extract pity, I wondered. Do I expect someone to rescue me? Not him, I thought. Not really.

I applied the brakes after 110 unreadable pages. In the meantime, I had filed two consecutive magazine stories of such stupefying obscurity that my editor suggested, demurely, that I needed a vacation. Maria Lorca eased me off Captagon with injections of Valium. My appearance scared her. So did my muttered responses to her questions. If you don't mind, she said, I'd like to get a little blood work done. She caught the fear in my eyes and said, I'm sure it's nothing too dramatic.

Food: health: life. I was gnawing a Sabrett's hot dog when I saw him walking towards me, crossing Astor Place near the cube sculpture. We slowed down as we neared each other and stopped at the wrought iron railing of the Community College, performing a kind of waltz glide, him with his back to the fence, me angling around to face him, and though we stopped it seemed as if we were still moving, around and away from each other. I threw the hot dog away.

You wanna talk things over, he asked. I could see he wanted to. I shrugged.

What's to talk about, I said. I smiled, but not much.

He swallowed, lowered his eyes. He took a few steps away. I looked back and he looked back.

Obviously, he said, I'm not capable of giving you what you need.

I don't think you're capable of giving anybody what they need, I said.

He spun around and stalked off. Bad theater, I shouted after him.

I guess I'm happy enough, I told M., tilting a glass of champagne. Happy, and empty.

You can't have everything, M. countered. Never happens.

And I do have wonderful friends, I said.

And a job, M. reminded me.

Yes, I said. And prestige.

And, he coaxed, what else?

Well, I said, in the same bright voice, Maria Lorca seems to think I've got hepatitis.

M. bristled. I think you better tell me about this, he said. We settled the check at the Spring Street Bar in the usual manner. I worriedly pulled a twenty from a mash of singles while M., always quicker on the draw, slipped a crisply folded hundred from the pocket of his pink and white Armani shirt and held it indifferently until the bartender plucked it from his fingers. We paced up to Broadway in nervous complicity. M. hobbled, his bad knee reacting to the fickle cool of an ocean breeze gusting up from the toxic harbor. I felt a rush of remorse for years of dumping my problems on M., in this case overstating them for dramatic effect.

She just said my antibody count is in a funny place, I said, clearing my throat as if to change the subject.

M. halted to light a Marlboro against the wind. The butane lighter sparked and flickered and finally sent a long rope of flame into the bluish mist. M. expelled an anxious stream of smoke and said: How funny is it?

We resumed walking, in silence, and reached the side of an unattended parking lot where very few cars, all highly polished, glistened under floodlights. I spotted the white Mercedes before he did.

Oh gee, I said. Look at that.

Please, he wailed. Don't. Not here.

But I was already halfway across the lot, gliding up to the grille of the Mercedes. I leaned with my back against it, posing as if I'd stopped to light a cigarette. I reached expertly behind my back and snapped off the hood ornament, pocketed it, and walked through the lot to where M. stood on the Broadway side of the enclosure. I had been vandalizing Mercedes hoods for over a decade.

I don't want it, said M., who owned at least a dozen of these nocturnal trophies.

Who said it was for you, I said.

It must have been the metal star in its circle, more than the letter I mailed him that week and the typed addendum I sent on a three by five file card immediately afterwards, that set the whole business going again. In the letter, I spelled out everything he'd done wrong, all the ways he'd invented to hurt me, and the most damning thing of all, that he knew all this would destroy my ability to function, I'd lose my job and end up penniless again, because unless I arrived at total ruin he couldn't feel stronger than me. And, I wrote, you've almost managed it, but I won't sacrifice myself for you, I need to build my own life, whereas you only know how to play games. If you had loved me, I might have considered changing things, I might have given up ambition to be with you, but you don't want me, you want to witness the spectacle of my destruction. I'm on drugs now, I wrote—lying, since I'd just gone off them—and drinking myself sick every night—that part was true, though it wasn't really his fault— and even though you've never made love to me my doctor thinks you've got hepatitis B, the worst kind, and I've gotten it from your feckless kisses, or maybe from eating off the same plate. So you've not only crapped up my working life, you've also ruined my health. I hope you're satisfied, but I suppose you're not, because you've never been satisfied with anything short of total catastrophe, and since I'm still alive, you've obviously failed.

I sealed the letter in a legal envelope left over from a long-ago temporary job at the Mystic Steamship Company in Boston, and even found a stamp, buried under a morass of canceled checks and Chemical Bank statements. This seemed a decisive augury

because I had never previously managed to locate a stamp in my
apartment, which was why I'd never written home in ten years.
You write the letter and there's no stamp, to get a stamp you have
to walk to the post office, I've always hated going inside. Everyone
in the post office stinks of expectation and petty concerns. They
think their postal transactions will save their lives and solve
impossibly complicated problems. Or they imagine they'll receive
something crucial, like a tax return or a package full of useful
objects. Yet nothing anyone has ever received at the post office has
prevented them from dropping dead or developing a brain tumor
or having teeth fall out, my father used to get his hearing aids
by mail and none of them ever worked, the only thing that ever
happens in the post office is waiting, waiting for some disgrun-
tled, overweight mental defective to weigh a package or inform
you that whatever you've stood in line a half hour to retrieve isn't
there and never was there, the thing to do is to buy enough stamps
to last until the rates go up, but of course the rates go up before
you've used half your stamps, and then you need to buy supple-
mentary postage, so the whole stupid comedy starts all over again.
Which is why the phone has eliminated personal correspondence,
except in cases like this one, where I really didn't want to talk to
him, and suspected his phone would be unplugged if I tried to.

I dumped the letter in a mailbox on Second Avenue. The feet of
the mailbox had been unscrewed, either by vandals or perhaps by
the post office itself, to undermine confidence. Maybe he won't get
this, I thought, until years from now, when it won't mean anything.
He won't even remember who I am. I won't remember who he was,
and he won't remember who I was, either. It will just be a strange
piece of mail. And he won't receive it anyway, because he won't be
living there, and Gregory isn't the type to leave a forwarding address.

The addendum, on the file card, read: In spite of everything,
you have a beautiful soul, and I would do anything for you if you

were in trouble. For this, I bought a stamp from a machine at the discount center on Ninth Street. I mailed it from the same defective mailbox, wondering if he'd get the postscript before the letter, and what sort of confusion that would cause.

And then I bumped into him a few days later, and pulled the Mercedes star from my pocket. Here's your birthday present, I said. I got the real present yesterday, he smiled, meaning the file card, the postscript, the apology.

II

At the carious onset of the dream time, Gregory went to Maria Lorca for a blood test. He did, it turned out, have hepatitis, which accounted, Maria Lorca thought, for his continual exhaustion, though she also wanted a biopsy on his lymph nodes, since many people with chronic hepatitis never experience fatigue but just have it rummaging around through their livers, whereas these swollen nodes, Maria Lorca told him, might be the residue of his long-ago IV drug use, or a side effect of hepatitis B, but there was, she said, a marginal possibility of lymphoma. He reported this accusingly, as if he would've been perfectly healthy if I hadn't sent him to the doctor.

He immediately saw himself as a cornered creature. He needed bed rest and complete quiet, but he needed to keep going, keep working, or else he'd have no money. He'd lose his apartment and starve to death. Or else his job would kill him. Either way, he'd die.

You've got to quit, I begged him over the phone.

I know, he said, but how can I?

You're supposed to be recovering, in bed. Resting. You're not even supposed to move around.

I don't have any insurance, he whined. I'll have to move home. Or move in with you.

Would you rather be dead, Gregory? I mean, you don't have too many choices here.

I'd rather be dead anyway, at this point. It's just been one shitty thing after another.

I'll take care of you, I said, instantly regretting it.

That's just what I've been avoiding, he said, as I knew he would.

But Gregory, I said, this is an emergency. Maria Lorca says you have extensive liver damage.

She *told* you that? Does she realize I could sue her for divulging information?

I paid your goddamned bill with her, I said, if you can't afford to pay her how do you think you can afford to sue her? Anyway, I'm involved in this too, you know, I'm infected. I have to know how to take care of myself.

I'll bet you even resent her for looking up my asshole, don't you.

She's a *doctor*, Gregory, she needed a stool sample, I don't really consider her a love rival. I mean, grow up, will you?

I am bisexual, you know.

I know all about it, I said. You and the Emperor Tiberius. I'm sure Maria Lorca would prefer someone closer to the top of the food chain, in any case.

Oh, great, he said, now I'm nothing but scum to you, now that I can't fuck you.

You've already fucked me, every way but in bed. Why are you dragging this down to some idiotic emotional level, anyway?

Go ahead, he said, get it all out. I won't hang up on you. You'd just call right back anyway.

You'd have unplugged the phone, Gregory, I know your little ways.

You always think of me in the diminutive, because you're so big and important. If you only knew what people really think of you.

What people. Your friends?

Everybody except the four or five people who can stand you. Everyone says you're a raging drunkard and a liar and a mediocrity who thinks he's a genius. That you have so little self-respect you've lived in a pigpen for ten years. That you pretend you're this moral paragon when the fact is you've never had the opportunity to sell out. You've never paid back a loan, and you've never picked up a check. That's what people say.

Anything else?

You've also got bad breath, Gregory concluded.

Obviously not bad enough, I said, since you've given me hepatitis.

Hepatitis antibodies, Gregory told me. Pugg has full-blown hepatitis.

Lucky Pugg, I said. If I was Typhoid Mary I wouldn't brag about it.

Thank God I never fucked you, Gregory said. I knew if I ever did you'd destroy what's left of my sanity.

What makes you think there's anything left? You've been insane as long as I've known you.

Since meeting you, he assured me. I was fine until then.

I'm sure there's a mountain of used syringes to back that up, I said.

Thanks to people like you, he said. People I took pity on because I thought something decent might be buried under all that bullshit.

You should've been an archaeologist instead of a waiter, I said. Maybe it would've paid better.

Go ahead, rub it in, he said. It makes you feel so superior.

I'm actually not enjoying this, I said.

I find that hard to believe, he said, like everything else you tell me. I wonder why that is.

Because, I said. You're that rare thing, a skeptical drug addict.

You're the one on drugs, he said, classical Freudian projection.

I'm not on drugs, I said.

You're drunk, he said. Same thing.

Yes, I said, I am drunk. I'm often drunk lately. When the person you love treats you like shit you have to make your own fun.

Your idea of fun is self-destruction, he said.

So's yours, I said. And you go a lot further with it than I do.

We'll see, he said.

A few days later, Philippe lost control of himself in a definitive manner, fortunately not with the gun, first smashing a row of bottles with a fireplace poker he happened to have in the basement, then bashing a waitress in the kidneys with some detachable part of the espresso machine. Then he broke a chair over the bartender's head, raged through the kitchen overturning stacks of dishes and cookware, threw a colander full of bubbling french fries into the cook's face, grabbed a meat cleaver, started with it for the dining room, then, evidently, restrained by considering the legal consequences of assault with a lethal weapon, dropped the cleaver on his foot, unfortunately catching it on the blunt end, and finally he slung an unopened can of Amstel Light at Gregory's back, causing no serious damage but inspiring Gregory to walk off the job.

For the next six hours, Philippe called Gregory's apartment, begging him to return, and Gregory kept calling me, reporting each outrageous string of insults, threats, bribes, and, incredibly, emotional appeals that Philippe resorted to, citing their "years of intimate friendship." Gregory sounded greatly amused by Philippe's desperation, which escalated as the dining room of the restaurant filled, though after several hours of more or less complete inanity, Gregory gave me a code to use to get through to him, Ring twice, he said, hang up and ring again. I suddenly wondered if during the many periods when Gregory wouldn't talk to me, someone else had been getting through, using the same code. He had more or less admitted to screwing Pugg, and I suspected too that he'd been screwing one of the waitresses. I knew the waitress was in love with him. She had come into the gallery one day when Gregory was working there, and had looked at him with such dewy eyes I wanted to vomit. She was also dewy from heroin, Bruno later told me. In any case, it pleased me to learn that the waitress had hepatitis as well as Pugg, even though they'd gotten it from Gregory, since whatever he'd done with them he wouldn't be doing again for a while.

Once he'd actually quit at the restaurant, Gregory fell into a panic and made me promise to take care of him. If I did, he said, he'd make everything up to me. What's more, he'd never treat me badly, ever again. I would see right away what a different person he could be.

You should only get addicted to things you can afford. Cigarettes kill slowly, softening up the tissues for the inevitable neoplasm. Alcohol turns your liver the green of rare cheeses. One morning you discover a lump, a swelling, a mysterious discoloration.

When Gregory came, not to move in, but to "rest" in my apartment every day, returning to his own in the late evenings, we fell under a spell. The barricades between us toppled, and a strange quiet settled in. He came every day without fail. It no longer mattered if he came an hour or two later than promised, because that gave me free time. And I knew he'd eventually appear. I cooked his breakfast. After eating he spent hours doing the *Times* crossword, while I sat at my desk, chipping away at my weekly article. Often he laid the paper aside and went into the bedroom and slept.

Somewhere in the middle of the day there would be another meal, and then later another, and then at ten or eleven or midnight I walked him home, or halfway home, or else he decided to walk home by himself We had a rule, that when I walked him I had to phone when I got back, and if he went by himself he called me when he got there. We seemed extraordinarily fragile to ourselves. The dozen blocks between our houses held all the world's strangeness. The air was a dense medium full of monsters, flesh, drugs, and danger.

The hours between midnight and four were my own, and the hours of sleep. Gregory didn't want me to drink, so I did it secretly, dumping the evidence outside when I went for the morning paper. I dreamed about lost dreams. I suddenly had what I had wanted all along. A daily presence, someone who took my constancy for granted. I dealt with his laundry, paid his bills, massaged him when he ached, protected him. We never talked about the earlier time. He had had some kind of falling-out with Pugg. I stopped seeing Victor late at night. I dropped my gym classes. We were completely alone. The days were running longer and the weather was glorious, but we never left the house. The apartment had the dead atmosphere of a sick ward. I changed the phone number again.

Gregory couldn't work, so he looked at pictures. We passed through the blanket bazaar on Second Avenue on the way to his place, shopping for porn. He knew the magazine models by name, the agencies they worked for, knew which look was featured where. We spent our spare money on jumbo packages of *Jock* and *Powerhouse* and *Stud*. Some showed oral and anal penetration, others had alternating color and black-and-white spreads of individual boys and men undressing and playing with their genitals. There were specialty publications featuring nipple and cock torture, whip action, stuff with chains, boards, and pulleys. Anything anyone had thought to do, there was a magazine about it. Soon there were little skyscrapers of porn in the apartment, awaiting Gregory's scissors.

He began to refer, sarcastically, to sodomy; from the absurdly uncomplicated dramaturgy of the magazines, the idea of sodomy as a bad joke entered the schizobabble we exchanged in private. Gregory would indicate a large object and ask if I thought he could get it up his ass, or up my ass. Eventually, he only needed to point at something with a certain look on his face. This stayed funny for a while, but he kept joking about it long after it lost its charm. Let me just stick this refrigerator up your ass. Would you mind easing this bathtub into my asshole? Do you think your ass can handle the file cabinet? We hardly touched each other. In such straits, even the surreal verbal intimacy of someone who offers to shove a bookcase up your can may seem indicative of an interest in your body.

He enjoyed being contagious. He didn't need his usual defenses, since nothing could lead very far. So he became kind, reliable, and loving. The total stasis of our days corresponded to what I thought a "real" relationship might consist of except for the quirk that we left each other to sleep. He claimed he could never sleep in anyone else's bed.

He'd lost weight. How much, I couldn't tell. A lot. He was pale, careful about his movements, almost simperingly gentle. He didn't want to have the X-rays and the biopsy Maria Lorca insisted he should have. He said they cost too much money. When I said I would pay for them, he still refused. I knew what he was thinking.

He was there for me now, all the time. And yet he remained absent. I sat at my desk making false stabs at going on, he sat in his chair penciling letters into the crossword boxes. We spoke in lowered voices, always about practical things. Are you hungry. Can I get you anything. Did you want some music.

I lost the habit of talking to Libby and Jane every night; there was nothing to report, nothing to arrange into anecdotes. And the act of speech had come to seem dangerous. I didn't know my own thoughts. Life assumed a regular, lifeless pattern. At night, when I walked him home, the streets carried too much noise, too many colors. I wanted things to stay dim and gray and soundless, spectral, unthreatening. He intoxicated me and made me full, and at the same time he had lost all reality. I often forgot to call him to tell him I was safely back in my apartment, even when I had nothing except him on my mind.

I can hear him breathing in the next room. I wrote: How on earth did I get involved with him? I had just returned from Colombia, where I had been acting in a low-budget movie—I'd gone down there and stepped off the plane with $8 in my pocket and no precise address for the hotel, the airport was pitch black and the daily thunderstorm had just finished flooding all the potholes on the road into town. I found Rainer at the Hotel Plaza de Bolivar, at a table in the courtyard where the palms and the ivy were still dripping; Rainer looked up from his storyboard and laughed. Wouldn't you agree with Edith Sitwell, he said, that the laughter is always in the next room?

In the meantime everything is so changed I might have come back twenty years ago. Yesterday I knocked off my piece for the magazine and came home, Gregory had washed the floors and tidied up the kitchen, we smiled at each other and he said, Welcome home, darlin', kissed me on the nose, and then resumed reading a back issue of *October*, lying on the bed with his head propped up on the pillows and his fat bare feet crossed at the ankles, I started fiddling around with papers in the study to give him some solitude, naturally I couldn't get anything accomplished, I could hear him lighting his cigarettes and crossing and uncrossing his legs and inhaling exhaling and after an hour he got up and walked into the kitchen, started making dinner, asked me about my day, what I've written, made some jokes about Conceptual Art, then some of his asshole humor: he showed me the bluefish we're having and mimicked cramming it up his keister. I kept thinking, If he didn't have that goddamned face I would've gotten rid of him months ago. But he does have that face. He's being stoical about his hepatitis. He doesn't complain but why should he since both our lives revolve around his illness. We talked for a while about how to renovate the apartment; Gregory made some sketches. He said he needed to borrow back the pictures he gave me, for Bruno's group show. And asked if it would be all right to sell them, since he's not making any money. We ate dinner. Illness hasn't affected his appetite, he still eats like a horse. Then we sat around smoking cigarettes and drinking coffee until he decided to go. We went together as far as Second and Seventh and then he said, You don't need to walk me tonight, I want to think for a while, I'll phone you when I get home.

I stopped in the Reno Bar and drank a beer, feeling guilty because he might be trying to reach me. When I came in he hadn't left a message so I phoned his place. No answer. I suddenly wondered how long I'd been in the Reno Bar, thinking he'd had plenty of time to get home. I waited a half hour and called again, when he didn't answer this time I freaked—I don't know what I was thinking, but I found myself running downstairs and racing across Ninth Street Over to First and all the way down into Loisaida, the air had gotten muggy and my face was sweaty. When I got to his place the super was standing out on the sidewalk, reeling drunk, I pushed Gregory's buzzer and waited and waited while the super stared at me like a staggering moron, this went on for ten minutes and finally he said, You wanna go in? and unlocked the door for me. I went upstairs and knocked on his door.

I could hear music inside, I expected to hear him coming out of the bathroom or getting out of bed, but nothing happened. I stood there pounding on the wood until my fingers hurt, then I noticed a keyhole under the doorknob, They hadn't removed the old lock panel after putting in a deadbolt. So I got on my knees and squinted into the opening. The fights were on inside, my eyes kept watering so I only got a blurry picture. I could see most of the futon and part of his desk and the space between, the place was all lit up and the stereo or the radio was on at a low volume. From my side of the door, it didn't look the way you'd leave a place if you were going out. But I also had the feeling he wasn't inside. I kept blinking, trying to clear the picture, the edges of things kept getting wet. I rapped on the door again and strained to hear if there was any movement inside. I imagined him crouched in the alcove or hiding in the bathroom. I couldn't identify the music at all, I knocked again, I suppose I thought he'd been murdered, and then I realized I could only find out by breaking down the door and I wasn't ready to do that. I stood up and left the building, suddenly paranoid about running into him outside. What would he think I was doing there?

Why wasn't he there? He calls me even if he stops somewhere on his way, so I won't wait up for his call. I ducked into the cocktail lounge on the corner, a real shithole, and took a stool at the bar, with a clear view of the side window, but far enough back so he'd have difficulty recognizing me if he glanced in while walking by. I ordered a beer. The bartender was a perky old dyke with a henna crewcut who would gladly have bored me to death with a little encouragement. There were a couple of obvious hookers further down the bar, a fat man in a rumpled suit nursing a beer at a table, and some Spanish punks playing video games in the back. Patsy Cline on the jukebox, falling to pieces.

I knew I expected to see him going by with someone, someone he'd arranged to meet well in advance. And what if they came in here? I drank the first beer and ordered a second, and then a third. I started feeling pleasantly stupid, remembering that Gregory couldn't drink alcohol, and wouldn't have any reason to enter this particular bar. He couldn't have sex with anyone, either; and why else would he be bringing someone home at two in the morning? Maria Lorca had already vanquished the idea that Gregory was taking heroin, and I now saw myself spinning a pointless web of suspicion from overworked nerves and the sheer uneventfulness of his convalescence. Maybe he met Bruno in the street, maybe he took a walk. It's not like he has a secret life, if I see him twelve hours out of twenty-four. I treat him like my child, and so he becomes a child.

I finally convinced myself to leave, and hailed a cab on Houston Street.

I had to see W.'s photographs at an opening on Fifty-seventh Street. Gregory hates W. because he thinks W. exploits sex, but says he wants to come along because he's going stir crazy, Please don't, I said, since you have such strong feelings against W., I want to enjoy myself. Besides, Gregory wants to bring the odious Pugg along, now that they've reconciled. I said I really didn't feature listening to the two of them kvetching about the moral outrage of W.'s pictures since I happen to like them and W. is a friend of mine. Gregory said, I'm always willing to have my mind changed. I said I'd just as soon he took the opportunity to change his mind on another occasion, but then he promised to behave himself. And I finally thought, Well, it's a big concession on his part to be seen in public with me, he's so paranoid about it. We went up in a cab, and got jammed into the elevator with several people I knew. Then we spilled out into the gallery, which was so crowded I could barely breathe.

Pugg was already there, in the front gallery, where W. had installed some light boxes. Pugg and Gregory instantly formed a cabal. Martha happened along; I introduced Gregory, ignoring Pugg. Martha said: It's a beautiful show. Gregory said: I hate this stuff.

And he went on, delighted with himself explaining to Martha how exploitative and retrograde W.'s photographs were. He wore his most seductive smile, and talked in that sculpted voice that's so ingratiating, and Pugg stood around gazing at him rapturously, as if he'd never heard anything quite so brilliant. Martha tried arguing back, but she is no verbal match for Gregory. I left the three of them there and ploughed through the place smiling at people and waiting to get lost in the crowd, as far away from Gregory as possible.

I found Jane somewhere in the mob, looking nervous, as though she were worried about the fire exits. Why haven't you called me, she asked. I said, Because Gregory's at my house every night until midnight. So call after midnight, she said. What's going on with you two, anyway? I'm nursing him back to health, I said, and I guess it's working, because he's here, badmouthing W., I think I'll throttle him.

We should talk, Jane said. Like, tomorrow.

I really do feel like killing him, I said.

That will change, Jane said.

I circled back to the front room, rubbing shoulders and sleeves with the rich and famous, and found him still holding forth. Martha had managed to separate herself, so Gregory and Pugg were contently snickering in a corner. I'm leaving, I told him, accentuating the singular, but of course he followed me to the elevator, with Pugg trailing. I couldn't look at him. I got on the elevator hoping the crowd would separate us, but it didn't. We rode down to street level in hostile silence. Outside I flagged a cab right away and jumped in, the two of them tumbled in beside me. We rode thirty blocks without a word. At last Pugg asked me some trivial thing about W. I managed a civil answer, knowing the whole episode had been about pissing me off I wasn't going to play it the way Gregory wanted: he hoped I'd say something nasty to Pugg, giving him an excuse to leave me and spend the evening with his friend.

We got out at Tenth Street and Second. I had some doubt that Gregory still planned on having dinner with me, but just before the cab stopped he snapped into a sort of married tone: Do we have enough food in the house, he asked, and then he asked Pugg if he wanted to keep the taxi. So we left the creep with a few dollars and walked to the Korean place on Second and Fifth.

We did the shopping. I could barely speak to him, but kept telling myself, Let it go. But I lost it at the check-out. Behind the register an incredibly bovine, chubby Korean girl looked at each item in my basket as if she had never seen any such thing in her life. After ringing up one item, she would take the next thing out, look it over idiotically, then call to someone in the back of the store and ask for a price. She seemed completely stoned. Finally I said, under my breath, Oh for Christ's sake, and the girl snapped out of her trance, blushed, apologized; I felt the kind of guilt you feel for hitting a child. On the street Gregory said, icily, How could you do that?

My God, I thought, he's so diabolical I'll never know how to explain it to anybody. Don't . . . *start*, I said through my teeth.

I can't believe you, he said, you, who claims to care so much about other people, and supposedly have so much compassion, could humiliate a poor working girl—

Look, I said, I think maybe it would be a great idea if you'd just go home, Gregory. Just go home right now. Because I'm not going to listen to this, and I'm not going to stand still for you telling me how to behave, particularly right after . . . especially not right this moment, okay? Just go home and spend the evening at your own place, and buy yourself something to eat with your own money.

Don't do this to me, he said. If you want to talk something

over, all right. We can talk it over. But don't turn a conversation into World War III, because I'm telling you something and you ought to be, we ought to be far enough along in this relationship to say things to each other without turning it into some final epic drama . . .

How dare you criticize me, I said. How dare you tell me how to behave.

It went on like that until we got to my apartment. I realized that sending him home would simply involve more unpleasantness over the telephone, and we had already bought dinner. Upstairs, he renewed pleading on behalf of the cashier. I told him he'd behaved like a pig at W.'s opening.

Aha, he said, so that's what this is all about.

No, I said, that's not what it's all about, but while we're on the subject, how dare you go to somebody's show and spend the entire time there blabbing about how much you hate his work? You pleaded with me to go there, you weren't invited or anything.

I was with Pugg, he said evenly, we were in a very discreet part of the gallery, we weren't talking so anyone else could hear us. Believe it or not, he said, I didn't go there to make you uncomfortable. Quite the contrary.

It occurred to me then, that as long as I desired him I would never prevail in that kind of confrontation. Because the argument had nothing to do with the strings being pulled. It also dawned on me that Gregory was a complete sociopath. This perception was of no help whatever.

I got him a $500 emergency grant for his medical expenses. I took out a $1,000 interest-free loan from a benevolent organization to pay his back rent. Gregory then applied for a $3,000 grant, from a foundation that supported mid-career artists having temporary setbacks. At first Gregory acknowledged that his chances of getting this money were slender. But as time went by, he developed an irrational, intractable conviction that his application would be approved, and began speaking of the grant as assured money he was waiting for. Before long, this $3,000 replaced all other income-producing plans for his immediate future. If it didn't come, he said, he would have to pack it in. He didn't say as much, but that meant returning home to Connecticut and his mother, and starting again from square one.

He just didn't see any other possibilities, although both of his pictures in Bruno's group show were sold, and two other galleries had asked him for work. He went through the motions of ordering prints from some of his slides, and got the works fabricated and delivered, but his attitude was lost posthumous, he no longer felt involved with these pictures, or with making art at all. The reception of his work was, as he'd predicted, quite sensational. Enough, at least, to stir interest from three museums and a half dozen collectors. This attention did nothing for him. Or perhaps it did: it scared him, and he was already scared beyond his ability to cope. I later realized that to stand behind something he had made would have forced him to reveal an identity to the world, abandoning the masks that were his only real works of art. He wanted to be seen but he wanted to be invisible. I came to understand that he had only told the truth when he said he wanted everything.

12

He promised at last he'd have the X-rays taken. Maria Lorca phoned the prescription into the lab on Third Avenue, right around the corner. Last night Rainer called from the Gramercy, he's bringing Willie's ashes home to Australia. We went there this morning for breakfast. Rainer is going through the worst moment of his life, but he was very patient and nice with Gregory and kept up a stream of absurd chatter, much of it about sex and the things he used to enjoy. I could feel Gregory's Savonarola complex rising darkly between his ears while Rainer described sex with a rubber queen from New Jersey. We ate in a truly horrible outdoor cafe near the hotel and Gregory left us there, claiming he had some errand. Rainer talked about suicide, not in a depressive way, but lightly, even warmly. No call for help there. I'm certain he's planning to do it.

At two o'clock, Gregory showed up at the magazine office. I hadn't quite finished writing and he stood at the entrance of my cubicle, leaning against the slatted glass with his upper lip stretched out against his hands, which were clasped on the top of the divider: the picture of despond. His entire body whined. When I finished we went to the accounting office for my check. The checks hadn't been signed. We had to sit there. Gregory's impatience sucked all the air from the room. I have never seen anyone suffer so insistently. He makes Camille look like Esther

Williams. Next we walked to the bank, another martyrdom of waiting for him. Finally I handed him the money and told him, Just take this and go over there, okay? I can't eat lunch with you, I just can't take being with you right now.

That's so unfair, he cried. You promised to have lunch with me. How can you be so selfish, you know how upsetting this is.

He's become such a sodden bag of cringing need. I desperately wanted some oxygen, to walk alone in the streets, to look at the sky and think about anything except him. We went to a coffee shop on Broadway. He ordered a cheeseburger. I said: It's you that's unfair. You know your fucking horrible behavior is making me sick, why can't you leave me in peace for one bloody minute.

He calmly consumed every morsel of food on his plate, then pushed it away and became indignant. He stood up and walked out of the place. I took the check to the register, paid it, and found him outside, loitering near a trash basket at the corner. Are you getting these X-rays or what, I said. He looked at the money I'd given him. I need more than this, he said. They're $75.

No, I said, they're $50, I asked them.

Maria ordered a second set, Gregory said. The duplicates are $25.

I dug out $25 and slapped it into his hand.

Are you gonna walk me over there?

All right, I said, thinking that he was probably frightened out of his wits.

At the door of the lab I said, I'll come in and wait for you.

It's all right, he said. Don't bother. I'll be fine.

Are you sure, I said.

I love you, he said.

He went in. When I got to my apartment, lay down for a minute, and smoked a cigarette, I pictured two things. One was Gregory pressing his chest to the cold rectangle of an X-ray plate. The other was Gregory walking into the lab, sitting down in the waiting room, watching three minutes pass on the wall clock, and promptly walking out.

He brought me a bunch of jonquils this afternoon. He said he'd traded a picture with Bruno's friend Roger, and Roger had insisted on giving him some money as well, even though Roger's piece is a painting and worth more. He did the shopping too, which left the afternoon free. Pugg is back in the picture. Gregory thinks it's only a matter of days before he'll have to get a job, hepatitis or no hepatitis. Pugg wants them to start a loft-cleaning service. This seems impractical to me, first of all because Pugg's an obvious dope, but also, Gregory's still sick. Maria Lorca says he shouldn't do anything whatsoever for two months. We would both be better off in the Soviet Union, at least he wouldn't risk losing his apartment because he's sick.

Gregory decided he was well again, if only because he felt poisonously bored. One morning he announced his recovery and said he would spend the day looking for a job. Some hours later he called me from a pay phone, in tears, and said he'd spent his last dollar getting uptown, and had gone to the wrong address and missed the appointment he'd made, now he was stuck at Fifty-ninth Street and feeling sick. I told him to take a cab to the house. As I paid the cab I saw the stricken, humiliated look on his face, and knew he was lapsing back into the bleary hopelessness he'd lost during his illness.

Look, I said, I'm not your enemy, I'm not trying to add to your frustrations. I'm helping you, I've given you every spare penny I have.

This isn't a reproach, I'm glad to give it to you. But you can not mope and complain all the time because it's bringing me down. You can't tell me every time a problem gets solved that you suddenly have ten more that are too much for you to deal with. If I get any more depressed I'm not going to function anymore and then we'll both be in deep trouble because I won't get any work done and there won't be any more money coming in. Can't you at least see that?

I knew you'd eventually throw the money thing back in my face, he said.

I'm not throwing it in your face, I'm telling you something. I've been supporting you to relieve some of this anxiety of yours, but the more I do for you, the less you seem willing to do the one thing I need, which is, Gregory, for you to at least pretend you have a positive attitude, and stop whining about how persecuted you are.

In other words, he said, you want me to lie, and pretend I'm happy, when I'm crumbling apart right in front of you. You know, I'm not the kind of person who can scream and jump out the window, but in fact I'm cracking into pieces.

That's what I don't understand, I said, for six weeks you've been in a really good mental state, you've been able to rest and not worry about your bills or anything, and now you're acting the way you did before. I mean I thought we'd worked some of this out with each other.

Do you realize what it's like, he said, pounding the sidewalks for hours and hours and going through these job interviews, being interrogated by these hideous people?

Yes, I do, I said, and when I did it I didn't have anyone waiting at home to see that I got enough to eat and that my rent was taken care of, but you do. I just don't see why that doesn't take the edge off for you.

Surely, Gregory said, you understand how mortifying it is for me that you have to take care of me.

I don't have to, I said. I've been doing it because I wanted to. So why turn it into some sick guilty thing.

I can see, he said, that you're not interested in how I feel. You know how you want me to be, and if I don't coincide with that, you get pissed off.

Gregory . . . I'm not asking you to be *cheerful*, I'm not asking you to pretend everything in your life is wonderful. I'm not asking you to be anything. I'm just asking you to . . . lighten up a little bit. Before I murder you.

At the very moment when I thought we had come to trust each other, old complaints resumed, with renewed malignity. I asked Martha to hire Gregory, as she needed an assistant; he returned from the first afternoon's work in a bitter mood, lamenting that she'd gone out for a sandwich and coffee without offering him anything, that her photographs were corny, that looking at them all day had had a really negative effect on his brain. Another day, when he'd helped fetch a bookcase from Libby's apartment, he noted that one of Libby's cats *smelled*, as if this plainly reflected something terrible about Libby's whole way of life. His second day of employment with Martha ended even before Martha arrived at her spare apartment in the East Seventies: once again he phoned from somewhere uptown with his last quarter, speechless with horror, and while I waited for the cab to arrive Martha called asking where he was. She had been delayed fifteen minutes in traffic. *Do you know what I felt like*, Gregory asked insanely, *sitting there on her stoop, with everybody who walked by staring at me as if I was some kind of criminal?*

Nothing suited him. A mutual friend hired him to wait tables in a small restaurant on First Avenue. Gregory resigned himself to it with poor grace, and warned me that I'd now be seeing much less of him than before. For two weeks he made himself scarce. On the phone he dissected his co-workers. They were stupid and frivolous and amoral and all taking drugs. It was now summer and business was falling off, he said, so he was making practically nothing.

Richard's rented this house in Sag Harbor, and he pestered me for weeks to come out, so I did. I realized if I listened to Gregory whining for another second I would strangle him. His new enemy is Kenneth, who used to be his friend years ago and now runs this restaurant, Kenneth went back to Gregory's place one night after work and they got stoned, according to Gregory Kenneth said a lot of nasty things about me. Kenneth is something of an airhead, but I recognize Gregory's technique of keeping people he knows alienated from each other. He complained so much about Bruno that I stopped speaking to Bruno for a while, he didn't want me and Bruno exchanging notes about him. And it turned out that he and Bruno had remained friendly the whole time. Now it's Kenneth persecuting him. Kenneth made him work an extra hour one night when some friends of the restaurant wanted a table. Kenneth made remarks about Gregory's bad character. Kenneth told Gregory that Gregory was losing his looks.

I've called him every day. Every day he tells me things are fine, he misses me, and so forth. His voice has the same incredible power over me it's always had. Soft and cuddly like a child's voice, a caress. He says his days are really flat without me. He's having dinner tonight with Pugg. Pugg is still on about the cleaning service. Gregory's making nothing at the restaurant, et cetera.

The house is so peaceful I could settle in here and forget everything. I cooked dinner, which took hours because I kept having little drinks with Richard. The evening was full of sexual innuendos and jokes, and it didn't surprise me later that Richard slipped into

bed with me, declaring that he wanted to try a new condom brand.
I felt weird about it at first, but life is short and lately not so wonderful, after all. I doubt if we'll ever do it again, anyway.

It would really destroy Victor if he ever found out about this,
Richard assured me. Not because I did it with somebody but
because it was you.

So he's betrayed Victor and I've betrayed Gregory. Is that really
true? Or do people like to poison themselves and each other with
morality when the slightest pleasure makes it possible to breathe
for a change? Richard says both partners in every gay couple he
knows cheat. Most of them stay together out of fear and then
desire bursts out in these odd moments. Let's face it, he says, being
scared about this disease, after a while, it's like we're in prison.
Worse than prison because even really disgusting mass murderers
who are in prison are allowed to fuck their wives and create children, when they ought to be electrocuted. When you think your
peak years of sexuality have to go by with no action, Richard says,
it's really fucked. I'm sure, he says, all this frustration is building
up everywhere like an H-bomb, all this energy seething away
inside people. It makes you sick in your mind, he says, thinking
you fuck somebody so you die. Its sick.

I wondered if Gregory happened to be screwing Pugg at the
same moment Richard was screwing me. I can picture it easily.
Maybe those two really love each other, but Gregory can't live off
Pugg. Who knows what tiresome drama I've been cast in. But he
sounds so sincere on the telephone. Misses me, and all that. He's
probably feeling the pinch. But what if it's real, and he does love
me, and he's just too crazy to cope? Don't I have an obligation to
him? I've made him rely on me, now he needs me. Maybe he's
trying his best, and everything does go wrong for him, as soon as
he sees a chance of having a real life, something comes up, he gets
sick, he gets stopped by his money problems. . . .

But then again, he got that $500 from the grant, and the $1000 I borrowed for him, and I'm always shelling out tens or twenties nearly every day, where does it disappear? Life's expensive, but I take care of his meals, his transportation, I paid for his work to get made up, it's a pretty good deal for him, really.

The night I got back to the city I phoned Kenneth's restaurant. He's not here, Kenneth said, I've had to let him go. But why, I asked. Well, look, Kenneth said, I'm running a restaurant, I'm not a psychiatrist. You know, every time I talk to him he tells me how degrading it is for him to wait tables, how much he hates this work, he says this to the waitresses and they think it's a big drag having to hear that all the time. He's really fucked up. He owes the waitresses a lot of money and he owes me $40, too.

Libby called and said Gregory had phoned her and said I'd left money for him for the week but he'd somehow lost it, and then she lent him $50. He just came over, she said, looking terrible, I invited him in for a cup of coffee but he acted jumpy and just grabbed the money and left. He'd also hit up Jane for cash, and Roger, the painter, said Gregory had showed up at his door asking for $10. I gave him the ten, Roger told me, but the creepy thing was, he'd gotten into the building without buzzing my apartment, it's a security building, you know? Gave me the creeps, there he was right outside my door.

I couldn't locate Gregory. He wasn't at his place. I didn't have a number for Pugg. I phoned anyone who might have seen him. Bruno said Gregory had come to the gallery looking like shit, and begged him for money. Then Doris told me he'd visited her and wheedled $100 out of her. He told her he was losing his mind. He didn't know if he could continue living in the city. Everything was driving him nuts. Next, it turned out he'd sold Roger's painting to a collector I knew, for $400. She gave him the $400 outright, but two days later he phoned up and asked to borrow an additional $100. So there has been quite a volume of financial activity going on in my absence. No word from him whatsoever.

He seemed to have disappeared from the city. I considered calling his mother, in case he'd gone home to Connecticut. While I was still thinking about it, his mother called me, asking for him. He'd given her my number as the place he was living. He doesn't really live here, I told her. Do you know where he is, she wanted to know. I've been trying to locate him for several days, I said. Is he in some kind of trouble, she finally asked. Yes, I said, I think he probably is. I knew it, his mother said.

13

I find it difficult to tell the rest of this story. Incidentally, I am not sure that it is one. Such a continual accumulation and disintegration of things can hardly be called a story.

After Gregory's disappearance his mother called me every day, and sometimes his sister called, a few times I heard from his brother as well, furthermore there were several calls from a social worker connected in some strange way with the mother, this person lived in the city and felt he could help Gregory if only Gregory would agree to meet with him. Gregory's mother sounded quite odd, a mixture of resignation and hysteria. At times she would say, I just know he's dead somewhere. I'm his mother, I can feel it. At other times she opined, I wrote him off a long time ago. I can't afford to feel anything about him.

When the sister called, she cautioned me that the mother was emotionally unstable, hyperbolic, hypocritical, a born liar, and had always favored Gregory over the other siblings, that Gregory had been the mother's golden child who could do no wrong. And, the sister said, the fact is, Gregory's a loser, he's never been able to get anything together. Now, I suppose, he's all strung out on drugs somewhere. It's happened plenty before, the sister said, but he's so sly and manipulative and my mother worships him, the last time he lived at home he had her convinced I was the one on drugs. Actually, the sister went on, my mother has been on drugs for twenty years, Libriums, ever since my father left, if the truth be known my mother threw him out, he made our lives totally miserable. The brother told me that the sister was emotionally unstable, a pathological liar, and a drug addict. He also said that Gregory had been "unnaturally close" to the mother, had in fact slept in the mother's bed "long after the normal age for that," but further claimed that Gregory had always been industrious and cheerful about working, a truthful person with tragic problems caused by the mother and the sister, and that it was "quite unlike Gregory" to complain about his lot.

I began hearing strange reports, that Gregory had been sighted in the West Village, or uptown, Victor spotted him one afternoon on Second Avenue, "racing to get somewhere," Victor had greeted him but Gregory had shot him a frightened look and kept going. The telephone at his apartment had been disconnected. Bruno attempted to learn whether Gregory still lived there, and once saw him near the building, "moving quickly down the street" with "a very large black person."

I felt the way I imagine an air crash survivor feels. Horrified, but weirdly liberated. Richard took me out of town for several days, back to Sag Harbor, abruptly severing the increasingly importunate communications from Gregory's mother and Gregory's sister and Gregory's brother, all of whom had decided to blame me for Gregory's situation. When I returned I discovered that my apartment had been looted, three huge bookcases emptied, the typewriter and answering machine gone, and within a few days, I heard from certain people who had sighted Gregory on Second Avenue, with his own blanket, peddling books and magazines. He had told Roger, the painter, *This is actually a lot of fun.*

I later heard, through Bruno, that Gregory's sister and brother had tracked Gregory down in the streets, restrained him with help from a third party, shoved him into a car and forcibly removed him to Connecticut, where his mother committed him to a hospital. Several months passed, and then I heard that Gregory and Pugg had been observed in the Temple of Dendur at the Metropolitan Museum, "looking very symbiotic." Shortly after this communication my phone began ringing every night, just after midnight. I would listen to the blankness on the other end; sometimes I heard music playing. These calls continued for several weeks, then stopped.

This story, if it is one, deserves the closure of a suicide, perhaps even the magisterial finality of what is usually called a novel, but the remnants of that faraway time offer nothing more than a taste of damp ashes, a feeling of indeterminacy, and the obdurate inconclusiveness of passing time. People come, people go. If I were to offer a picture of how things are now, I would need to tell the story of Libby and the stain. If now were then it would seem unduly cynical, but time has ruined all the feelings that would make it so. And I myself have changed decisively enough to recover pity without taking a bath in it.

Two years after the events I have described, I happened to be with Libby in a bar near the theater district. We had gone to some wretched performance given by a mutual friend, and afterwards drifted into the nearest saloon, a welcoming place full of amiably plastered regulars. This reminds me, Libby said, of the places I used to go in the sixties to pick people up. Oh, I said, the sixties, they were actually sort of wonderful when you look back. Yes, Libby said, at least one had adventures then.

But, I said, when I went to bars I'd never wear my glasses, because they ruined my looks.

Me neither, Libby said, and it used to get me into trouble.

I know, I said, I'd get this whole heated thing going with some guy across the room, and by the time I saw what he really looked like it was too late to change my mind without a scene.

I had a lot of peculiar near-sighted experiences, Libby said. One night I was sitting at the far end of a bar, I think it was the Grassroots Tavern on St. Marks Place, drinking a gin martini, and I noticed this very sexy guy down at the other end of the bar who seemed to be cruising me. So, you know, I started smiling suggestively, and doing things with my face that you do to attract people, but he kept staring in this uncommitted fashion, so this went on, and I had another drink, and finally I thought, Obviously I have to make the first move with this one. So I screwed up my courage and stood up, and started walking down to his end of the bar. And, as I got closer . . .

Don't tell me, I said. When you got there you realized he was hideously ugly.

Actually, it was worse than that, Libby said. Because when I got up close to him, he turned out to be a stain on the wall.

I never saw Gregory again. Although I believed, for quite a long time, that I would hear if something bad happened to him, I'm not so sure any more. We live in a time when bad things happen so frequently, to so many people, that it's an entire vocation to keep up with the bad news. To tell the truth, I don't think I would want to know.

Last week I quit smoking, and this afternoon I had my hair cut.